Pride Publishing books by Catherine Curzon and Eleanor Harkstead

Pride Publishing books by Catherine Curzon

Pride Publishing books by Eleanor Harkstead

Captivating Captains

THE CAPTAIN AND THE FATHER OF THE BRIDE

CATHERINE CURZON & ELEANOR HARKSTEAD

The Captain and the Father of the Bride
ISBN # 978-1-83943-971-1
©Copyright Catherine Curzon & Eleanor Harkstead 2021
Cover Art by Erin Dameron-Hill ©Copyright April 2021
Interior text design by Claire Siemaszkiewicz
Pride Publishing

THE CAPTAIN
AND THE
FATHER
OF THE BRIDE

Dedication

From both of us,
to all of the Captivating Captains' fans!

Chapter One

Leo held Liv's hand as he watched the solicitor flick through the file on his large mahogany desk. Leo had never been to the reading of a will before, never been inside a solicitor's office before, and Liv had gamely agreed to come with him for moral support.

He was amazed to see the green-shaded lamp on the solicitor's desk, as Leo had only seen them in films, yet it seemed that here they were a perfectly normal part of real life. The room was so quiet, all sound muffled by the thick carpet that ran through the wood-paneled offices. Leo's breathing and his own heartbeat sounded twice as loud, and although they were in the middle of London, he could barely hear the traffic or pneumatic drills that had been so ear-piercing when he was outside.

The solicitor shuffled some papers. It wasn't even as if Herr Schreiber, captain of Cologne industry and the most colorful man ever to leave North Rhine-Westphalia for a life on the ocean waves, had been

Leo's relative. He had merely been a client whose yacht he had skippered around the Mediterranean. A very rich, rather eccentric client, but a client nevertheless. And in his own way, a friend.

Gunther Schreiber's death, coming as it did in the arms of his cabaret-singing lover in the eighty-first year of his life, hadn't been unexpected. In fact, rarely did the platitude *he died doing something he loved* ring so true, but for Gunther Schreiber, being in the arms of his latest muse was exactly how he would have ended his own final Chapter. Leo had no doubt about that, and for the same reason, his sadness at the death of his late client was tempered with a sense of satisfaction at a life well-lived and filled to the brim with the fizz of champagne and the hum of the super yacht's engine.

The last thing Leo would have expected was to find himself sitting in this vast office with its scent of leather and wood polish, his best friend at his side as they waited for the last attendee to arrive. What could possibly be in the will of Gunther Schreiber that would concern Leo Maxwell? Perhaps a little token to mark their happy sailing. One of the handmade yachts from Gunther's salon, or perhaps one of the paintings that had decorated the walls. Leo hoped it wasn't that, because he doubted he'd be able to afford the insurance premiums to protect those priceless works.

This is probably a mistake. Or he's left me something completely random, one last prank to send me on my way.

Yet Mr. Brockett of Brockett, Brockett and Holliday had been very clear in his letter that Leo should attend the meeting in person. *A meeting to discuss the last will and testament of Gunther Jost Schreiber*, said the neat type on the thick ivory paper with its green and gold

8

lettering, *at which you will learn something to your advantage.*

Mr. Brockett tapped his pen on the cover of a buff file on his desk. He looked over his half-moon spectacles to the door and pursed his lips. Leo was surprised by the frames of his glasses as well—was the office furnished entirely from the contents of an antiques shop?

Telling himself the experience was fun and not terrifying, Leo grinned at Liv.

"All right?" he whispered, his voice absorbed at once by the deadening effects of the muffling carpet. She nodded, the high brunette ponytail on top of her head bouncing with the motion. Then she smiled and squeezed his hand.

"I *am* sorry," Mr. Brockett offered. "I'm sure Mr. Beaucock will be here very soon. I understand he's a very busy man. A fellow solicitor, you know."

Beaucock? Seriously?

Trying to avoid laughing, Leo asked, "Is he Gunther's nephew or...? He told me he'd never had any children."

"A very distant connection," he replied. "Herr Schreiber's only living relative."

Leo nodded. "I see. Are any other of Gunther's friends coming? Those ladies on the yacht..."

Leo hoped Mr. Brockett would know what he meant by that. The ladies came and went, and Gunther had always been very fond of them. Surely at least one of them would trot in on their patent-heeled shoes and inherit Gunther's villa in Cannes?

"I'm not at liberty to disclose any details, but I can assure you that Herr Schreiber has been most generous in his provisions. He stipulated that the parties each be informed in a strict order and according to strict instructions." Brocket chanced a thin-lipped smile. "I'm sure you understand."

Liv gave a little snigger and murmured, "So all of Gunther's girls don't bump into each other?"

Leo put his hand over his mouth, trying not to laugh. "I've seen that happen! Someone called Heidi threw someone called Marisol into the sea!"

"Oh God, we saw it all when we were crewing for Gunther," Liv told Brockett. "He got more action than any of—" She was silenced by the sound of the door opening, the gesture ushering in a cloud of potent aftershave ahead of the new arrival.

"Jesus Christ, this place is out in the bloody boondocks!" a voice announced. "Hardly the beating heart of legal London, is it? Beaucock. Pleasure to meet one of the *real* old guard!"

Leo turned in his seat. There before him was a man dressed in pinstripes, a sneer taking up most of his long face. Leo instinctively held Liv's hand tighter. He gave the new arrival a polite nod, even though he would much rather have run away. He'd met people like Beaucock before, monied pillocks who would hire him to skipper their eye-wateringly expensive yacht and treat Leo with contempt as the *hired help*.

"Morning," Leo said to Beaucock. "How do you do?"

"I've had a hell of a morning in the very best way." Beaucock planted his feet a shoulder-width apart and held out his hand to Leo. "Let's just say that's one more Premier League player whose license won't be snatched away by the so-called forces of law and order for a tiny bit of harmless speed. They see a Ferrari and they think it's payday. Well, not today!"

"Mr. Beaucock specializes in motoring cases," Brockett explained as Conrad waited for Leo to take his hand. "High-profile ones."

"Teflon Con," Beaucock said with obvious pride. "Conrad Beaucock."

Leo shook Conrad's moist hand. "I've never met one of Gun's relatives before. Nice to meet you. I'm Leo Maxwell, but some people call me Max." Leo grinned at Liv. *Some people* being Liv. "And this is my friend Liv."

Conrad gave Liv the sort of look a man might give a new car, appraising her in one glance.

"Good to meet you, Leroy." He released Leo's hand. "And *great* to meet you, Liv."

"It's *Leo*," he prompted. Yes, Conrad really was *that* type, the kind who consigned people to a bin marked *inconsequential human being* within seconds of meeting them. And Leo had bought a smart tweed three-piece just for this meeting. His oilskin jacket and wellies hadn't seemed quite the thing to wear. He didn't even have to look at Liv to know that she wouldn't be impressed. Men like Conrad were all too easy to come by in the yachting world, and they were as far from Liv's cup of tea as it was possible to get.

"Capricorn," Conrad replied as he took a seat. "Don't tell me you're into that bullcrap?"

"Leo is my *name*." *Is this guy for real?* "I can't even remember what my star sign is. I don't particularly care." Leo glanced at Mr. Brockett and the file on his desk. Conrad rubbed his hands together, then looked at his watch with such theatrics that Leo knew he was waiting to be asked what was on his wrist.

So Leo wouldn't ask.

"Let's get this baby read," he told the solicitor. "My Rolex tells me I can give you an hour."

A Rolex. More like a load of Bolex.

Leo shook his head. *Conrad Beaucock, you are a tosser.* "I'm sure Gun would be over the moon to know you've managed to squeeze the reading of his last wishes into your busy schedule. It's not very respectful to the old boy."

"It's not like he's here to complain, is it?" Conrad sniggered. "Get over yourself. Who are you anyway?"

"Mr. Beaucock, this is Mr. Maxwell. He skippered Herr Schreiber's yacht around —" Brockett began to explain.

"So you're a taxi driver without a taxi, yeah?"

"I'm RYA Yachtmaster Offshore certified, actually." *So there.* "And, more importantly, I was Gun's friend."

"We both were," Liv said, taking Leo's hand again. "And we miss him."

Leo grinned at her, the days of larking about in the sunshine rushing back to him. "Life's going to be a lot quieter without Gun around!"

"Not mine, mate." Conrad sneered. "My life's going to be a lot louder once I bank that check!"

"Why, are you buying a drum kit?" Leo quipped. Was that a childish riposte? *Oh, tough titties, I don't care.*

Brockett cleared his throat and opened the file.

So this is the moment, then.

The mystery of the meeting was about to be solved and Conrad Beaucock was about to inherit everything Gunther hadn't given to his girlfriends. And after five minutes in his company, Leo knew that he didn't deserve a penny of it.

Gunther had kept an exquisite ship in a bottle on board. He'd spotted Leo admiring it and had waxed lyrical about it. Maybe *that* was Gunther's bequest?

"Now," Brockett began, "this is a rather complicated matter. Herr Schreiber's posthumous wishes have been carried out by a will, as you might expect, and a trust. Due to the sensitive nature of some of the bequests, it's been necessary to be rather...exacting. To ensure that the documents could be sealed, as Herr Schreiber wished. I hope you'll understand?"

Leo glanced to Liv, who gave him an encouraging smile. He listened intently as Brockett began to read, the will and trust documents a dense tangle of legalese and arcane wording that soon had Leo lost. Conrad, *Teflon Con*, looked as though it was all old news to him, the flash lawyer in his pinstripes and pointed shoes. He was a world away from Gunther, white-bearded and lounging in kaftans and silk slippers, like a cross between a hippy and Father Christmas.

"And now we reach the bequests," Brockett said eventually. "There'll be time afterward for questions, but I'd appreciate it if you would allow things to proceed. The ladies were somewhat ungoverned during this portion, but do try to cooperate."

"Of course," Leo said.

Heidi, Marisol, Anook and Tjitske came to his mind in a flurry of big hair, long nails and metallic bikinis. They had always been ungoverned on the deck of the yacht, so Leo couldn't imagine them being any different in Mr. Brockett's office. What a scene that must've been.

Brockett reached down beneath his desk and, to Leo's surprise, produced a laptop. He lifted the lid and danced his fingers across the keyboard, then turned the screen to face his audience. There was Gunther again, large as life and beaming with happiness on the deck of the *Aphrodite*. Behind him Leo could see the crystal-blue ocean, a horizon stretching off into infinity.

Leo sniffed back a tear. He missed that wide smile. He glanced at Liv, knowing she would feel the same. "There he is, Gun the man!"

Liv didn't answer, but her eyes were filled with tears. Then she looked at Leo and smiled as she said, "I loved crewing for Gunny. He promised Dad he'd look after me like my own family, and he always did. And you too, Max. It was like having a big brother!"

Conrad made a sound of annoyance as Brockett reached around to press a key on the laptop. The screen came to life and Gunther raised a glass of sparkling champagne to the camera.

It must've been breakfast time.

"*Digga!*" Gunther beamed. "If you're watching this, as they always say in the movies, I must be off charting new waters. Let me tell you now, no tears. My Mäuschen is in my arms once more, and I am a happy man indeed."

"*Mäuschen,*" Liv mouthed with a smile, a tear making its way down her cheek.

Leo patted her hand. With a grin, he said, "Do you think his Mäuschen is telling him off for all those girlfriends he had? I wondered why we had that storm last week! But they'll be making up now."

"So, Leo — *Max* — and Conrad, hello!" Gunther took a sip of champagne. "Here are my bequests. The last of many! To my good friend, Leo, the captain of the *Aphrodite* and the man who steered us all safely home, I bequeath the ship in a bottle that was the first gift given to me by my beloved, much-lamented Mäuschen, when I had not a mark to my name."

"Aww," Liv whispered, and Brockett paused the film. Gunther's *Mäuschen*, as he always called his late wife, had died long before Leo's path crossed that of the millionaire, but he felt as though he knew her all the same. Her pictures decorated the surface of the yacht's piano and hung above the fireplace, showing a small, smiling woman with wild blonde hair. He wasn't even sure what her real forename had been. When Gunther had reminisced about his late, adored wife, she had always been *Mäuschen*.

The tears Leo had tried to sniff back wouldn't be stopped now. The image of Gunther on the screen blurred as his tears rose. "That's so sweet of Gun, he loved that little ornament." As if Gunther could hear him, Leo told the image on the screen, "Thanks, Gun, it means a lot. I'll look after it, don't you worry."

"I didn't know it had been a present from his wife," Liv said, handing Leo a tissue. "Now I understand why he treasured it like he did."

Leo took the tissue and dabbed at his eyes. "He was such a nice bloke. I miss him."

"A ship in a bottle?" Conrad snorted. "From a millionaire? That's a slap in the face! Sucks to be you, Leon!"

How could Gunther have been related to this twazzock?

"Once again, it's *Leo*." Leo had the feeling that at any minute now, Conrad would be doing an impression of a lion. "Got it, Connie? I never expected to inherit anything from Gun, and that little boat meant more to him than all his money. I'm so chuffed he trusted me to look after it."

"Gentlemen, if you would?" Brockett pressed the key, and Gunther spoke again.

"My second bequest to you, Leo, is the yacht you skippered so well. Now, I know you'll say *the yacht? I can't take her!* But you can. All I ask in return is that you love the *Aphrodite* as much as I did, wherever she may take you."

A strange feeling of unreality came over Leo, distorting the light, distorting the room, until he felt as if it were a stage set. His own yacht. His very own. "The *Aphrodite*? That massive yacht? You'd have trouble fitting *her* into a bottle!"

"The— Can he— Wait a minute!" Conrad snarled. "The whole fucking yacht? To *him*?"

"Have you even *seen* the *Aphrodite*?" Leo rolled his eyes.

"I've seen it!" Conrad replied. "I Googled the bloody thing, and you're not getting away with this!"

And there was Gunther, smiling at them from the screen. Leo felt protective of the eccentric, affectionate man. "He was my friend. Doesn't that mean anything to you? These are his last wishes, for heaven's sake."

Leo's glance fell to Conrad's Rolex. His shoes were probably handmade, too, like his suit and his shirt. Did Conrad really need Gunther's yacht when it looked like he could buy one twice the size himself?

"Play it, come on," Conrad commanded. "Let's hear it."

On the screen, Gunther sprang back into life. He took a sip from his glass. "And all that remains is the cash. Leo, *Aphrodite* needs a skipper, but a skipper needs someone at his side. For fifty-two years I had my Mäuschen, and all the money in the world could never replace her. So I've given most of mine away."

"He's *what?*" Conrad gasped.

16

"But I kept back one million. Now, I told my Mäuschen that I would marry her when I made my first million, and six months later, I did both." He leaned forward little. "Leo, you're too kind and too gentle a fellow to sail alone. The *Aphrodite* is yours to keep, but if you find and wed your own Mäuschen in the next twelve months, consider the million pounds your wedding gift. If not, let someone else enjoy the money instead. I haven't seen little Conrad in thirty years, but twelve months is more than enough time for the good Mr. Brockett to track him down. Herr Brockett, do your worst. Find our Conrad and give him *his* bequest, my collection of nautical memorabilia. As for the cash... Only time will tell!"

Leo listened as Brockett reiterated the contents of the video in his dry legalese from the documents in front of him, but Leo couldn't take any of it in.

He kept trying to say *'a million pounds'*, but no sound came out of his mouth.

A million pounds.

There was so much he could do with the money. Charities he could help. Maybe he could set up a sailing school.

Finally, Leo managed to croak, "A m-million pounds? R-really?" But what was that about the Mäuschen? Leo asked Brockett, "There's a catch, isn't there? What does he mean, *wed your own Mäuschen*? Does he mean marry a *woman*?"

Brockett cleared his throat, his lips set in an unreadable line. After a second he nodded.

"The partners here have spent a long time debating on exactly what Herr Schreiber meant and we believe that he intended for you to take a wife. He was very clear in his choice of language, and to all who knew him, *Mäuschen* was widely known to refer to the gentleman's wife." He glanced toward the screen. "Obviously you're more than welcome to seek alternative opinions, but—"

But that would cost a king's ransom.

Conrad's head whipped around, and he jabbed his finger toward Leo. "You put him up to this! He was an old man and you— He was probably demented, and this fucker planted this stupid idea in his head! That money and that boat are mine! You heard him, I'm the only relative!"

Leo raised his hands in defense. "I didn't! Bloody hell, I didn't do a thing. We just went out on his yacht and had a fab time. That's *all*. How dare you accuse me of manipulating him, you flash bastard? And as for Gun being demented, maybe if you'd bothered to take time out from Brylcreeming your hair, you might've known he was as sharp as a pin right up to the day he died. This is *all* news to me. I had no idea *what* was in Gun's will. Not a clue!"

"And you heard Gunther," Liv added. "He hadn't seen you in thirty years, you can't expect—"

"Expect?" Conrad roared. "I expect you to hand over that money! Meet a bird and marry her in the space of twelve months? Oh, come on! You'll promise some tart a few thou and get a ring on her finger sharpish, that's what I'd do, that's what any man would! Some cheap bit of skirt, fifty grand, nondisclosure and wallop, you're a millionaire! Well not on my watch, sunshine!"

Except I'm gay.

What a precipice to be on. *Of course* Conrad would do it, it was a mercenary move, but could Leo abandon his principles? What would people say? *But you came out, you rode about on a float at Brighton Pride, you're gay and now you're marrying a woman?*

Leo looked at the screen. Gunther. *Oh, Gun, why didn't I just tell you I'm gay?*

"I— I— you never know what could happen in twelve months," Leo said. *I might suddenly become un-gay. As if that's likely.*

But Liv lifted their joined hands. What would he do without his best friend? The woman who'd joined the crew wracked with seasickness and homesickness and found her sea legs in next to no time? Thank God she was here.

"There's not going to be *some tart,* as you put it," she told Conrad boldly. "Leo and I have already talked about marriage, but we wanted to take things at a sensible pace. That's what you do when you're in love, Mr. Beaucock."

Leo blinked.

What did… Did Liv just…did she really just say…?

Leo brought their joined hands to his lips. That bizarre feeling of unreality came over him again as he said, "Oh, yes, we're in love. We met on the *Aphrodite.* Who *wouldn't* fall in love on that yacht? We talked about getting married and now…well…now we can afford your dream dress, just like you wanted! My beautiful bride."

Thank goodness Mum made me join the school drama club.

"Oh, Max!" She beamed, then dashed her hand against her tear-filled eyes. "You'll have to ask Pops, but I know he'll say yes!"

Brockett closed the laptop. "Well, Mr. Maxwell, the yacht is currently in Monaco, I believe, but it will be safely back in our waters within the month. I believe

Herr Schreiber kept a berth in Brighton? That's where the yacht's bound for. There'll be some paperwork of course, but I believe that concludes our business for to — "

"Balls does it!" Conrad snarled. "That's my boat and my mill, and I'm going to get them!"

This was the man who got speeding footballers off the hook. Of course he'd contest the bequests. And it wasn't as if Leo had any money to spend on legal fees.

"I think you'll find they were Gunther's," Leo said. "And he could leave them to whoever he wanted. Maybe you should've joined us on the yacht? You missed some brilliant parties!"

"Gentlemen, madam," Brockett said. "Are there any questions? Of course I'm available to you if any arise once you've had time to fully consider Herr Schreiber's wishes."

"I don't have any at the moment," Leo replied, still playing his role of overjoyed fiancé. He hoped his beaming smile concealed his churning unease. Was this right? Gunther had loved his Mäuschen, wasn't it understood that Leo should marry for love? He shouldn't be marrying a woman he didn't, couldn't, love. Not as a husband, anyway. Of course he loved Liv, she was his friend, but it wasn't quite the same thing.

He felt like he was watching someone else shake hands with the solicitor and walk out into reception, as though he had become a spectator in another man's surreal life. All he wanted to do was escape, but at the door of the lobby Conrad Beaucock stepped in front of him.

Leo clenched his jaw. *You're just like the bullies at school. But sadly I can't kick you in the balls.*

Feigning his breezy tone, Leo asked, "Sorry, Conrad, do you want something?"

"I know a bum bandit when I see one," Conrad told him in a low whisper. "And if this ends up in court, I'll dredge up every dirty little secret you've ever had. *Comprendé*, gay boy?"

A shiver of fear ran down Leo's spine. Perhaps it was wisest to drop it now. Let Conrad have the yacht and the money—but not the ship in the bottle. Avoid upsetting friends who would wonder why his sexuality had suddenly changed. Avoid upsetting his parents, who would hate to see his dirty linen flap on a line in court. Not that there was much dirty linen in Leo's life, but anything could be twisted by a ruthless bastard like Conrad.

And yet, Gun had wanted Leo to have the money. He'd wanted Leo to be happy. *Why the hell should Conrad win, the utter shit?*

"And I know a complete fucking bastard when I see one," Leo whispered. "I'm not surprised Gun left you some rusty portholes and a pile of novelty lifebelts. You don't deserve anything else."

"I'll see you in co—" Conrad began, but Liv stepped between them.

"Yeah, you will," she said. "And Leo's soon-to-be father-in-law just *happens* to be pretty shit hot when it comes to the law. I'm a Greville-Hall, as in the same Greville-Halls who've been at Bedford Court Chambers for the last three hundred years." Liv put her hands on her hips and told him coldly, "Google it, Teflon Con, because we're coming for you. *Comprendé*?"

Leo struggled to hide his surprise. When Liv had told him that her father worked in law, he'd never imagined he was as grand as that. Still, playing his role, Leo said, "Yeah, my soon-to-be father-in-law will eat you for breakfast! He's the best!"

Conrad puffed out his chest and declared, "May the biggest balls win!"

Leo winced. "There's an image I really don't need in my head, thank you very much." Then he looped his arm through Liv's and said, "What do you say to lunch, my gorgeous fiancée?"

"I say yes! We've got wedding plans to make." She beamed, pushing open the door and sweeping them out into the London afternoon.

Chapter Two

Leo took Liv to a café in Soho. All the chairs and tables and crockery were mismatched, and the walls were covered in postcards and photographs, scattered at random. He loved it there, with its citrus scent from the freshly squeezed oranges and the tarted-up fry-ups they served.

Back on familiar turf, the unreality that had distorted Leo's view faded and he felt himself again.

"Are you sure, really sure, you want to do this?" Leo asked Liv. "It's so fab you suggested it, you're amazing, but are you *sure* you want to be Mrs. Maxwell?"

"After meeting that absolute arse?" She flicked her fringe back from her eyes. "I'm certain of it. We'll get married, you'll get your money and after we've made it look halfway realistic, we'll part amicably and quietly get divorced. I'm terminally single, Max, it's not like there's anybody else coming along, after all!"

"But what if your dream man comes along and you're Mrs. Maxwell and you never get to be with him? I couldn't do that to you, Liv." Leo fiddled with the napkin that was rolled around his knife and fork. "And I feel guilty about deceiving Gun. I know he's dead, but that clause means I have to marry a woman who I love as much as he loved his Mäuschen. Then again, I don't want Conrad to have the money. I don't think Gun did either, to be honest."

Liv smiled and took his hand. "I'm not looking for a dream man. I've had it with men. I'm going to concentrate on my poorly little seals instead. Honestly, Max, you're my best friend. We wouldn't be deceiving Gunny, he just didn't know you prefer men!"

An idea flashed into Leo's mind and he slapped the table, excited. "Let's do it! Let's get married and give all the money to your seals!"

Liv's seals. They'd become her whole life since she'd started work at the little sanctuary on the edge of Brighton. In fact, Leo already had a suspicion that she put most of her meager salary back into the collection tins.

Liv's mouth fell open, then she shook her head. "You can't! I mean…no! It's not for my seals, it's for you!"

Leo shook his head. "Do you remember when the dolphins followed us, and Gunther was running up and down the deck, kaftan flowing in the breeze? He loved it! So why not give it to the seals? Honestly. What could the charity do with that kind of dosh?"

She puffed out a long breath of air and shook her head. "Pretty much anything. We've only room for three long-staying patients at the moment but we could expand that if we had the funds… We'd be able to get the new clinical kit we're fundraising for and the sanctuary boat needs an overhaul too so we can actually get to the poor little things when they need us.

I'm doing it in my spare time, but I'm not sure how long Dad's going to be willing to keep handing over cash for the restoration project!"

"There we are then!" Leo squeezed Liv's hand. "I mean, I *could* sell the *Aphrodite*, but I'm not sure Gun would've wanted that. Maybe I can hire her out, or I can take paying passengers up and down the coast when I'm back home? And that money can go to the seals as well!"

"But you're the skipper. Would you really be happy buzzing up and down the coast with the whole world out there waiting?"

Leo ran his hand back through his hair. "I've seen a lot of the world, but I'm never in one place long enough to meet anyone. Do you know what I mean? I've been wondering if I could do something else, so I wouldn't have to be away most of the time. I was lying in bed this morning, and I was thinking, *I'm thirty-two and I'm still sleeping in my old bedroom, and it's still got a frieze of teddies in little boats on the walls.* I'd love to get my own place. But I dunno, maybe I could live on the *Aphrodite!*"

"Well, lovely old Gunny did, with his gals." She laughed. "I can't take all that money, you know, but you could always make a donation when you cash your check."

"Come on, you deserve the money," Leo insisted. "This is your idea. Maybe the..." Leo lowered his voice, the word feeling decidedly odd in his mouth, "...million, minus the fees for our quickie divorce! How does that sound?"

"No." Liv shook her head. "I couldn't. You'd still need to have some money of your own to live on."

Leo shrugged. "I'm still going to be the skipper! I'm not giving up work. All right, tell you what, I'll give you half of it, then I'll put the rest in the bank and give you more bit by bit."

Liv smiled and told him, "We'll see. Do you think you'll live on the *Aphrodite*, then? Everyone should live on a boat. I thought Pops was crazy when he first talked about it, but it's amazing. I love it."

Pops. The sainted, adored father whom Leo had yet to meet and who, he now realized, would need to be convinced by their subterfuge. Unless they could confide their plan in him and —

"We need to convince Pops this marriage is for real," Liv told him gravely.

Bang goes confiding in him.

"We can't tell him about the will, can we? He'll know at once what we're up to." Leo quailed. How long would it take for her father to realize they were scheming? But then, there had been a couple of occasions when he'd been hanging out with Liv and old ladies had cooed, "*awww, what a sweet couple!*" They'd tried not to laugh in response, but maybe they could pull it off.

Maybe.

"If he knows, I don't think he'll go along with it," she replied. "And we have to be super convincing, because he's really sharp. I'll prepare the ground, then we can get you and him together?"

"Yeah." Leo glanced up as their plates arrived, but he suddenly wasn't hungry. *Will Pops report us? Are we breaking the law?* "He won't twig—some people think I'm straight." *From a distance. On a dark night.*

Liv furrowed her brow. Her eyes swiveled up, her expression growing thoughtful.

"I'm pretty sure I never told him you're gay. He won't twig. Just be butch." She grinned. "I mean...unless you gay guys emit some sort of invisible signal to each other. Even he can do butch when he needs to, you should see him in court!"

"I can do butch! *I'm the captain! Stop playing silly buggers with the water pistols or I'll throw you overboard!*" Leo laughed. He could do this. He just had to fox Pops' gaydar. Somehow. Leo started to saw into his sausage. "Your dad's gay? I mean...excuse the sausage, but..."

She paused, her fork halfway to her mouth. "Did I never tell you? Yeah, he's super gay!"

"Well...you and Pops *do* live in a yacht in Brighton marina, so I should've guessed!" Leo abandoned his sausage and moved onto his fried egg and hash brown. "But no, you never said! Does he have lots of hot boyfriends?"

"Oh my God, I totally need to fill you in on my soap opera of a childhood, don't I?" Liv grinned. "How do you not know all this? Let's go for a roast on Sunday, and I'll give you a lesson on Liv, ready for when you tackle Pops. But no, he doesn't have a lot of boyfriends at all, and he should. He's lovely. A proper gentleman barrister."

Leo could picture him, white-haired, sitting in a high-backed leather armchair by a fireplace. Not that he'd have an armchair or a fireplace on his yacht, of course, but Leo knew the type. The men who pottered about marinas in the way other men pottered about in their sheds.

"Okay, roast on Sunday, and we'll bring wedding magazines to look at! You're going to look gorgeous!" Leo reached across the table and tweaked Liv's cheek. "Pops will cry, his boyfriend will cry, it'll be adorable."

And Pops' boyfriend would be like him, white-haired, genteel, the sort of old-school gay man who peppered his conversation with Polari and had once been on first name terms with Quentin Crisp.

"Just think, he'll be in court right now little suspecting that his only child's just got engaged." Liv gave a saucy wink. "To a yacht-owning millionaire."

"See, when you put it like that, I'm a very eligible bachelor. Except now, of course..." Leo took her hand and stroked it affectionately. "I'm spoken for, by the beautiful Ms. Greville-Hall. Oh, Liv...did that feel weird, me doing that?"

She nodded and laughed. "Totally weird! But thanks for trusting me, Max. It means a lot. I've never had a friend as lovely as you."

"I haven't had one as lovely as you either." Leo withdrew his hand and returned to the sausage. "And if I had been straight, or you'd been a bloke, I'd have asked you out on a date. But as it is, we're friends. Special friends."

"And with men like Conrad Beaucock hanging around, we're going to need all the friends we've got!"

"There's another word beginning with 'C' that would suit him as well!" Leo chuckled. "We'll win. We've got Gun on our side. Remember that squall when *Aphrodite* was keeling, and his girlfriends were panicking, and he got all emotional and promised he'd never let us down? He won't now either, I'm sure of it!"

She picked up her glass of orange juice and said, "To Gunny and Mäuschen, may they have calm seas and open skies!"

Leo held up his glass too. Leo was certain that the old roué would've approved. "To Gunny and Mäuschen!"

Chapter Three

Leo decided to salute Gunther with another drink and headed to The Hervey in Mayfair. The plush hotel had been Gunther's favorite place to stay when he was in London, and the hotel's bar was where Leo had first met him, his interview turning into an inebriated crawl through the hotel's selection of Weissbier. And Gunther and his Mäuschen's wedding reception had been held at The Hervey, many years before. It had been a special place for Gunther, so where else to raise a glass in thanks?

Leo ordered a long glass of German beer. He held it up and toasted Gunther and his Mäuschen. "*Prost!*"

It was an extraordinary, unexpected gift, but the clause was a headache. Gunther had been well-meaning, it was just unfortunate that when Leo had said "*She's not my type*" when Gunther had made an attempt to matchmake, Gunther hadn't picked up on the fact that *not my type* meant *not a man*.

Marrying Liv was so devious, but who would give up the chance to acquire that money? Especially when it was going to the sanctuary. That made it all right, surely? It was to do a good thing.

But as Leo's gaze wandered about the bar, he saw couples — apparently genuine couples — and as they laughed, as they gazed at each other with casual affection, Leo felt a pang of despair. Even if his marriage to Liv was over fast, they would have to pretend they were in love. They'd have to kiss on the lips in front of everyone at the wedding, and how would they share a bridal suite? Maybe they'd make sure they booked a room with a sofa and a spare blanket.

And what about *Pops*, giving away his little girl with pride, not knowing that she'd already scheduled her divorce. And what would happen when that divorce was played out? What if Liv's plan, so simple and clear, hit a massive, ragged pothole?

Could the divorce be enough for Conrad to mount another attack? No marriage, no Mäuschen, no million pounds?

But it would be too late then, wouldn't it? The marriage was the only caveat. There was no stipulated length of time that the marriage had to last.

Leo held up his half-empty glass. "Oh, Gunther... I wish I'd told you the truth."

But why be miserable? Gunther had given him a chance that very few people ever got. A million pounds. He should be happy.

Leo put his glass down on the mat and glanced over at a man in a tux who'd just walked into bar. *He* looked happy, at least.

As that thought slipped into Leo's head, the man reached up and unknotted his bow tie, letting it fall loose against his chest. He was already unfastening the top few buttons of his shirt when he said to the barman, "Balvenie on the rocks, please."

"Coming right up, sir," the barman said.

Leo propped his head up on one hand. *Balvenie on the rocks.* It sounded more elegant than his beer. And the man was really handsome in a mature sort of way, like a character from a film. The low light of the bar caught a couple of silver strands in his dark blond hair. But he had to be straight. A woman in a floor-length satin gown would appear at any second, wouldn't she?

What brought all these people to a hotel in Belgravia on a spring evening, Leo wondered? Who was the man in the unfastened bow tie, seemingly content as he waited for his Balvenie on the rocks?

But he hadn't ordered a second drink, for his yet-to-appear satin-clad companion.

The barman placed a glass on a mat in front of the man. "Will there be anything else, sir?"

Leo glanced to the door of the bar and back again at the man. He chanced a grin at the man.

"That's the lot, thanks," he said with a smile. "Stick it on room four-two-three!"

The barman nodded and went over to the till.

Leo raised his glass to the man and said, "Cheers!"

"Cheers!" He lifted his glass too. "Here's to propping up the bar!"

"You're propping it up very elegantly!" Leo said. It was true as well, there was something in the man that seemed perfectly suited to looking artfully rumpled in very expensive hotels.

"It's a skill that takes years to perfect." He held out his hand. "Archie."

Leo edged his way along the bar and settled one stool away from him. He took Archie's hand and as he shook Leo noticed the signet ring on Archie's little finger and the classic watch on his wrist. The cologne he was wearing, somehow spicy yet fresh, sent a shot of desire through Leo. He was reminded at once of the urbane men he'd see, hair tousled on the decks of their yachts as they sped over the sea. They'd head to a marina, where champagne corks popped and laughter rang on the air until sunrise.

"Leo," he said.

Something about Archie was making Leo wonder about that first impression he'd had of him being straight. What was it? An inflection in his voice, perhaps, or the way he was smiling at Leo, or even his neat sideburns, that made him wonder, *maybe this man isn't straight at all*. And now Leo wondered if he should be talking to him, because he was spoken for by Liv. He couldn't go about meeting men in hotel bars if he was trying to convince the world he was happily marrying a woman. And yet...he was on his own, toasting his late friend Gunther. And what would Gunther have done, if he'd been on his own in a bar and someone so gorgeous had walked in? *I'll be like Gunther. The man marked his seventy-fifth birthday with a carpe diem tattoo across his tanned chest.*

"I hope you don't mind me saying, but I *really* like your togs." Leo tipped his head to one side as he looked Archie up and down with undisguised interest. "Very suave. *And* exciting. Have you just been having a fight with Blofeld?"

Archie widened his blue eyes then dropped his voice to a whisper to confide, "You've found me out. Nearly had a rather nasty run-in with a laser beam, but I escaped in the nick of time, as ever."

"I hope your trousers didn't get scorched!" Leo chuckled. He gave the trousers a lingering look, as he wondered what treasures they might conceal. Then he caught Archie's glance and smiled.

"They didn't, but I lost the keys to my moon buggy." Archie took a sip from his glass. "Luckily, I have a room booked for tonight."

Leo laughed. "You're staying here?"

"Room four-two-three."

He nodded, then asked, "You?"

Leo shook his head. "Wish I was! But no. I was just raising a toast to a departed friend. And I had a meeting earlier, hence my attempt to look smart." He gestured to his brown tweed suit and dark-blue silk tie, hoping the handsome man in the tux would like it.

"I think you look *very* smart. I feel like I should fasten my tie." Archie smiled. "But I won't."

"An unfastened tie suits you," Leo told him. "Very louche. You suit louche."

"Then I'll leave it just as it is." Archie rested his elbow on the bar, a gentle look dancing in his eyes. "I'm sorry about your friend."

"Thanks." Leo wrinkled his nose. There was something about the kindness of a stranger that ran the risk of him blubbing. "He died happy, and very old, and he had an awesome life. And...I'm just saying *thank you* by splashing out on his favorite posh beer!"

Leo raised his glass again, as if the shade of Gunther was there beside him. And for all he knew, perhaps he was.

Archie clinked his glass against Leo's and smiled.

"To good but absent friends."

"Hear, hear." The whiskey in Archie's glass glowed in the light, and Leo felt a warmth from him that he didn't want to turn away from.

Carpe diem, as Gunther would've said.

Or carpe noctem.

Seize the night.

Leo brushed Archie's arm so lightly it could be mistaken for an accident, but it served as a signal too, if Archie was ready to pick up on it. "So...are you here alone?"

"I'm escaping from a frightfully prestigious and frightfully boring awards bash," Archie admitted, glancing back toward the lobby. "Do you want to get a table? Easier for me to lie low!"

"Yeah, why not?" *This is going well...* Leo picked up his glass, then realized there was little left but foam. "I need a top-up, I'll just— Can I get you anything?"

I'm going to be a millionaire soon, I can buy a drink for a gorgeous stranger.

"This one should keep me going for a while yet." Archie picked up his glass and nodded toward a vacant booth. "I'll grab that for us. Pop your drink on my room." He smiled and raised his eyebrow. "I'm in four-two-three."

Leo ordered a glass of white wine. When he gave Archie's room number to the barman, excitement bubbled through him. *That eyebrow raise.* It played in Leo's head on a loop as he watched the barman deftly pour his drink into a metal measuring cup, then into his glass. No man raised their eyebrow like that unless they were unambiguously asking, *fancy a naked romp?*

Yes. Yes I do. I need a thrilling, naked, sweaty romp in the arms of a handsome stranger with sparkling eyes.

Because how long would Leo have to keep up the lie for, that he wasn't gay, that he and Liv were in love? This might be his last chance for quite a while to feel strong, manly arms around him and feel the gentle rasp of evening stubble against his skin.

As Leo headed to the booth, he couldn't take his gaze from Archie. The light caught the silver in his hair, and there was something about his bearing, assured but carefree, that drew Leo to him like a magnet. He imagined the unruly sea breeze in Archie's hair, his blue eyes fixed confidently on the horizon as the sails filled with wind and carried him home.

The booth looked so snug and welcoming, like a bunk at the end of a rainy day. Leo slipped in and sat beside Archie.

The candle on the table in its clear glass holder leaped, then settled, throwing out its intimate glow.

"You've picked a very nice spot," Leo whispered, as if he were sharing a secret.

"I didn't think you'd mind somewhere a little more private," Archie told him. "You're here alone?"

"Private is good." Leo raised his eyebrow in just the way Archie had raised his. *Fancy a naked romp?* He combed his hand back through his hair. "Yeah, I'm here alone. In case you're wondering, I'm single. And I don't have any plans for this evening, unless...?"

Archie gave a languid nod then picked up his glass and asked, "So how about we single guys make plans together?"

Leo moved a little closer to Archie, closing the gap between them before he lightly placed his hand on Archie's knee. His heart was pounding, his voice hitching with anticipation as he asked, "*These* sort of plans? Bedroom sort of plans?"

Archie cocked his head to one side, the faintest hint of a smile playing at his lips as the candlelight danced in his blue eyes. Then he put his mouth to Leo's and kissed him, slow and deep.

It was what Leo had hoped for, the sort of kiss from the sort of man that would send desire shooting through his body. He ran his fingers through Archie's hair, exploring him, as he slid his other hand up Archie's thigh, brushing against Archie's hardness.

Their kiss deepened and Archie closed his hand over Leo's, twining their fingers together. *If only* — But there wasn't any time for an if only, not tonight. Leo was going to take his chance.

Leo broke from their kiss to beg, "Take me to bed, please, Archie." Then he brought his mouth back to Archie's and kissed him again, stroking Archie's erection.

Only when they had to break for breath did the kiss finally end, their joined hands still caressing Archie's body. After a moment he pressed his forehead to Leo's and purred, "Let's go."

They got out of the booth, Leo holding his jacket carefully over his groin with one hand, the other twined with Archie's as they left the bar and headed for the lifts. He couldn't help but grin at how ruffled Archie's hair was. And how much more disordered it'd be by the end of the night.

What an epic final fling this would be.

They walked through the polished, shiny reception, over the marbled floor and past the gilt-edged furniture and ridged columns. The brass doors of the lift opened smoothly, and they stepped inside.

They were alone in the lift, and once the doors were closed, Archie took Leo in his arms again. He teased him with nuzzled kisses against his jaw, his lips trailing heat and desire. Leo leaned back against lift's wall, pulling Archie against him, sliding his hand down to Archie's buttocks. They were so firm to the touch, and Leo gave him an appreciative squeeze.

Archie's answering moan sent a thrill through Leo, a surge of heat that darted straight into his blood. He *had* to be a top, didn't he? Leo was usually pretty adept at reading the signals, but he'd known Archie for less than an hour. All the same, something in his physicality told Leo that he was right.

What a night they were going to have.

Chapter Four

The lift doors opened onto an impressive corridor that looked more like it was in a country house than a hotel. And there was no lingering smell of cooked breakfast, unlike in the hotels Leo usually ended up in when he was traveling.

Leo squeezed Archie's hand. "You have excellent taste in hotels."

"We secret agents don't believe in slumming it." Together they walked along the corridor, passing closed doors on either side on their way to four-two-three.

"I should hope not!" As they headed toward Archie's room, Leo told him playfully, "What if I told you I'm in the secret service too? I'm the captain of an innocent-looking cruiser traveling around the Mediterranean, but we're picking up and decoding signals. You see, I'm rather good at that... I can be quite a strict captain sometimes, but I'm very sweet, really. However you'd like me."

"Sweet *and* strict?" And there was that teasing, suggestive eyebrow again. "I *knew* you'd be fun."

Lowering his voice, Leo took a chance as he said, "I'm very good at knots, too. Would you like me to give you a personal— very *intimate*—demonstration?"

Would Archie be into that? Leo hoped he might be. It would be fun for them both.

Archie slipped his hand beneath Leo's tie and let the silk rasp against his palm. All the time he held Leo's gaze, desire flashing across his blue eyes. Then he closed his fist around Leo's tie and pulled him into another kiss.

"Consider permission to come aboard well and truly granted," he murmured. "*Captain.*"

Heat rushed through Leo's blood at the sound of that word on Archie's lips. *Captain.* He could've stripped off in the corridor and flung himself at Archie right away and not cared if anyone saw. But as impetuous as Leo was feeling, even he would draw the line at public sex.

"Show me your quarters," Leo said. "I hope they're shipshape. I like a tidy bunk."

"I'm looking forward to finding out exactly what my captain *does* like." Archie touched his key card to the lock and there was a metallic click as it opened. "Besides me in this tux."

"You're about to find out," Leo replied as they went into the room.

It wasn't often Leo saw a chandelier in a hotel room, but it wasn't often he embarked on sexual adventures with men he'd just met, either. The room had a high ceiling and ornate decor, and a huge bed with a beautiful antique metal frame.

And it was very tidy.

"Your captain approves," Leo said, hands clasped behind his back. "Very tidy quarters and an excellent bed."

To tie you to.

The door closed behind them and they were alone at last. London might've been a world away, its noise and bustle a mere memory in the calm surroundings of this opulent room.

Leo took Archie by his lapels and pulled him to him, kissing him deeply, his heart beating fast.

It beat faster still when Archie put his arms around Leo's waist and settled his hands against his bottom. They caressed and squeezed, his fingers tracing the contours of Leo's body through his tweed trousers.

Leo responded with a groan of desire into their deepening kiss and stroked his hand between them to cup Archie's erection and feel it properly.

Oh, he's big.

He felt Archie smile against their kiss, heard a hint of a growl in his plummy tones when he asked, "What's the verdict, Captain?"

"I wondered where that bowsprit had got to!" Leo joked. He took his hand away, his voice gentle as he said, "Now we're alone... I'd like you to undress for me."

"Do you want to make yourself comfortable?" Archie asked, stroking his hands down over Archie's bottom. "So I can take my time?"

Leo nodded. "Take as long as you need. I like unwrapping my presents slowly." He glanced over at the elaborate silk-upholstered armchair by a fireplace decorated with cherubs and cornucopias. "Seems like a nice spot to be your audience."

"Oh, I can tell you're going to be a lot of fun." Archie landed a soft slap on Leo's bottom. "Take a seat, darling."

"Cheeky!" Leo chuckled. He prowled across to the armchair and draped himself across it, one leg up over the arm as he leaned back. He unfastened his tie and tugged it first one way, then the other, his gaze never leaving the hot, rumpled man in the tux. "Are those shoulders as broad as I think they are?"

"I like to think they'll do." Archie kicked off his shoes and socks as he replied, his bare feet sinking into the luxurious carpet. There was more than a hint of mirth in what could be arrogance, a glimmer of mischief shining in his eyes. He didn't break the charged gaze between them as he peeled off the tux with exquisite slowness, letting it slide down to fall onto the floor behind him.

This is quite a show.

Leo curled his arm up behind his head, cushioning it against the armchair in an attempt to look unflustered when all he could think of was how bloody exciting it was to be alone with this man. Archie was standing in front of him in his shirt, his toned body all too obvious to Leo. Those shoulders weren't the result of padding and careful tailoring, and his arms... It took all the determination Leo could muster to stay where he was and not spring across the bedroom to devour this wonderful new man.

"I'm not disappointed," Leo said. "I think you should take off your trousers next."

"Anything you say," Archie purred. He reached around to unhook his cummerbund and let it fall. Then he unbuttoned the immaculately tailored trousers and slowly eased the zip down, teasing Leo.

Leo ran his tongue over his lip. "Very nice zip action," he said.

"I'll put that on my CV." Archie stepped out of his trousers and kicked them aside.

Once Leo had recovered from just how tempting Archie's crisp, white shorts were—and not only because of the suggestion of something incredible inside them—his gaze fell to Archie's legs. Now *those* were thighs. And the shape of his calves, curved and strong...

"Has anyone ever told you you've got gorgeous legs?" Leo asked, toying with his hair as he tried his best not to leap from his chair. "Because you have."

"Maybe...but not as nicely as you just did," Archie told him with a saucy smile. He lifted his arm, one silver cufflink catching a flare of low light before he unfastened it and threw it toward Leo. "Look after these, Captain."

Leo caught it with one lazy stretch of his arm. He couldn't resist looking at the cufflink, nestled there in his palm. "What a lovely little thing," he said.

"I hope you mean the cufflink."

"Oh, if I was talking about your cock, then I'd be saying *what a lovely great big thing*," Leo assured him with a grin. Archie greeted that with a laugh and threw the other cufflink toward Leo, then began to unbutton the few buttons of his shirt that were still fastened.

Leo put the cufflinks in his breast pocket, then he shifted in his seat, watching Archie's show. Slowly, slowly, more of Archie's chest appeared. He looked after himself, that much was clear. He was sculpted, perfect.

Leo swallowed. "It's nice to see a seaworthy chap like you. I'd have no qualms about having you on board."

"Shirt on?" Archie asked. "Or off?"

Leo swung his draped leg and said, "Oh…will you roll up your sleeves?"

And without questioning it, Archie did just that. There was the face of the elegant vintage watch again, while his forearms were as sculpted as the rest of his body. And tonight, he was all Leo's.

"Will you come over here?" Leo asked, his voice soft. Archie cocked his head to one side and smiled, then crossed the floor to stand before Leo. The spicy scent of his cologne was intoxicating, just like the blazing blue of his eyes.

Leo reached for Archie and laid his hand flat on Archie's stomach where it was visible through his opened shirt. Leo sighed to touch it, then he began to run his hand upward, stroking Archie's chest.

"Even more lovely than I'd hoped," Leo whispered.

"And all yours." Archie leaned lower and brushed a kiss to Leo's mouth. "However you want me."

Leo toyed with Archie's shirt, aware of a twitch from Archie's erection inside his shorts. "Can I ask…how do you want *me*? I'm an obliging sort of captain."

"How do I want you?" Archie purred, teasing his lips against Leo's. "Happy, hard and very much the boss. For now, at least."

Leo laughed as he stroked down Archie's torso and tugged at the waistband of the shorts. "For now? Do *you* like to be the boss sometimes, Archie?"

"Well, y'know…maybe now and then. But not tonight." He dropped to his knees in front of Leo's chair and stroked his hand over Leo's thigh until he could cup his erection through the stiff tweed. "Tonight, you're the captain."

A thrill shot through Leo. He affectionately ruffled Archie's hair as he said, "Take me in your mouth."

Archie met Leo's gaze again as he slowly unfastened his straining trousers. He slid his hand inside, curling his fingers around Leo's erection as he freed it.

"Now *that* is quite something."

Leo groaned at the contact, trying to stop his hips from rising into Archie's touch. How was he going to last when Archie did anything else to him?

"And it's all for you," Leo murmured. "It's all because you're so bloody hot."

Archie ringed his fingers around the base of Leo's erection. Then he drew the tip of his tongue along the length, teasing circles when he reached the tip.

Leo combed his hand through Archie's hair. "That tongue of yours…it's the sort of tongue that could get a man in trouble."

"I hope so," Archie murmured. He took the very tip of Leo's erection between his lips, and Leo felt the stroke of his tongue again.

Leo's grip tightened in Archie's hair. He didn't mean to, he didn't want to hurt him, but sharp bursts of pleasure were playing through his body, radiating out from the touch of Archie's tongue, and Leo was so aroused that he couldn't stop.

"You're good, you know," Leo moaned. "Bloody good."

Archie slid lower until Leo's cock was fully in his mouth. Then he began to rise and fall on him, his lips tightening and his tongue lathing against Leo's body as he moved. There were the little moans too, purred sounds of pleasure from deep in Archie's throat.

Leo hadn't been lying when he'd said it. Archie's mouth was magical, drawing Leo on but simultaneously holding him back, teasing him, making it all last longer.

Leo moaned, and in reply, Archie tightened his lips just a little more. He closed his hand over Leo's thigh as he moved faster.

How the bollocks could I have thought this man was straight?

Leo moved his hips, just a little, with Archie's movements. He knew what he was doing. *Oh, he really, really does.* The thought of romping with Archie in that huge bed burst in on Leo's mind and he pictured him on the bed, those blue eyes sparkling at him, inviting him, teasing him.

And with that, Leo's hips jerked and a sensation like falling and flying together took over his body as he came.

"Y-your captain is very pleased…" Leo murmured, valiantly trying to keep up their little game. Archie blinked up at him as he rocked back on his knees, releasing Leo's softening erection with a teasing slowness. Then he drew his tongue over his lips and smiled.

"You have the most wonderful cock, you know," he informed Leo. "I could've happily done that all night."

"That sounds like a pretty good way to spend a night!" A tremble ran through Leo and he reached for Archie's hand. He twined their fingers as he said, "That was amazing."

"You're absolutely beautiful," Archie told him. "But I've a feeling you must know that?"

Leo blinked at him. He could feel the heat of a blush building in his face. "Oh, stop it!"

"Why?" Archie shook his head, offering Leo a grin. "If you're gorgeous, why shouldn't I tell you? You. Are. *Beautiful.*"

Leo chuckled and brought their joined hands to his lips. He kissed them softly. "I like it when handsome men say things like that to me. Especially when it's *you.*"

What a perfect distraction Archie was from the cares of Leo's day. From his smile to his body to *everything*, he was just what Leo might've wished for and never expected to actually have. Everything he couldn't have now.

"What would you like now, Captain?"

"I want to undress you," Leo said. "I want to see what's in your shorts."

"Be my guest," was the murmured response.

Leo brought his mouth to Archie's as he swept the shirt from his broad shoulders and down his sculpted arms. His eyes were closed as their kiss deepened, but Leo explored him by touch alone, all those firm muscles under soft, smooth skin. And what cheeky, pebbled nipples he had too, which Leo tweaked as they kissed.

He loved the gasps and moans his touch drew from Archie, each filled with more need and desire than the last. Archie's fingers combed through Leo's hair, twining in the strands as they kissed again and again.

Between kisses, Leo whispered, "How long can you bear to wait?"

"As long as you can bear to make me," Archie assured him.

Leo laughed. "That might not be very long if I'm totally honest! But your captain will try his best."

"You know…" Archie's lips slid over Leo's jaw until he could catch Leo's earlobe with his teeth, "Unless you have to rush off, we have all night."

"You'd like me to stay?" Leo swirled his hand in a circle across Archie's back. "I'd love to. Now, secret agent Archie, I hope you've got johnnies?"

"My sponge bag's in the bathroom. It's got everything we need."

"I'd better go and get it." Leo pulled up his zip and got up from the armchair, giving Archie a kiss before heading into the bathroom. He spent a moment admiring Archie's toiletries in their classic packaging. They looked very at home in the bathroom, standing near a bath with lion's feet.

Leo spotted an unzipped sponge bag on the side and peered into it.

We'll be needing these.

Leo left the bathroom, the sponge bag tucked under his arm. "Your captain has inspected your cargo. All is well."

"Perfect!" Archie was standing beside the window, holding two glasses of white wine, condensation beading on the chilled surfaces. He held one out to Leo. "Now, I *think* you said something about seeing what's in my shorts?"

"I want to know *all* about what's in there."

Leo put the sponge bag down beside the bed, then he went over to the window took the glass from Archie. He moved behind him, one arm around Archie's waist and his chin on his shoulder. He pressed a kiss to the back of Archie's neck and stood there for a moment, breathing in the warm scent of him. Outside the sky was darkening but London bustled on, lights appearing at windows across the skyline. In each of those rooms there must be another story, but none could match theirs, Leo was sure.

Leo came around to stand next to Archie. He sipped his wine, smiling at the disheveled man. "To us," Leo said, and clinked his glass against Archie's. As Archie touched his glass to Leo's, he reflected that maybe disheveled wasn't the right word at all. As he was now, clad only in his shorts, watch and of course the gold signet ring, he looked as though he'd been styled by someone. Even his disordered hair, still mussed by Leo's fingers, managed to look artful.

"To us." Archie smiled then took a sip from his glass. "And lots of fun, don't you think?"

"Oh, yes. Lots." Leo drank his wine, sharp and fruity at the same time. "Once you've finished your wine, I think it might be time you tested my knots, don't you?"

"Do you really want to wait that long?" Archie walked the tips of his fingers down Leo's back. Then he took a leisurely sip and said, "I'm terribly keen, Captain."

"That's just what I like to hear from my crew," Leo said. "Let's go over to the bed. If you're good, I'll let you have some wine once you're tied up."

"Depends on what you mean by *good*." He slapped Leo's bottom again. "But I'll do my best."

"That's the kind of *good* I like!" Leo told him as he went over to the bed. "But those hands of yours need securing so I know where they are."

Archie unfastened his watch and put it down on the bedside table, placing his glass beside it. Then he settled his hands on his hips.

"Shorts off? Or would you rather do the honors yourself?"

Leo folded his arms, admiring the straining shorts. He raised one eyebrow and gave a curt, one-word order. "Strip."

And on Leo's instruction, Archie slid his thumbs beneath the waistband of his shorts and brought them down.

Leo couldn't hold back the gasp that escaped him as he saw Archie's extraordinary nudity revealed to him.

And that cock.

It delivered what it had promised and more. Girthy and long, standing proud. The sight of it fanned Leo's erection back to life.

"Fucking hell, you're magnificent," Leo said.

"It's very kind of you to say. I do my best," was Archie's fruity reply. Then he laid down on the bed, louche and irresistible. "Captain, I'm ready for you."

"You definitely are." Leo took off his shoes and socks and joined Leo on the bed. His heart hammered, sending a tremble into his voice as he commanded, "Arms up behind your head. Grab the headboard nice and tight."

Archie reached up and wrapped his fingers around the metal headboard. He tensed his arms, peacocking for Leo. And with arms like that, why not?

Leo bent down to kiss his biceps. "That's it. That's perfect." He leaned over Archie, his tie still dangling unfastened around his neck, and said, "Take my tie. With your teeth."

With a playful growl, Archie caught Leo's tie in his teeth. He turned his head and drew the tie from beneath Leo's collar.

Leo ruffled Archie's hair. "Thank you." Then he took the tie from Archie's mouth, kissed him with a quick tease of his tongue, then bound Archie's wrists to the bedhead.

Leo stroked Archie's chest, admiring the view of the tethered, aroused Adonis before him. "How's that feel? Too tight, too loose?"

"It feels perfect." Archie quirked his eyebrow then tensed his arms against the silk tie. "How do I look? Will I do, Captain?"

"You'll do, oh yes…" Leo planted a kiss on Archie's chest then roamed over his skin to meet his lips. He teased Archie, taking his lips away before returning them, kissing him deeply.

"Leo…" he gasped, the word somewhere between a whisper and a groan.

Leo still kissed him as he caressed his way down Archie's body and closed his hand around Archie's erection. Leo moaned as he assessed Archie's size, then he stroked his hard length. Archie's hips jerked toward him and he rolled his head back against the pillow, his full lips parting to exhale a decadent sigh.

Leo could happily listen to that sigh forever. He took great delight in stroking again and again, wanting to hear Archie sigh once more. Leo watched Archie's face, seeing his closed eyes, his lips still parted. Then he tensed his arms, his back arching, and there was that sigh again. It sent fresh heat soaring through Leo's blood.

Leo kissed his way around Archie's face, running his tongue over his neat, graying sideburns. He pressed his mouth to Archie's ear and whispered hotly, "Do you want me naked, darling?"

"Yes," he breathed, watching Leo through dreamy eyes.

Leo couldn't resist teasing his captive audience. He gave Archie one last smooch then he escaped from the bed and stood at its foot. Very slowly he slipped his jacket down from his shoulders, then unbuttoned his waistcoat, turning away from Archie a little to draw out his anticipation.

"I'm quite a shy captain, really," Leo cooed in a voice that was anything but.

"Well, I know all about shy," Archie teased. "I'm all sorts of retiring."

Leo threw his waistcoat across the room. "See? I'm a wallflower..." Then he began to unbutton his shirt, turning his back to Archie as he watched him over his shoulder. He looked magnificent against the white sheets, just a hint of a winter tan still on his skin. Then there was that erection, standing proud from his body.

Leo turned back just as he undid the final button, then he threw his shirt open with all the vim of a stripper. He nudged his shirt off and dropped it at his feet.

"Does your captain please you?" Leo asked Archie as he started to undo his trousers.

"My captain is bloody perfect," Archie told him with a smile. "Thank God you decided to stop for a beer."

"Best beer I've ever had!"

Leo swiped back his fallen fringe then went on unfastening his trousers. He didn't turn away this time, instead fixing his gaze on Archie. He brought his shorts down with his trousers and in one swift movement, Leo was naked.

"Hellooo," Archie smiled, giving the fruitiest greeting Leo had ever heard. "Ready to board, Captain?"

Leo put his hand on one hip and posed for Archie. "Very. And you? Or is that a pointless question?"

"I'm very, very ready," he replied, shifting sensuously against the covers. It was another touch of peacocking, and Leo wasn't about to complain.

Leo went over to the bedside table and unwrapped the box of condoms that he'd found in the spongebag. "A box of twelve? Well, we won't be getting any sleep tonight, will we!"

He removed one from the box, and got back onto the bed, bringing some lube with him. A box of twelve condoms, Archie tied to the bed and the whole night before them. It was certainly going to be one to remember.

Before he did anything else, Leo rubbed Archie's arms. "There. We don't want them getting stiff. Unlike a certain other part of your anatomy."

Leo kissed his arms, then he prepared Archie's erection. He straddled him, wholly aware of the strength in Archie's body and how it was restrained. Then he slowly brought his hips down onto Archie at the same moment as he sank into a kiss, his arms curling around Archie, holding him close, as their bodies joined in bliss.

There was such a fierce hunger in Archie's lips that it stole Leo's breath. He lifted his head from the pillow to chase Leo's kiss, the gesture filled with need. Leo began to move against Archie, rocking his hips as he pressed his mouth to Archie's. Their tongues darted and stroked, and Leo thought of nothing but this very moment with this man and the intense pleasure he gave him.

Archie matched the rhythm of Leo's hips with his own, thrusting against him as they went on kissing. He caught Leo's lip softly with his teeth, teasing into another kiss. Leo moaned. This man was full of surprises. As they kissed, Leo caressed one hand up to Archie's arms, soothing him as they moved together, bringing each other closer and closer to their release.

His arms were so wonderful to caress, firm and toned and sculpted. Archie's fingers were curled around the intricate headboard, holding onto it as he thrust his hips harder, every breath a sensuous moan.

Leo needed this badly. An all-in libidinous adventure, a good, hard fuck. Archie was an amazing lover, and as Leo's pleasure built, he wished it wasn't their one and only encounter. But it would have to be. And he would enjoy it as best he could, and not wish for the impossible.

"You—" Archie gasped the word against Leo's lips, "are bloody gorgeous. You feel wonderful—"

That fruity voice.

"You're a splendid fuck," Leo whispered. "You're amazing to have inside me."

"A splendid fuck…" Archie purred. He flicked his tongue against Leo's lips. "From one to another…"

"Bet you can go all night. A man can dream."

Pleasure curled up from the center of Leo's being, spreading into his limbs, filling him and taking him over with bliss. Archie seemed to intuit exactly the moment that Leo reached his peak and he quickened his pace and thrust harder, sending them tumbling into pleasure together.

Chapter Five

Leo sank down, his head on Archie's shoulder. He trembled as the last aftershocks of his pleasure worked themselves out and he breathed out heavily.

"Archie... Fucking hell, I can't move. That was intense."

"It was wonderful," Archie murmured through a contented sigh. He shifted beneath Leo then kissed his hair. "What a night..."

"I'll just untie you. Hang on a mo'." Leo reached up and with one lazy flick of his hand released Archie from his bonds. A second later, Archie's arms were around Leo, holding him tight. It was just what he needed, tenderness after their wild encounter.

Leo brushed his lips against Archie's cheek as he snuggled against him. His lovely, strong body, all warm and safe.

"So you liked being tied up?" Leo asked. "Your arms looked fantastic, by the way. So defined."

"I loved it," Archie told him breathlessly. "And I get the feeling you did too?"

"Of course! I've got to say, it's not like my go-to, routine sort of…y'know, *thing*. But it's fun sometimes, isn't it?" Leo said. "Big strong naked man, restrained. It's erotic."

Archie's gaze was heavy with contentment. He drew his fingertips down the length of Leo's back and replied, "And a lot of fun."

"Are you into that sort of thing usually?" Leo asked, trembling in the wake of Archie's fingertips. "Getting tied to the bed?"

"Would you believe it was my first time?" He widened his eyes. "But hopefully not *our* last?"

"Your first? Really? Wow." Leo swallowed, trying to find some way to answer that question without hurting the man. Archie wanted more, and Leo did too, but it could never, never happen. "Our last? You never know!"

Not a flat no. And it was true, maybe they *might* meet again. Maybe in a year's time when Leo would be the gay divorcee.

Archie curled his arm around Leo's neck and drew him down for a kiss. "You never know," he murmured. "And you look like the sort of guy who has a *lot* of silk ties."

"I've got a few, that's for sure." Leo did his best to smile. His first time being tied up, and he'd trusted Leo, and Leo couldn't even… It might not've worked out anyway. He was lovely and posh, and handsome and tremendous in bed. But it might not've worked out even if they'd had the chance. Leo kissed him passionately, wanting to give Archie as much pleasure as he could in the narrow piece of time allotted to them.

"What shall we do with our stolen evening?" Archie's strong hands swept down to cup Leo's buttocks. "It's still early."

"I think" — Leo paused as he glanced around the room — "we should drink some more wine and make the most of this bed."

"That sounds like a wonderful plan to me." Archie smiled, then glanced down at his chest. "Do you mind if I grab a quick shower? Or *we* could grab a quick shower, if you fancy it."

"A shower for two is definitely on the menu." Leo pushed himself up from Archie. "We're a hot mess!"

It felt perfectly normal to step into the shower with Archie, as though they'd known each other far longer than one evening. Leo would have met up again in a heartbeat if only he could have, but he couldn't. Maybe one day, though, when wills and bequests and marriages were all history?

Anything's possible.

They stood under the pulsing hot water, smoothing their hands over each other's bodies, exploring and enjoying. They fitted together so well that Leo couldn't believe all they'd ever have was tonight.

The man's perfect, for heaven's sake. He has sparkling blue eyes. And an amazing cock that he definitely knows what to do with. And arms — oh, the most beautiful arms.

"Leo the captain..." Archie put his arms around Leo's waist. He tilted his chin, considering Leo for a few moments. "How do you get a job like yours? I'm mildly envious, you know."

"I was recruited by a civil servant in a raincoat one day," Leo joked. "You know how it is, being in the secret service."

"Oh, absolutely," his companion nodded. "We'll probably have to escape by speedboat before the night's out. I'll do my best to be dashing just for you."

Escape.

Leo blinked in the falling water. There would be an escape before the night was out, but it wouldn't be together. It couldn't be.

How could I have known he'd want more?

Leo lathered up and rubbed bubbles over Archie's body, committing each curve and plane, each muscle, to his memory.

"You don't have to try hard to be dashing," Leo observed.

"And you don't have to try to be beautiful." Archie kissed Leo's jaw. "Or sexy." He kissed his lips, running his hands through Leo's wet hair. "Or to get me hard."

Bloody wills, bloody Conrad bloody Beaucock.

More like no cock.

Leo closed his hand around Archie's rejuvenated erection, a glorious column of promised pleasure. "You are one keen bloke, Archie. Not to mention a big bloke…"

Archie tipped his head back and closed his eyes as the water splashed over his face. Then he shook his hair and blinked, focusing on Leo again.

"I want you," he whispered.

Leo watched as the water rolled down Archie's face. "Then have me. Have me and enjoy me."

And forgive me, please forgive me, when I walk away.

Leo had had other lovers but as he and Archie kissed beneath the warm shower water, their hands caressing and exploring, he knew that none of them had captured him quite like Archie. How cruel that he should meet him when he wasn't even looking. What a bastard fate could be. And how perfect Archie was.

They got out of the shower and, still kissing, wrapped themselves up in the fluffiest towels Leo had ever seen, then they went back to the bedroom.

"To us." Archie picked up the wineglasses and offered one to Leo. "And our terribly decadent night of passion."

Leo took the glass and joined in the toast. But he added silently, *Our only night together*.

Leo was enjoying it, and Archie was enjoying it, and that was the main thing. Their one night was fantastic.

Leo sipped his wine, then he said, "You're so trim. Do you swim or something?" He dotted a kiss to Archie's broad shoulder.

And what a shoulder it is.

"I love to swim. I just empty my head—which isn't difficult—and plunge into the sea," Archie told him. Leo pictured it, Archie's strong arms cutting through the water, his toned back glistening in the sun. "There's something about swimming in the sea, don't you think?"

"The waves and the currents carrying you along…" Leo remembered swimming off Kefalonia last summer, diving from the deck of the *Aphrodite*. And now he added Archie to the memory, swimming toward him, his powerful arms turning through the clear water. A holiday they'd never have. "It's blissful, bobbing about in the sea."

"I always think best when I'm swimming and trying not to think at all," Archie admitted, then drew back the rumpled duvet and cast off his towel, throwing it onto the desk. "It's heaven."

Leo took his towel off as well and hung it over the back of a chair. He climbed into the vast bed and snuggled down beside Archie. With a wink he said, "Swimming is great, but sex is more fun!"

"I'm all for fun..." Archie reached across to put his glass down on the table. Then he kissed Leo's shoulder and said, "Especially with you."

Leo glanced up. His tie was still dangling on the bed frame, but he didn't want to use it this time. All the same, he left it there, a cheeky reminder of what had gone on earlier. He put his glass down beside Archie's, then he lay back on the bed and gazed up Archie.

He kissed Leo's shoulder again, then nuzzled his way up to his earlobe. "What's your favorite thing, Leo? What can I do for you?"

Leo circled his toes against Archie's leg. "Tying you up was fun, but I want to feel your arms around me."

And what arms they were. Archie took Leo in his embrace and kissed him. It was a long, slow smooch, and Leo reveled in it. As much as Leo loved being the captain and tying up men with fine arms, this was just as good.

Where have you been all my life, Archie?

And why is this all we'll ever have?

The kiss went on and on, their tongues exploring, stroking and caressing, and as it did, Archie danced his fingertips down Leo's chest. He took their erections together in his hand, the strokes assured and tender.

Leo tweaked at Archie's nipples, though it was hard to keep his fingers from slipping as pleasure swelled within him. He loved the sounds of Archie's sighs and gasps, the way they caught in his throat or slipped into their kisses. And he loved the touch of his lover's body where it pressed to his.

"I want you," Leo murmured. He wasn't the captain when he said, "Please, Archie."

"Oh, Leo..." Archie reached over to the packet on the bedside table. "You're just — you're lovely."

Leo kissed Archie as he prepared himself. The heat of their bodies and the sound of their breathing aroused Leo to a pitch of anticipation that made him tremble.

And that was before Archie slid his arm around Leo's waist. He stroked his fingers down the cleft of Leo's buttocks, teasing him.

Leo moaned at Archie's touch, longing for their bodies to combine again. Archie's fingers stroked deeper as he moved over Leo, easing his legs higher until he could feel the tip of his erection, promising the pleasure to come.

Leo brushed Archie's face, gazing into eyes bluer than any ocean he'd ever dived into before. "You're wonderful," Leo murmured. And there was that smile again, warm and affectionate and intoxicating. It was the sort of smile Leo would never tire of.

And it was a lovely smile to kiss, as if Archie transmitted joy through it. Leo wrapped his arms around Archie and looped his legs around Archie's waist, wanting to be as close to him as he could be. As Archie brought their bodies together again, he pressed his lips to Leo's ear and whispered, "We should come back here, don't you think?"

A moan fluttered from Leo's lips, drowning his answer. It was neither a yes nor a no.

As they moved together, Leo daydreamed that they could have more. What a lovely thought, to be one half of *we* with a man like Archie. The sort of man Leo always hoped to meet but had never thought he actually would. And now he had and...it was a dream.

A lovely, impossible dream, but it was real enough as Leo gazed up at Archie.

They moved together in the moonlight, a dance that was instinctive and felt perfectly natural. Archie knew how to make Leo sigh and Leo drew the sweetest moans from his lover in turn.

"You're perfect," Leo told him, his breath catching as pleasure washed through him for the third time that night.

"I'm really not," Archie whispered. He flicked his tongue against Leo's ear. "But you can keep saying it,"

That teasing tongue unleashed bliss, and Leo moaned as his body trembled with it, helpless in Archie's embrace. He was everything Leo was looking for and here he was in Leo's arms, both of them joined in bliss.

They kissed each other tenderly as they returned to earth, and Leo gazed at Archie's languid, content expression.

He would never, ever forget him.

As the night drew on, they laughed and kissed and snuggled beneath the duvet, drinking the bottle dry in their sanctuary high above the city. If Leo could've stopped the clock, he would have, keeping the passing hours at bay so he could steal one more minute in Archie's arms. But he couldn't, all he could do was enjoy his lover's caresses and pretend that he wasn't somehow about to be engaged to his best friend.

There was so much to do, and the wedding had to look real. Rings, and dresses, stag and hen nights, wedding favors, and Leo wanted none of it. But what could he do? Gunther's words were clear. He had to marry, not a man but a woman.

Leo curled up against Archie. He wished he could let him in on the secret, try to make him understand. Ask him to wait for him until after the clause of Gunther's will was fulfilled and the money had passed safely into Leo's hands. But he couldn't risk losing the money, especially not to Conrad. And would Archie even believe him? *You're gorgeous and we've had a great time, but I've got to marry my best friend. Can you hang on a bit?*

He'd given Archie a night to remember, just as Archie had Leo, one last fling before Leo took a wife.

And as Archie's breathing evened out into a soothing, sleepy pattern, Leo laid in his arms and watched him slumber. How he wished he could be there in the morning to kiss Archie awake, but he couldn't. All they had was tonight.

Leo began to fall asleep himself, but he forced himself awake. He had to go. He reluctantly freed himself from Archie's arms, and in the pale glow of the bedside light, collected up his clothes. With a heart as heavy as lead, Leo went into the bathroom and got dressed. Then he went over to the desk and wrote a note.

Thank you for a wonderful evening, you gorgeous man. I'll never forget you. I wish I could tell you why I can't stay. Maybe we'll meet each other again one day? Maybe you'll forgive me. I hope so. I wish it could've been different. Leo x

Then he crossed over to the door. He opened it as quietly as he could. Archie was stirring, and Leo tried to stifle his panic. He was a coward, he knew that. He shouldn't run out on a sleeping lover, but Leo could see no other way.

Leo went out into the opulent corridor and closed the door behind him, leaving Archie to his dreams.

Chapter Six

A couple of days later, Leo met up with Liv again for lunch. He'd bought with him some wedding magazines, full of women with crisp ringlets wearing long silk gowns. Yet all he could think of was Archie, waking in that vast bed to nothing but a note. God, how ridiculous to miss a man he'd only known for one heady night.

But I do miss him. Because I never got to know him.

As he sat down opposite Liv, he said, "My mum saw them. I felt more awkward than the time she found my copy of *Attitude* under the bed."

"I talk about you a lot at home already, so hopefully it won't get Dad's Spidey-senses tingling when he finds out we're more than friends." Liv spun one of the magazines toward her. "How're you going to convince your folks that you've suddenly gone straight? Or are you going to let them in on it?"

Leo stuck his hand inside his pocket and fiddled with the cufflinks that he'd been carrying about since he'd arrived home from London. Archie had more to curse him for than just walking off after their night together — Leo had accidentally taken his cufflinks home with him. *And where the hell is my tie?* Leo had fallen asleep on a step outside Victoria station, waiting for a train home. He must've dropped it because he'd been so tired. That poor, elegant length.

But Leo hadn't left the cufflinks on his bedside table, he took them everywhere, fiddling and fussing with the exquisite silver pieces, and seeing nothing before him other than Archie's face.

"I — I told her that sexuality is a spectrum," Leo explained. "That until now I'd thought I was gay, but I'd never met the right woman. And now I have and — and we love each other very much and we want to get married."

"Wow." She winced. "So...how're we going to do this? I really ought to meet them and you need to meet Pops. Maybe not today though, he's been in an odd mood all weekend. Super grumpy, which is not Pops' usual style at all!"

"Yeah, there needs to be a family do, doesn't there?" Leo grimaced. "My mum's going on about buying a new hat, and she's really excited about meeting you. She's confused, I think it's fair to say, and she said she'd handle Dad. I mean, it's kind of odd that me marrying a woman is weirding my parents out more than coming out. They just went, *Darling, we know,* but this? Well, it's got to be done."

Liv smiled and opened the magazine. "Dad's just... He's very *astute.* It's a barrister thing. I was wondering, maybe you could come over to the yacht for dinner one night and we can tell him together? What do you think?"

Leo nodded. "Good idea. And I can impress him with my yacht knowledge. It comes across as manly. I'll tell Mum and Dad not to say anything about the whole *being gay* thing to your dad. Not until after the wedding, anyway."

"Yeah, he's so out and proud that it might be wise." Liv nodded. "So what do your folks think about you owning a classic yacht? I'm guessing you're not going to mention the whole *million pounds* side of it?"

"I haven't said a word about the money," Leo replied. He flipped through one of the magazines too and found himself entranced by a fashion shoot for dads at weddings. So many hot silver foxes, and he'd found his very own. And had to walk away. "There's some bits and bobs they need doing around the house, and Mum really wants to go to Australia to see her sister, so I'll nudge some of the money their way and say it came from a client. It's not a lie, not exactly, but I'll never tell them about the million. As for the boat… Yeah, I've told them about that. They can't wait for me to take them out on it, but my dad's already fussing because he can't see how I'll afford the upkeep. I've got my savings until the legacy comes in, I suppose. Might pick up some work at the marina."

"You definitely *will*." She flipped over a few pages, revealing a splash photograph of extravagant floral displays. "All the weekend sailors are rocking up to get their boats ready for the nice weather, so there's loads of work to do. For everyone like Pops, who straps on a tool belt and gets down to business, there're dozens of super-well-off Londoners who leave their poor old boats to fend for themselves over winter! If you want some cash, that's where you'll find it."

Because unlike Liv and her pops, most people didn't make their yacht their permanent home, did they?

"Why *has* your dad moved onto his yacht?" Leo asked. He looked up from a saccharine-sweet photo of toddlers in puffy pink dresses and tiny powder blue suits running about holding balloons. Would they have to find stunt toddlers from somewhere to make the wedding more realistic?

Liv took a sip of coffee and said, "Because he's from eccentric stock, why else? He spent half his childhood on a narrow boat and the other half touring India in a VW camper. He's not your run-of-the-mill barrister."

"Certainly doesn't sound it!" Leo gestured to a photo of a happy bride and groom being showered with confetti. "So he and your mum, right, they got married, then he came out?"

"Noooo," she said, and he heard again Archie's fruity *helloooo* in the hotel room. "He and Mum were best friends. They met in Thailand when they were about thirteen. All the parents were off smoking weed and buying really dodgy kaftans, so Pops and Mum hung out together instead."

Leo chuckled. "Bloody hell! Did your grandparents know Gunther, by any chance? So your dad and your mum, best friends, and— Pops was gay all along? I mean, I'm imagining your stoner grandparents wouldn't have cared one bit if he was gay?"

"God, not a bit! You'll have to meet them when they get home from their hols, they're super cool. Off in the VW camper again as we speak." Leo's own family was pretty unremarkable in most ways, but somehow Liv's seemed to suit her. No wonder she had taken to the crewing life so well. "So, Pops went to uni, and Mum opened a glassblowing studio and they were still the very best friends, but there wasn't any romance. Pop was out pretty much from the off. They were like you and me, basically. But hippies, hence the name."

Loveday, aka Liv. That explains it.

Leo whispered across the table to her, "But without the fake marriage." He turned the page of the wedding magazine and was presented with a photo of a very happy, very pregnant bride. "Was your mum a lesbian, and your dad, how can I put it, made a donation?"

"Spot on! And I was the result!" She smiled, a little sadly this time. "He was always around. Always *Pops*, but I knew they weren't a couple. But so what if they weren't, they were still awesome parents. And then Mum died, and there was just me and Pops. And that's how it's been ever since."

Leo clasped Liv's hand over the table. "God, that's so sweet. What an adorable pair your parents were, even if they weren't a couple. I can't say my birth was particularly exciting, although the river nearly flooded. But it didn't! You know, we should live together, shouldn't we? Does that make weddings seem more realistic? There's so much space on the *Aphrodite*, there's two huge bedrooms so we can have one each."

"Oh, that'll be so cool!" She beamed. "And we'll be in the marina, so I won't be far from Pops, either! Hang on, I've got a piccie of Mum and Pops on my phone."

Liv took her phone out of her bag, but after a few seconds spent tinkering, she tutted.

"No I haven't. I'm still trying to fathom this new bloody phone out, but I'll get there. Anyway, you'll meet him soon enough."

"Bit nervous," Leo admitted. He held his smile for as long as he could, but he ran out of energy and gripped the cufflinks tight in his pocket. "A bit sad, actually."

She frowned. "Tell Auntie Loveday all about it."

Leo sniffed. "I—I met this guy the other night. He was..." He'd not said a word to anyone, how could he have? But he couldn't bring himself to tell Liv he'd gone to bed with Archie. It felt like a betrayal even though their marriage was pretend. "He was perfect. Like a living dream. He was so gorgeous, and we got on really well. He very obviously liked me, I very obviously liked him. But...but I had to walk away. Because of all this." Leo slapped the wedding magazine on the table in front of him. "I'm not letting Conrad win, and I *will* get that money, and I *will* do good things with it. Far better things than Conrad would. But it was so hard, Liv. I keep thinking about him, I keep worrying that I've hurt him, because I couldn't tell him any of this, could I? I feel like such a bastard."

Liv left her seat and came around the table to hug Leo. The irony was she would be a wonderful, loving wife to some lucky fellow. But not to Leo. To Leo she was a best friend, almost a sister.

"Did you get his number?" she asked. "This isn't going to be forever. If I had the money, I'd pay for you to challenge that bloody legal decision. Who're they to say Gunny meant a wife? We knew him, they didn't. He didn't mean a wife, he just meant someone to love!"

Leo put his arm around Liv. She smelled of flowers and sunshine. "You'll think I'm stupid, but I could've fallen in love with him. And I didn't get his number. I didn't leave mine either, I didn't dare. Imagine if he rang and someone heard and realized... Oh, God, if I had his number, it'd be a constant temptation. And it's not fair on you, is it? You're my fiancée."

"Sweetie, I'm not really. I mean, I am, but I don't mind if you cheat on me with hot men!" She kissed Leo's cheek. "But I feel super paranoid, don't you? As though Conrad's probably put a microphone in my handbag! Do you think he's the sort to sniff around?"

"Probably, we're talking about a million quid after all." Leo sighed. "He seems the type who'd bend every law he can to get at it, and he's the sort of lawyer who could!"

Liv resumed her seat. "Then we have to be really, really careful," she concluded, glancing around. "And get the wedding done as soon as we can, but not so quick it looks like it's too quick. And we have to hold hands. Sorry, chickie, but we do!"

Leo held his hand out to her. "Just as well we get along, isn't it? When the *Aphrodite* arrives, shall we just move straight in? That'll be convincing, like we were waiting until we could get our own place. And Conrad'll struggle to infiltrate it, unless he's got hold of some sort of mini-submarine!"

She nodded. "And I was thinking about rings. Shall we wait until we've told Dad? We'll get something quirky and vintage, doesn't have to be pricy. You pay in case Conrad's somehow watching but I'll give you the money back. And then there's the wedding. We can't let our folks shell out for a fake wedding bash, can we? I say we be awfully independent, have a little quiet ceremony then a good old knees-up somewhere? No big sit-down dos in stately homes?"

Leo sighed with relief. "Oh, thank God you've said that! No sit down, three-course champagne supper, a disco with a buffet will do. We could hire the Sea Scouts' hut. Wedding in the registry office with a few flowers? Yeah, and the ring... Why are weddings so complicated? We could go and have a look for one now, if you like? Just see what there is."

"And if anyone insists on throwing gifts or cash at us...let's tell them to donate it to the seal hospital? Good karma for us *and* my little patients."

"Yeah, perfect!" Leo swallowed his tea. Thoughts were pinging around his head like a ball in a squash court and he tipped too much tea into his mouth. He spluttered. "This is going to be...interesting."

To put it mildly.

Liv nodded. "When's the *Aphrodite* due in the marina? If it's pretty soon, I thought maybe we could cook supper for Pops on board and tell him we're engaged?"

"I'm expecting her tomorrow. I've been sorting out the berth." Leo had been so obsessed with the million pounds, the fake wedding, his lost love and the looming evil of Conrad that he'd forgotten to be excited about finally owning his own yacht. He smiled at Liv. "It's a fucking huge berth! I'm lucky they had one free. And Gun kept her in such good nick, we can move straight in. Wonder if his champagne fridge is still full? It's just so amazing she's mine." Leo glanced over his shoulder. *Why was that man reading his newspaper upside down?* "I mean, ours."

Liv clapped her hands together. "I'll move in once Pops knows we're getting hitched, so it's not a massive avalanche of stuff. I can't wait!" She reached out and caught his fingers. "Come on, lover, let's go ring shopping!"

Chapter Seven

Leo stood on the pontoon watching the skipper edge the *Aphrodite* into her berth. She really was quite a boat, and he still couldn't believe she was really his.

But the next thing he knew, he was signing a document to say he'd received her, and the skipper handed over the keys. Leo smiled when he noticed they still had Gunther's key ring, an enameled woman in a bikini. The crew climbed onto the pontoon, their kit bags slung over their shoulders. Then they were off, heading to their next adventure, leaving Leo to his.

Leo walked over the gangplank and wandered about the deck, running his hands over the masts and the furled sails, over the carving of the bosomy Aphrodite who hung over the prow.

Mine.

A beautiful piece of craftsmanship, and full of so many memories of his time working for Gunther. The parties, the music, the laughter, the lazy afternoons in the sun, the late mornings when they'd all had breakfast on deck courtesy of the world's most underworked cook.

Working for Gunther had never felt much like work.

Leo went down the companionway into the yacht and turned on the radio to hear to the chatter at sea and on shore, courtesy of sailors, the marina, the coast guard, and the lifeboat. Some of the conversation was about "*that bloody big boat that's just gone into the marina*," but as the hiss of voices blended in the background, Leo took the ship in the bottle from the shelf and sat in the plush lounge, alone, and gazed at Gunther's most prized possession.

Not the yacht, not a million pounds, but a tiny square rigger in a bottle, whose sails trembled as Leo held it on the palm of his hand.

Gunther had adored his Mäuschen, and Leo wondered if he would ever love someone as much. He could have fallen in love with Archie, but he'd had no choice but to abandon him, and it hurt to think of what he'd lost. Only a fool would walk away from a million pounds for the sake of a stranger.

And I'm not a fool.

I can keep telling myself that, Leo decided as he glanced around, spotting the little spaces here and there where items must have been taken to fulfil the bequest for Conrad Beaucock. The porthole ashtray had gone, so too had the little lighthouse lava lamp that had once stood in the window. Leo remembered that lamp in particular because he had always made sure one of the crew had the job of snatching it to safety whenever they encountered rough seas. And now it belonged to Conrad Beaucock, who would probably have already thrown the whole lot in the dustbin.

"Oi, Levi!" A voice rang out from the deck. It was sneering, angry. Could it be Conrad himself? Did thinking of him conjure him into being? "Anyone home?"

Leo steeled himself. He carefully put the ship in a bottle back on the shelf and poked his head out of the companionway. Conrad Beaucock, in his pinstripes, on Leo's deck. And next to him, a huge cardboard box, its sides stamped *Fragile.*

"Conrad? What the hell are you doing on my boat?"

"Dropping off this stack of tat that was delivered to my penthouse. Lava lamps? Fishing nets?" He gave the box a nudge with his foot. "You're welcome to it, mate. Maybe you can sell it off to fund the massive legal bill you're about to be hit with when I challenge this bollock of a will in court and get it thrown out!"

"Careful! Some of that's fragile." Leo dragged the box away from him. He opened the flaps and took out a ceramic duck wearing a rubber ring. "Do I need to sign something to say you've willingly passed your bequest onto me? Because if you're going to fling threats of legal action around, I don't want you claiming I nicked a singing trout or a light-pull shaped like a beach hut."

Conrad took an envelope from his pocket and thrust it toward Leo. "Here. This is a signed declaration that I've passed this shit back to you. You're welcome to it."

And I'm glad to have it back. This is where it belongs.

"Thank you," Leo said. He could see some friends of his who worked on the marina approaching, pointlessly coiling ropes and prodding fenders, their eyes fixed on Conrad. He'd been rude to them, Leo was sure, barging his way into the marina with the box of boat jumble. "Would you mind sodding off now?"

Conrad leaned closer and whispered, "Lawyer up, buddy-bumboy, and I'll see you in court."

Then he turned and strode from the deck, leaving an acrid cloud of aftershave in his wake.

Leo poked out his tongue and stuck up his finger at Conrad's retreating back. A childish move, but it was cathartic.

He took the ceramic duck and sat on the edge of the boat, swinging his legs over the side. Had Gunther bargained for Conrad being so litigious? Leo was going to have to watch his back, and his front, and everything else because Conrad was determined to bleed him dry. Not because he needed the money, but because he was a bully who always wanted to win. He'd already robbed Leo of the man of his dreams, and he was revving up to take his inheritance and leave him with legal bills he could never afford.

But Leo didn't like bullies. Conrad was no doubt hoping he would be scared of the legal fees and hand over his inheritance now, without a fight. Leo shook his head.

"I'm the bloody captain, you pinstriped turd," Leo said to the air. "And you're not going to win."

What if Conrad *did* take him to court though? Leo couldn't afford the vast legal costs that were bound to rack up, and the very idea of selling the *Aphrodite* to fund them was unthinkable. What if he'd thrown away a chance of more with Archie and lied to his family about the engagement for nothing?

I might still lose it all.

Chapter Eight

Leo adjusted fast to his new home on the yacht. He'd lived on it before, of course, but under sunnier skies. Yet there was lots to do to turn it into his home, rather than a museum to Gunther. Leo bought cushions and tea towels, and his parents dropped things round from home—his favorite mug, framed photos, his books and the clutter and odds and ends that made up a life.

To avoid going through his savings, Leo picked up some work on other yachts, priming engines and shinnying up masts to fix troublesome sails. He took a nervous owner out for a spin on their new boat and he leaned into the rushing wind, so glad to be moving across the water again, if only for a little while.

Each morning, as he drank his tea on deck, he heard the chorus of the seagulls, the chug of marine diesel engines heading out to sea, and the cheery roar of an old car. He spotted it eventually, a little black vintage MG zooming out of the marina, presumably belonging to someone else who lived on a boat there.

He still thought of Archie, though. One morning the cloudless blue sky matched the color of Archie's eyes, and Leo hurried inside the *Aphrodite* to press his face into the cushions, hiding from the memories it heaved up. He even thought he saw Archie once or twice, at a distance on the pontoons. The same assured bearing, the same dark-blond hair. Leo's heart beat painfully, but it was only his mind playing tricks on him. Archie was lost to him forever.

Everything seemed calculated to make him feel guilty, but nothing stung more than the excruciating lunch he and Liv shared with his parents at their home in Newhaven. It was all so lovely, so friendly, and it was all a lie. He was lying to his mum and dad, to himself, and Liv was about to do the same to her own father, the only parent she had. That thought tormented Leo as he stacked the dishwasher, watching his father tour Liv around his colorful garden. She was beaming as she followed, her ponytail bouncing high on her head, and Leo felt more wretched than ever. What a thing she was doing for him. She was the best friend he'd ever had.

"Well, Liv's lovely," Leo's mum commented breezily as she ambled into the kitchen. "I'm still surprised, but it's all happening, isn't it? You've got a yacht, you're engaged... Are you sure this is what you want, Leo?"

He saw Archie again, in the shower, water cascading over his toned body.

No, it's not.

But Leo nodded. "Yes. It's exciting. It just feels right, you know? Being with Liv. It feels *right*. I know you must think it's sudden, but Liv and I were friends for ages and one day we realized it was more. Took me by surprise! A very nice surprise, though."

"It's a big thing, love." She crossed the kitchen and patted Leo's shoulder. Though her tone and expression were gentle, he knew her well enough to know that there was doubt there too. And who could blame his own mother for that? "I just want you to be definite, that's all."

"I—I am. We are. Me and Liv. I miss her all the time when we're apart. She makes me happy. Complete." Leo felt as if he were listening to someone else's words. *Oh, Archie, I miss you.* "So…so getting married, it seems the natural step."

His mum pecked a kiss to his cheek. "She's lovely," she told him. "And so are you. We're so proud of you, Leo, whatever you do."

"Thanks, Mum." Inside, Leo shriveled with shame. How proud would they be of him if they knew he was lying to them? He gave her a hug, hoping she wouldn't wonder why it was the sort of clingy hug children give in the interval between breaking something and their parents discovering the shattered pieces. "You and Dad are the best."

"Liv's dad a lucky bloke. He's getting the best son-in-law he could wish for."

"We'll have to have a nice do, won't we?" Leo said. "Everyone meeting up. Lovely." *Oh, horrors, can't I just put up the sails and run?*

He hadn't even been tempted to pop over to Liv's yacht to introduce himself. In fact, he'd taken the long way around the network of pontoons to keep as far from Liv's dad as possible. The thought of meeting the man scared him witless—a barrister fixing him with his beady eye and spotting within seconds that Leo was nothing but a no-good liar.

"We'll have a barbecue," said his mum, flicking the switch on the kettle. "But you've got to meet him first. Let me know when you have, and we'll invite him over!"

"Barbecue? Great!" All Leo could see in his mind was the massive metal fork his dad used to turn the meat and poke steaks with as they cooked. If he wasn't careful, Liv's dad would be using it on *him*. "He's a barrister. Dad could ask him for tips about next door's leylandii."

"Give him my phone number," she said. "And tell him I can't wait to meet him."

"Will do! I'm sure he can't wait to meet you guys." Leo released his mum from the hug and said, "Could you do me a favor, though? When you meet him, could you just…not mention the whole *I used to be totally gay* thing? It's just, you know, sexuality is a spectrum and all that, but I'm not sure it's the sort of thing to talk about over the sausages."

A sausage of quite a different kind reared up at Leo, and he had to force away the memory of Archie's spectacular erection.

His mum's reply was a nod and the sort of noncommittal sound that did nothing to strike optimism into his heart. But things were what they were. Archie was lost and nothing Leo could do now would ever bring him back.

Chapter Nine

Leo set the table in *Aphrodite's* dining room for three. He tried to quieten his fear at the thought of Liv's dad's imminent arrival by remembering the wonderful parties that had once taken place in this very room. Gunther's shade would be pleased to see it being used for a gathering once more.

Although no one at Gunther's parties had ever been as nervous as Leo was right now.

He fiddled about in the galley kitchen, putting the finishing touches to the gigantic salmon he'd bought. No expense spared. He wanted Liv's dad to believe he was the sort of man who would look after his daughter.

Fortunately, the wine and champagne fridges were still nearly full with expensive bottles. How could Pops *not* be impressed by his soon-to-be son-in-law?

Five minutes.

Leo swallowed, his throat dry. He guzzled a glass of water and spilt half of it down his shirt, and nearly slipped in his sprint down the length of the boat to the bedroom to change. He hadn't wanted to wear the same outfit as he had on meeting Archie, but it was the first thing he saw in his wardrobe. He added a purple-blue tie.

Three minutes.

Leo paced up and down the length of the yacht, humming, swinging his arms, clicking his fingers, trying to work his nerves out of his system. He toyed with going up on deck, but something stilled him as he imagined Liv's *Pops* spying him from afar and deciding, through some unnamed skill, that his son-in-law-to-be was gay. Or that the marriage was fake, or *something*. What if being a barrister gave him some sort of magic power so he'd just *know*?

So many *what ifs*.

He froze when he heard footsteps on the pontoon.

Is it them? Is it him? I don't want to do this!

But Conrad's sneer appeared before him, floating disembodied like the Cheshire Cat's smile.

Leo *had* to see this through. It was a lie, but it was worth it to wipe that self-satisfied, arrogant smirk off Conrad's face.

"Come on, Pops," He heard Liv call over the sound of her shoes. "Wait until you get a look at Max's place *and* his cooking! Helloooo, Maxie, we're here!"

Where did Liv learn to do such a fruity hello?

Channeling his inner captain, Leo strode toward the companionway.

"Liv, honey! Give us a kiss and introduce me to the famous Pops!"

He saw two pairs of legs appear before they began to descend into the yacht. Something caught Leo off guard, and it took a moment for him to realize it was a scent.

The scent of Archie's cologne.

"Pops, meet my lovely Max!" There was Liv, standing right in front of him and behind her— *It can't be.* "Max, meet my lovely old Pops!"

I'm hallucinating. I must be.

Leo kissed Liv's cheek, hoping the few seconds it took would clear the apparition from his mind. But as he held out his hand to Pops, the man before him hadn't changed.

He was Archie. His dream man. Standing right there on the *Aphrodite.*

"Erm...Pops. Great to meet you. I'm...well, I'm Leo. Or Max. Leo Maxwell. It's a nickname, you see. Do I call you Pops as well?"

Archie took his hand, but his face was unreadable. Then he painted on a look of cheery greeting when he said, "Call me Archie. Pleased to meet you." He released Leo's hand. "I wasn't expecting— So, *Max*? Or Leo?"

"Just don't call him *daddy*," Liv teased. "We don't want people getting the wrong end of the stick, do we?"

A painful laugh escaped Leo. Was the boat moving, swaying under him? Is that why he was suddenly plagued with nausea? *Archie. Oh, fuck.* "No! Ha ha! No, we wouldn't want that! Fancy a drink? I think we could all do with a drink, couldn't we?"

"There's some bubbly in the fridge." Liv sidestepped around Leo, leaving him adrift, his gaze locked on Archie's. "Let's get it up on deck, shall we? Then we *might* have something to toast, Pops!"

What the hell do I have to celebrate? I went to bed with my best friend's dad!

"It's—it's a l-lovely evening for it," Leo stammered, as images of his naked limbs entwined with Archie's forced their way into his mind. "For a drink. On deck. Bubbles. For a toast. Lovely. Very nice."

And to think I hoped I might meet him again one day. But not like this. Nothing like this.

Archie took a deep breath. He looked even more gorgeous this evening, if that were possible, dressed in dark chinos and a pink shirt, his sleeves rolled up just as Leo had requested of him in the hotel room. The top buttons of his shirt were unfastened, affording a glimpse of his toned chest, but his eyes had lost their sparkle. Instead they were filled with something that seemed to hover between sadness and annoyance.

And who could blame him?

"I like your shirt," Leo said, as if trying to justify his gaze returning to it again and again. *Those arms. That chest.* But he quickly took another tack. The manly *I'm terribly straight* tack. As if Archie would believe him after what they'd got up to. "So what do you think of my little pad, then? Such a surprise to inherit her, but it means a lot. Where I met my future wife! I never thought at the time we'd one day call it home!"

Well, that's definitely not *a lie.*

"It's quite something," Archie replied with a studied politeness. Then he seemed to register something and asked in a tone that was every inch the outraged barrister, "Your future *wife*?"

Leo nodded, cursing his racing thoughts. "We...we're mad about each other. We... Sorry, I'm just so excited about it, we were going to tell you together and it just...popped out."

"Max!" Liv sounded at least as annoyed her father. "We were going to tell Pops over champagne! Why — Max!"

"Sorry, honey, it's just…nerves, you see." Leo held up his trembling hand. *Exhibit A, m'lud.* "We want to get married, me and Liv."

"Loveday?" Archie looked to his daughter. "Is that right?"

She held up the bottle of champagne. "We're in love, Pops, so put my Sunday name away! Let's go up on deck and get the champers poured, then you and Max can really get to know each other better!"

If only you knew.

Leo led the way back out on deck. He took a lighter from his pocket and was about to light the candles in little jars that he'd scattered about, when his heart squeezed in his chest. It was like that intimate booth he and Archie had—

I've burnt enough bridges. I may as well light bloody candles as well.

Leo gestured to the cushions he'd laid out and went on lighting the candles. He saw Archie again, in the shower, water cascading over his toned body. "Take a seat. Make yourself at home."

Archie settled into a seat, but Leo couldn't remember ever seeing anyone look quite so awkward as Archie did right now. *What must he be thinking? God, it doesn't bear imagining.* Leo, the fiancé who picked up men in London hotels?

God, no.

But there was no way Leo could explain. He winced as he sat down, Archie's cufflinks digging into his thigh. It wasn't *quite* the moment to return them.

"Lucky old Gunther always left his wine and champers well-stocked, isn't it?" Leo said. "You never know when you need to celebrate!"

"Don't sit down, Leo," Liv chided. "You're the hubby, so you open the bottle! Or Pops can!"

But Archie shook his head. "That's Leo's job, we're on his yacht, after all."

Liv handed the bottle to Leo then went and sat beside her father. She snaked her arm around his shoulders and asked in a soft voice, "Are you all right, Pop?"

"I'm fine." Archie smiled. "This is just...you're my daughter. It's a lot to take in. Congratulations, darling, I'm really proud to be your dad."

Dad.

Leo fixed his attention on the champagne bottle, gripping it manfully. And straight into his mind flashed an image of his hand around something else. Archie's magnificent —

He's my best friend's dad. I can't think about his cock.

Leo stood and peeled the foil from the bottle, then held it as far as he could from himself as he twisted and twisted the cork. It burst out, shooting off into the air, and as foam gushed over Leo's hand, a distant *plop* sounded on the air as the cork landed in the water.

"Quick, glasses!" Leo wheeled around, aiming the bottle at the champagne flutes on the little table. It was Archie who darted up to save the day, sweeping the glasses up and holding them beneath the flow of champagne. Liv gave a little shriek of excitement and clapped her hands together.

"My two favorite men!" she exclaimed.

"You've done that before!" Leo chuckled, in an attempt to engender some future son-in-law to future father-in-law *bonhomie*. Then wished he hadn't. And how would he get rid of the foam on his hand? He couldn't lick it off in front of Archie, could he?

"Full of surprises." Archie passed one glass to Liv and offered the other to Leo, his smile still fixed in place. Leo. The man who Archie must think was already cheating on his fiancée.

Leo glanced around and saw the ceramic duck in the rubber ring on top of the hatch where he'd left it. It was so incongruous there, but as Leo glanced at it, he saw Conrad's sneering face again, and he reminded himself of what he had to do. He and Liv *had* to get married. It was the only way.

"Archie—Pops—I would be honored if you would give me your blessing to marry your beautiful daughter, the woman I love."

Archie's gaze slipped from Leo's and settled on Liv. She cocked her head to the side and raised one eyebrow, the gesture unconsciously echoing her father. After a moment Archie lifted his chin and said, "She's the most precious thing in the world, Leo. Never, ever forget that."

Leo swallowed. Seeing them side by side, the similarity was so uncanny that he wondered how he hadn't spotted it in the hotel. The same color eyes, the fruity hello, the dark blond hair. Even that confident gait.

"I—I won't," Leo said. "I promise you, with all my heart, I'll look after her. I adore you, Liv. Will you marry me, darling?"

"Oh, Leo, you know I will!" Liv laughed and held up her glass. "A toast to the future!"

"To the future! To us! To everyone!" Leo clinked his glass against Liv's, then stretched to reach Archie's. Leo had a phobia when it came to toasts. He had to make his glass ting against every glass. And now, especially, he didn't want to leave any chance for bad luck to roll in.

"To a happy marriage," Archie said, not looking at Leo until he had no choice, then he darted a quick, cold glance in his direction.

He hates me.

Leo sipped his champagne, trying to decide what to do. Would Archie tell her? Should he tell Liv before Archie had the chance? *By the way, your dad gave me three orgasms in the space of one evening.* But the marriage *had* to look real. Even now, out in the twilit marina, someone might be watching, Conrad, or a hired hand, waiting for the truth to reveal itself.

"Leo, darling, would you like me to bring supper up?" Liv asked. "You and Pop can get to know each other?"

"Oh!" Leo had been hoping for a moment to slide off, but he knew it would be all too obvious that he was deliberately avoiding Archie if he insisted he go instead. "That would be great, darling, thank you. You know where everything is, don't you?"

"I lived on this boat for a year," Liv reminded him with a chuckle. She ruffled Leo's hair as she rose to her feet. "Don't worry!"

Leo caught her hand as she passed him, and pressed it to his lips. "Thanks, honey!"

Waiting there in the evening sun for Liv to go below deck was like waiting for a bomb to drop. The air, warm and balmy though it was, was seething, and Leo could see Archie's jaw tighten as soon as his daughter put her back to them. Once she was out of sight he turned to Leo and whispered, "What do you want?"

"Right now? Dinner," Leo replied. "And...and to get married. To Liv. I don't want anything else."

Other than the chance to wipe away Conrad's smirk. And the ability to turn back the clock to our night together and live it over and over again forever.

"Don't be smart with me," Archie warned, his voice sharp. "I don't want my daughter to marry a man like you. You'll break her heart, we both know that."

"I won't hurt her. I *won't*," Leo whispered. *If only I could tell you the truth.* "I love her. What happened between you, me… I shouldn't have done it. I made a mistake and I'm sorry. And it will never happen again so long as I'm with her."

"You betrayed her. And you expect me to believe it's never going to happen again?" He shook his head. "How the hell could you do that to Liv?"

Leo saw so much bitterness, so much hate in Archie's gaze. And he would have to suffer it, play the bastard. "I know I did. I'm not proud of it, okay? You have my word, I won't do it again. I feel like the worst man on the planet, and I'm going to make it up to her. I will treat her like an empress on this floating palace, I promise. She's the most wonderful woman I've ever met. The moment I met her, I…I felt something for her, and it's only grown. I love her, Archie."

The anger in Archie's eyes flickered into something else then, an ineffable sadness that wrenched at Leo's heart. He looked away and ran his hand back through his hair, then murmured, "I won't have her upset. She's been through enough in her life."

And when you walked into that bar, Archie, I felt something for you.

Leo nodded. "I know. She told me about what happened to her mum. I'm so, so sorry you lost your friend like that. I know Liv has days when it comes back to her. It happened on the yacht once. Beautiful sunny day, and everyone was laughing, but…she was the only one who wasn't. I knew something was up. Our Liv's nearly always happy, after all."

"I want you to promise me that you'll never tell her." Archie turned his attention back to Leo. "And I want you to mean it. She can't *ever* know, Leo. And you and I have to forget what— I don't trust you and I don't want you anywhere near her, but I can't stop it. But you *never* hurt that girl, understood?"

"I promise," Leo replied. "I promise you, Archie, I'll never tell her and I'll never, ever hurt her. One hundred percent faithful to her from now on, cross my heart and hope to die." *But forget our night together? No. Never.*

"Leo!" Liv called. "Come and help, I can't carry everything!"

"Duty calls!" Leo got up, relieved to be escaping at last. He couldn't blame Archie one bit. In fact, he was quite frankly surprised Archie hadn't bloodied his nose and hurled him over the marina wall and into the open sea.

Leo jumped down the companionway and hurried into the galley, where Liv had dished up the dinner perfectly.

"See, we make a great team, don't we?" But as Leo smiled, all he could think of was how much he'd hurt Archie. The last thing he wanted was to go through life making people hate him. *I'm not Conrad fucking Beaucock, am I?*

Leo helped Liv carry the dishes through to the dining room. He'd put the ship in the bottle in the middle of the table, to remind him of Gunther and how much fun they'd all had together on the boat. Certainly more fun than Leo was having right at that moment.

"Grab your dad, I'll grab the wine and we set sail for dinner!" He gave Liv a kiss on the cheek, just in case Archie had decided to come indoors, or anyone was watching through the uncurtained portholes.

"Pops is a bit...*off*," Liv whispered. "He's usually much more chilled than this, but I wonder if work's been a bit full-on. He'll love you, don't worry."

More like he'll rip my head off my shoulders and throw it to the sharks.

Leo put his arm around Liv's shoulders. "I'm so nervous around him, it doesn't really help to give a good impression, does it? I'll calm down eventually. Just...you know...worried about getting found out."

"He's an absolute peach, you shouldn't be nervous." She rested her head against his shoulder. "But we've been a little team of two for so long, I think it's just taken him by surprise. I'll go and bring him down."

That's not the only thing.

"Okay... I'll pour the wine." As Liv went to get her dad, Leo fiddled about with the corkscrew, which was designed to look like a pirate with an eyepatch and stripy jumper. It would've made him laugh, usually. But not today. There was nothing at all about today that even made him smile.

But they were about as deep as they could get now. The parents had been told and the plan was in full swing. There was no turning back from here.

Leo couldn't remember a more uncomfortable dinner than this. He tried to fill the air with anecdotes about sailing on the *Aphrodite* with Liv and all the crazy things that had gone on. While being scrupulously careful to ensure that Archie understood Leo had always kept an eye out for Liv, and that she'd loved every minute of it.

Whatever he said, though, he knew Archie would never change his opinion of him. As far as Archie knew, Leo had done the dirty on his daughter, and he would always hate him. And there was nothing Leo could do.

Liv coaxed Archie into the conversation bit by bit, even if Leo knew full well that he was only joining in for his daughter's benefit. Still, under her questioning he told Leo of the restoration of the yacht on which the two of them now lived, and despite himself Leo couldn't help but picture Archie hard at work on a home for his daughter.

And now she'll have to leave it and move in here, just for the sake of the lie.

Leo went off to fetch the pudding, and as he headed along the corridor, he heard someone knock.

Rage engulfed him and he stormed to the companionway, ready to confront *Conrad fucking Beaucock.*

But once he got there, another face peered down at him.

"I'm looking for Liv," the man said. A very square-jawed man with stubble on his cheeks.

Has someone ordered a strip-o-gram?

"And you are?"

A brawny hand attached to an arm like a tree trunk plunged into the yacht, and Leo nervously took it to shake. "Rob Cooper. I'm starting work at the seal sanctuary tomorrow. I was looking for Liv, but her neighbor said she was over here. Nice boat."

"Come on in." Leo eyed him carefully. He wasn't a spy, was he? But as Rob came aboard, Leo noticed his T-shirt, which had a faded design on the front for an otter sanctuary in Dorset. Not even Conrad was *that* careful when it came to detail, surely?

Leo led the way to the dining room. He dreaded to think what Liv and Archie had been discussing while he'd been gone.

"Well, Liv, I was going to bring you pudding, but instead I've brought you —" *A hot man!* Leo winced. *Oh, fuck, I can't be camp anymore!* "Rob. I've brought you Rob. He's your new colleague. Rob, this is the lovely Liv, and this is Archie, her dad."

Rob grinned and shook hands with Liv and Archie. "Great to meet you!"

"Rob! Paula said you weren't getting in until tomorrow!" Liv said, beaming. "So lovely to meet you! Have you just arrived in town?"

"Yeah! I've just met my landlady, thought I'd come out and see the sights, and here I am."

And his sights are definitely on Liv.

"Have you eaten yet? We're just having a little celebration, actually." Leo put his arm around Liv's shoulders. "We're just toasting our engagement."

"Congratulations!" Rob said, but it sounded slightly forced. Almost as forced as Archie's smile. What a bloody night this was turning into.

"Have a drink and some pud." Liv nodded toward the chair beside Archie. "And welcome to Brighton!"

"Thanks!" Rob said. He patted Archie's shoulder. "So nice of you to welcome me like this!"

Leo went to the galley to retrieve pudding. His usual showpiece was a decadent Queen of Puddings, but given the circumstances, he'd made a pavlova this evening instead.

He brought it back and served up, playing the perfect host as he dished up the pudding and refilled glasses. All he wanted now was for the night to end so they could all just pretend this hadn't happened. He willed the minutes to tick past, but the clock seemed to have stopped.

And that was before Liv piped up to tell her father, "Leo's folks've asked if you want to pop over and have lunch. That's right, isn't it, Leo?"

"Yeah. A barbecue." *Sausages.* Leo shook his head sharply. "Dad loves doing a barbecue. Mum's really keen to meet you, Archie, so...yeah. Family barbecue. Won't that be nice?"

No, it bloody won't.

"I'm really busy at work at the—" Archie began, but Liv furrowed her brow as though to say, "*I beg your pardon?*" "It'll be lovely. I'd love to."

"Great. Mum wants me to give you her number. You can let her know when you've got a gap in your hectic schedule and...yeah. Family party time it is!"

Rob was swallowing his pudding in loaded spoonfuls, eating like a JCB excavating a ditch. But a twitch on his face betrayed that he'd noticed something. It was hardly surprising. The tension hung thick in the air like sea fog in November.

"I'll give her a call tomorrow." Archie drained what was left in his glass. "So, Rob. You're seal crazy too?"

"I love British mammals," he said. "Used to rescue hedgehogs in the garden when I was a kid, then we went to Ireland on the ferry on holiday and I saw seals and dolphins, porpoises and whales. So beautiful. I was converted at once. Studied Marine Biology at Southampton. It's great to have the chance to move over to Brighton and look after the seals. I'm a diving instructor as well. Helps with the rescues and helps pays the bills!"

"We're a tiny little sanctuary really," Liv told him, twirling a length of hair around her finger. "But we do a lot of good work. And we really do want to grow and do more."

"You will," Leo said, and patted Liv's hand. "You'll do amazing things." *And this is why Conrad can't win.*

Rob's eyes sparkled as he smiled at Liv. "I can't wait to get down to business. I *love* seals. You know when you see them sunbathing, flipper out like this" — and Rob, of course, demonstrated, flapping his enormous arm and generating a palpable draft — "and it looks like they're waving! Can't wait for the pup season, those little fluffy cuties."

Did the sanctuary really need Gunther's million? Because at this rate, they'd be selling charity calendars like hotcakes if they could get Rob topless, cooing over a seal pup.

"You'll have to give me your address." Liv took out her phone. "I'll call tomorrow, and we can wander over to the seal hospital together if you like? I'll introduce you to everyone."

"I'd *love* that. I'm staying in Kemptown, it's not too far." Rob told her his address, smiling at Liv all the while. Leo glanced at Archie, wondering what he made of the new arrival. His arms were folded across his chest, his whole body seemingly as tight as a coiled spring. Leo searched for something to say but there was nothing there. He was completely out of small talk.

"Do you know of any boats on the marina for rent?" Rob asked. "I wouldn't mind living down here myself. I'm happier afloat, to be honest!"

Liv beamed and replied, "There're a couple that I know of. Nothing as grand as this, but what is? You know, Max, I didn't tell you this, but when *Aphrodite* first came in Dad was waxing his bonnet and he said to me, "*who the hell's this flash bugger, then?*" And I had to tell him it was my best friend!"

Even more reason to hate me.

"I should explain." Leo grinned at Rob. "I'm not a billionaire or anything. I'm a professional yachtsman, and this absolute character called Gunther — well, he left me this yacht after he passed away. He was a really great guy. I never expected to live in a yacht like this!"

"That's pretty cool! I was impressed when I saw it. Biggest boat in the marina, isn't it?"

Leo didn't even bother to look Archie's way, because there was no way *he* was impressed by Leo. Not one bit.

"I don't know," Leo replied. "I suppose it must be one of the bigger ones. It'd be too much if I was living here on my own, but the *Aphrodite* will become Liv's home too. Not bad, really!"

Waxing his bonnet.

"She will." Liv nodded. She reached out and took Archie's hand. "Once I'm sure Pops is going to be okay without me."

Leo hadn't expected that. He'd anticipated her moving in sooner, not later, but he knew she must have a very good reason and he suspected it was something to do with Archie's rather cool reception to him. And she'd never know the reason behind it.

Oh, God, what if Conrad finds out?

But there was going to be a wedding. That's what the will stipulated. It didn't say anything about premarital cohabiting, so Conrad could get stuffed.

"Whenever you're ready. There's no rush," Leo said, his hand over Liv's on the table. "And it's not as if we'll live that far away from each other. We're practically neighbors."

And Leo realized that when he thought he'd seen Archie from a distance on the marina and put it down to his imagination, he now saw that it hadn't been at all. He really had seen him. And he would go on seeing him for months with no way to escape.

It was Archie who ended the party and, no doubt for Liv's sake, he even waited until a decent hour to do it. With a stretch and a somewhat theatrical yawn he declared, "Well, it's been a lovely evening, but I'm afraid my old bones need their bed. I'll leave you youngsters to it!"

Leo pushed back his chair. "Lovely to meet you at last, Archie. I'm sure I'll see you again soon." *Unfortunately.*

Rob pushed back his chair as well. "Bloody good meringue. I'll see you tomorrow, Liv."

"You will!" She kissed her father's cheek and for a moment, Leo thought she might kiss Rob too. Instead she patted his arm. "I'll be home in a little while. I just want to help Leo tidy up. You make sure the kettle's on, Pops!"

"Of course I will." He smiled and kissed her cheek in return. "Good luck tomorrow, Rob. And, Leo... thanks for supper. Cheerio, then!"

"Bye!" Leo ushered them out along the corridor, in the style of an ardent youth keen to be alone with his lover. "Goodbye, everyone! See you all soon!"

And as Archie walked away into the night, he seemed somehow further away than ever. Yet he hadn't been so close in days.

Once they were gone, Leo closed the hatch and gestured toward the sofa in the lounge. "Erm...post-match report time?"

"Isn't he *gorgeous*?" Liv exclaimed, her cheeks rosy with wine. "He's like... *Thor!*"

"Sexy Rob," Leo said, giving full rein to his camp now because he could. "He *so* fancies you!"

With that, Liv's smile turned into a flamboyant pout. She flopped down onto the sofa and declared, "But I'm an engaged woman! And he has arms like bloody great big gorgeous tree trunks!"

Leo sat down beside her. He tugged at his hair in frustration. He couldn't tell her what had happened with her dad. Not a word of it.

"The seals really need the money," Leo reminded himself. "That's what we need to focus on. That sort of money doesn't drop out of the sky onto seal sanctuaries very often. We can't... We've *got* to hold the line."

She gave a firm nod. "I don't think I should move in yet. You don't know Pops, but he wasn't himself tonight at all. That's not how he is. I thought he'd be all, *call me Pop, let me show you the MG*, but he looked like he was seething half the time!"

"Yeah, I noticed. I suppose it's a shock." *For everyone.* "He'll come round, I'm sure! But he's not my greatest fan at the moment. There's nothing in the will to say we have to live together before getting married, anyway."

"And I don't want you to think he's one of those weird overprotective dads, because he isn't. I mean, he let me sail off round the world on Gunny's crew, after all." Liv rested her head on Leo's shoulder. "I'll have a chat to him. Do you think I should start wearing my ring now?"

"Yeah... it might help." *Or it might drive Archie up the wall.* "I'm sorry I blurted out the thing about getting married before we'd got the champers on the go. I was just... rattled. Erm... I've got the ring here."

Leo had kept it in a miniature treasure chest that was encrusted with shells and had pride of place on the coffee table. He took out the ring box and opened it, the diamond chips sparkling in the light. For a moment, Leo stared, thinking only of the way Archie's eyes had once sparkled at him. But he salted that memory away.

"I'll do this properly." Leo squeezed out from the sofa. He took the ring out of its box and dropped down onto one knee. He'd had more enjoyable experiences ripping off plasters. "Liv, Loveday, will you do me the honor of becoming my wife?"

"I will, sweetie." She leaned forward and kissed Leo's forehead. "For a little while."

Chapter Ten

Leo spent the next couple of days working, getting covered in oil, scraping the skin off his knuckles against barnacles, and shopping for curtains. It was as much fun as he could have without undressing, and all the work wore him out so he slept as soon as he got into bed. He had no time to stare at the ceiling and think about how miserable he was sleeping alone. And work was a welcome distraction from the churning of his stomach when his thoughts wandered.

He'd always shared everything with Liv, and it was driving him up the wall that he couldn't tell her about her father. She was worrying about him, but Leo knew that what he had to reveal would hardly make her day. In fact, wouldn't she be so shocked that she'd call the whole charade off? And everything would be wasted for nothing.

* * * *

Leo wandered up to the seal sanctuary to meet up with Liv once she'd finished her shift. It was a modest enterprise, with a small pool for the convalescing seals, a hut for their shelter and some sheds containing feed and supplies. As Leo walked through the gate to the visitors' area, he was greeted by a wave from a sunbathing seal, and a splash as its friend dived into the water.

Leo waved back to the seal, then he called, "Liv? Liv, are you about?"

"Are you saying hello to our little Roxie?" Liv emerged from one of the feed sheds. "Look how well she is! She was a poor little soul when she came in, but she's lovely and healthy now. She's been teaching Rob all about seals."

Rob appeared from the shed, brushing his hand through his hair. He'd swapped his otter sanctuary T-shirt for a brand-new Brighton Seal Sanctuary one, and it still wasn't quite big enough for him. "Roxie's great! This is the best job ever! How are you, Leo?"

Why haven't they brought any feed out of the feed shed?

"Oh, I'm good, thanks," Leo replied. The shed look rickety. One bad storm and it'd lose its roof. "Just thought I'd swing by and see the seals before escorting my fiancée home."

"They're super happy to see you too!" Liv stood on tiptoe and pecked a kiss to Leo's cheek. "Have you been on the marina today? Pops had a day off to do something manly to the MG. Has he been making a horrible noise revving it up all afternoon?"

Leo did his best to chuckle. "Pops owns the MG? Yes, I did hear it revving. And backfiring!" *Like a lot of things at the moment.*

"I'm not really an only child." She gave a comical pout. "Dad's got an MG too. He likes getting his hands oily, I think. All his pals are on the golf course, and Dad's there in his overalls, covered in oil with a massive smile!"

Leo's brain constructed a film reel for him, complete with seductive music. Oily Archie, shirt off, holding a big spanner.

"Sounds more fun than the golf course, definitely!" Leo remarked.

"Nice little MG," Rob said. "Doesn't surprise me your dad drives one of those!"

"Let me get this right." She laughed. "My sister's name is MGA Mark 1, I think? Leo, maybe you should ask him for a ride? Sort of like a bonding thing?"

I already have.

"I'm not averse to riding a vintage machine," Leo said. "Well, there's no harm in asking, is there?"

But to his horror, Liv was already taking out her phone. "I'll call him and see if he wants to take you for a pootle tonight. Are you free for pootling?"

Say no! Say no! But suddenly words emerged from Leo's mouth that he couldn't put back in again. "Yeah, I can go pootling with Pops."

She gave a bright smile then stepped away and pressed the phone to her ear, leaving Leo and Rob to entertain each other in her absence.

"This is such a great place," Rob said. "Everyone here's so committed. They really care. I've just been having a look at the roof of the feed shed. Needs making sound. Got a mate who's a roofer, he's always busy but he might be able to fit it in. Free labor, but we'd need to pay for materials."

Get stuffed, Conrad, you don't need the money like the sanctuary does.

"That'd be fantastic if he—"

Leo froze. There was a man on the viewing platform, snapping photos on a camera. Was he a fan of British marine life? Or was he— *What if Conrad's sent him to spy on me?* And wouldn't that be good, a photo of Leo beside a hunk like Rob?

Of course he's gay, he's talking to a muscly man in a tight T-shirt!

Leo took two steps back from Rob. "Erm...sorry. Where was I...? Erm...yes. Materials. Well, you never know, donations come in all the time, big and small."

He looked back at the platform. The man with the camera waved at Roxie and Cyrano, her new friend, a seal who'd been at the sanctuary for some time. Then he turned away and left. Leo tried to suppress a shiver.

Did the spy get what he wanted?

Things didn't seem to be going much better for Liv either. Even at a distance Leo could see that the conversation with Archie wasn't a happy one. Her face was ashen and sad, one hand gesticulating as she spoke with obvious agitation into her mobile. A new pang seized Leo now as he watched his best friend argue with the father she adored and who adored her too. They'd always been so close, he knew that from the year he'd spent crewing with Liv, and how close she'd come to giving it all up thanks to homesickness and the gnawing absence of her adored *Pops*, yet here they were at loggerheads.

Because of money.

Because of me.

Leo went over to her and patted her shoulder. He mouthed, *"Are you okay?"* Although he knew she wasn't. She held up her hand and shook her head, then said to her father, "Pops, don't be like this, please. I *know* it's a surprise — it was a surprise to us — but just go for a drink. Please?"

Leo put his arm around Liv's shoulder. He couldn't tell her, could he? It was just too embarrassing. *I had a night of passion with your dad and walked out on him. He hates me because he thinks I'm a philandering git.*

And even if he did tell her, he still couldn't tell Archie the truth about the fake marriage. The lie had to be watertight, and that included hiding the truth from their parents.

He could just hear the murmur of Archie's voice, but the words were too indistinct to make out. Instead Leo was guided by Liv's reaction when she gave a sigh of relief and said, "Oh, Pops, you're such a lovely old thing. I'll tell him. Seven'll be perfect. Love you, see you later!"

Phew. Sort of.

Leo gave a thumbs-up. "Drinks with Archie this evening, then?"

She pushed the phone into the pocket of her jeans. "Drinks and it's up to whether you want to pootle in the MG or on the *Loveday*." Liv poked her tongue out at Leo. "Named after me, of course!"

Rob had wandered off, looking busy with a huge brush.

"Of course!" Leo glanced around then he lowered his voice. "There was a man here just now, with a camera. Did you see him? I think he was photographing me talking to Rob. I think Conrad's sent someone to watch us."

Liv frowned, then shook her head. "If he had, do you think they'd stand there with a camera right in front of you? Where is he?"

"Maybe, if he wanted to intimidate us? I don't know how these things work." As Leo pointed toward the viewing platform, he felt rather stupid. It could've been anyone. "He was over there."

She nodded, then tightened her ponytail by giving the band that held it a sharp yank toward her skull. "Well, let them look so long as they put some money in the tins. The seals won't tell them anything anyway!"

"You're right." Leo scuffed his shoe against the concrete. "I'm sorry, I'm being paranoid, aren't I?"

As Liv answered, she held up her hand, as though admiring her engagement ring. "I wouldn't put it past him, though."

"We need to be *so* careful." Leo kissed her cheek affectionately. But it felt strange knowing he'd kissed her dad as well. He couldn't compare the two, though. Liv gave a little tinkle of laughter and dropped her head to his shoulder.

"We need to set the date," she said.

"Erm...isn't June the traditional month for weddings? That'll do, won't it?" Leo shook his head. "Sorry, *that'll do*... It doesn't sound very romantic, does it? Liv, you're the best mate anyone could have, willing to go through all this. But it'll be worth it. This place'll be even more amazing, I promise."

"The sooner the better," Liv whispered. "Then we can start thinking about the d-word!"

Leo winced. "You can have the ceramic duck in the rubber ring, but I *insist* you leave me the pirate corkscrew!"

Chapter Eleven

Leo arrived at the *Loveday* just before seven. It was a beautiful vintage yacht, with a white hull and varnished wood on the decks. Leo stood on the pontoon and called, "Permission to come aboard?"

Then wished he hadn't, because Archie had said just that as he'd laid there tethered to the headboard, seconds before they — *Stop bloody thinking about it!*

"Granted!" Archie strolled up onto the deck, casual again. His bright blue shirt matched the hue of his eyes, though they were hidden behind sunglasses, and his face was strained. "Hello, Leo. Welcome aboard."

Leo hopped across the gangway. He held out his hand to shake. "Great to see you again, Archie. Just admiring the *Loveday* — gorgeous! Like her namesake."

"Just so there's no misunderstanding, this is entirely for Liv's benefit," Archie said as he shook Leo's hand. "So are we driving or are we sailing?"

There was a question. As much as Leo liked the idea of going for a drive with Archie, being trapped inside a small car with him might not be comfortable for either of them. Whereas if they were on a yacht together, they could stand forty feet apart if things got awkward, one in the bow, the other at the stern.

"It's a nice evening for sail. Bit of a breeze, not much cloud. And I'd love to see how *Loveday* handles." *And you'll see that I can actually do something right. I know how to manage a yacht, if not my own life.*

Only when Archie's jaw tightened at his innocent comment did Leo realize how his sentiment might have sounded.

How does your daughter handle?

"She's not as grand as the *Aphrodite*, but we love her," Archie replied. He pushed his sunglasses up into his hair. "Let's get out to sea."

"I'll get your sails up," Leo said, scrambling up to unfurl the mainsail. Then he realized what he'd said and glanced back at Archie. "So to speak."

At this rate he'll throw me overboard.

Archie wasn't looking at him though, busy instead with his beloved yacht. Maybe they could just say nothing for the voyage then return safely to dry land. That was probably the best Leo could hope for.

Leo concentrated on hauling up the sails, and although he was used to being the skipper, he worked to Archie's orders. He slipped easily into his role of crew, telling himself that Archie was just another yacht owner, not the man he'd gone to bed with and deceived.

The sails filled with wind and Leo came to sit with Archie in the cockpit as they took *Loveday* out to sea.

"Liv said you did her up yourself," Leo said. He tried not to dwell on the fact that Archie looked incredibly handsome at the wheel, with the breeze ruffling his hair. "I've seen a lot of yachts, you know, and she's beautiful."

"She was rotting when I got her," Archie said. "One of my law profs gave her to me for a pint of beer and a Sunday roast."

"Sounds like a good swap!" Leo ran his hand over the wood. It was so smooth and glossy, and he pictured Archie's strong hands meticulously sanding the boat down.

"Took a lot of work, but it was worth it in the end. The idea was that I'd sail round the world on her one day," Archie explained. "You know, retire early once Liv was all settled... Maybe that day's closer than I expected."

"Maybe." Leo toyed with the end of a coil of rope, tying and untying the end on itself. So Archie would take himself off around the world? That was one way to avoid how awkward — *how bloody difficult* — everything had become. But what would he do when he found out about the divorce? "I took a yacht over to the Caribbean. That Atlantic crossing was really something. You've got to do it at least once in your life. It's incredible. And when you see land after days and days at sea... Not much beats that feeling."

"I've heard a lot about *Max* from Liv." Archie slipped his sunglasses down to shield his eyes again. "I can't pretend I wasn't surprised when things suddenly lurched into romance. Anything I need to know about that?"

Leo swallowed as he geared himself up for his lie. "It just sort of happened. One second we were laughing, the next we were kissing. And it felt right. Thing is, you know I've been with men before, I'd always thought of myself as gay. But...but sexuality is a spectrum, isn't it? It surprised me and it kind of *didn't* surprise me. We were friends, but there was something more."

Archie nodded once but said nothing. Leo could feel that his eyes were on him. Was this how it felt in court, faced by Archie in his full regalia, being questioned and watched, scrutinized even?

The wedding wasn't far away. And the divorce wouldn't be long after that. And once it was all over, once Gunther's million was in Leo's bank account, it would be finished. He'd never have to spend time with Archie again.

But despite everything, the thought left him indescribably sad. He watched Archie's hands on the wheel and remembered how they had felt on his body. And he'd never feel them again.

"I've still got your tie," Archie told him eventually, shattering the silence. "You forgot it."

The rope Leo had been fiddling with fell from his hands. *He still has it? He didn't throw it away?* "My tie? I thought... I thought I'd lost it at Victoria when I got the train. I..." Leo dug into the pocket of his jeans and pulled out Archie's cufflinks. They caught the evening sun and glistened in his palm. "I...I still have these. I didn't mean to leave with them, I found them in my pocket. I keep...I keep carrying them around with me," he admitted.

"I think you and I need to talk, don't you?" Archie ruffled his hand through his hair. "Because I'm still carrying your tie in my briefcase."

Leo nodded, his gaze fixed on Archie's. He returned the cufflinks to his pocket and shifted closer to him. *Should I really do this?* But even Conrad would struggle to conceal a spy on someone else's yacht. "Don't hate me for saying this, but...but I still think about you."

"I feel— She's been my whole life for so long and — this would break her heart. I want Liv to be with someone who loves her. You're cheating on her before you're even married."

"I *do* love her," Leo protested. "I love her, but I keep thinking about *you*." And nothing he had just said was a lie. What a relief, to be honest with Archie in something at least.

"If I'd known— I thought you were single," Archie told him helplessly. "What were you *thinking*?"

Leo didn't say anything at first. He felt ashamed, because in a way he had gone behind Liv's back. They were supposed to make the marriage look real, and what had he done within hours of them coming up with the plan? He'd flung himself at a handsome man. And he'd hurt him. Again and again, he'd gone on hurting the man.

I wish I could tell you the truth.

"I've only ever been with men. Just *once* before I was married, I wanted just to be sure— so I went with a man again. And I lay in bed beside you once you'd fallen asleep and I felt so guilty..."

"So— Hang on. You slept with me to prove to yourself that you'd rather be with a *woman*?" Archie sounded horrified. "Jesus, Leo, really?"

"I—I don't mean it like that." Leo shook his head. "I mean, this is all so unusual for me. The thought of never having a man's arms around me again... I just wanted to feel a man's embrace, once more."

Archie fell silent, the only sound now the soft hiss of the waves. What could either of them say though? Nothing could even *start* to make this right. And the divorce would make an already hellish situation so much worse.

Leo stared off at the sea. There should've been something comforting in it, there usually was, but nothing could salve this. Archie had every reason to hate him, based on what he thought was true. But if he knew the reality, he could still hate him for that as well, leaving him with nothing but a note and a tie.

"For Liv's sake, we have to try and get on." Archie turned his head and, despite the sunglasses, Leo could feel his gaze again. "And God knows how, but we have to put that night behind us. I meant what I said, though, Leo. I don't want even a *hint* of you hurting her. Be the husband she deserves."

Leo nodded vehemently. "I will be. You have my word. I *won't* betray my wife. I promise you, I *won't*. And let's forget what happened between us. For Liv. Shake on it?" Leo held out his hand to him. Archie clasped it in his own, and they shook.

But I'll never forget it. Not for a moment.

Then they sat in silence together, the only sounds the *swoosh* of water against the hull as the *Loveday* coursed through the waves and the occasional flap of the mainsail as the wind gusted. Leo went up to the bow to tighten the jib, but as he chanced to look up, he saw something ahead of them in the water.

"Skipper!" he shouted down the length of the yacht to Archie. "Skip! There's something ahead in the water!"

"What is it?" Archie called back, lifting his sunglasses again.

"Debris of some kind." Leo leaned out over the water, trying to get a better view. "Looks like discarded fishing nets. Off to port."

Leo was still looking at it, trying to work out what the mass of knots was ahead of them. It was moving, but then it was being carried by the tide, so there was nothing odd about that. But wasn't there something gray, mottled —?

Without a second's pause, Leo bounded down the yacht and nearly tripped on a piece of rope. "Archie, there's something caught in it. I think it might be a seal."

"I'll call Liv!" Archie took his mobile from his pocket and swept his finger across the screen. As he spoke to his daughter, Leo kept his eyes on the seal. It was small, just a pup, tangled in what looked like nets and flotsam and it was barely moving at all.

Oh God, don't be dead.

Leo grabbed the boathook as they came closer to the net. He could try to pull the net up, but even as he pondered this, he realized it could only make things worse if the net was too big and heavy. It was full of debris. Who knew how long the island of junk had been drifting about, catching everything in its path?

He patted his pockets and found his penknife. A sailor was never without one. Someone would have to go in and cut the seal free without getting tangled themselves.

"How's he looking?" Archie called, the phone still pressed to his ear. "It's going to take Liv at least half an hour to reach us!"

Leo groaned, tugging at his hair in frustration. "I don't think we can bring the whole net on board, you know. It looks huge, and there's plastic sheeting and bottles and crap all caught up in it. I think someone'll have to go in. I've got my knife."

Archie put his phone back in his pocket and told Leo, "Someone reported this poor little fellow this morning, but they lost sight of him. He's on his own out there." He was already unbuttoning his shirt, his words urgent. "I know it goes against everything they always tell you living beside the sea, but she thinks we should bring him on board rather than wait for her to get to us."

"Since this morning? Bloody hell, how long as he been caught in it?" Leo feared the worst. Even seeing Archie's impressive bare chest again wasn't as cheering as it could've been. "I'll helm while you go in. I'll radio the coast guard, too, let them know the nets are here."

Going in. Leo knew that what Archie was about to attempt was dangerous, but what other choice was there besides leaving an innocent life to a horrible fate?

"I'm not entirely sure how we're going to do this, but..." Archie stripped down to his shorts then held out his hand. "Can I borrow that knife?"

"Of course." Leo forced himself not to look down at Archie's shorts. A dam in his head was straining to keep back the memories from their night together, and one glance at those shorts and— He passed the knife to Archie. "I'll hold *Loveday* steady, then we'll get the seal on board, then you. Good luck, Arch. There's not many people who'd do this, you know."

"I don't even know if he's alive, but we can't leave him out there." Archie handed his sunglasses to Leo, then descended the yacht's ladder into the water. He took his time, no doubt to ensure that the lapping waves remained as undisturbed as possible, but still the stricken pup wasn't showing any signs of life.

Please be careful, Archie!

Leo focused his attention on holding the yacht steady, knocking the wind out of the sails to keep the *Loveday* where she was. He watched the sails, he watched the water for a change in the wind, and most of all he watched Archie.

He approached the seal slowly, and as he did, Leo saw the pup's eye move. Just a little, perhaps, but enough to tell him that it was still alive, if only barely. At the sight of Archie, it gave a feeble twitch of one flipper, as though trying to signal for his attention, but Leo got the distinct impression that there wasn't much hope left in the little body.

Leo kept the yacht as still as he could, desperate not to spook the seal as Archie made his attempt. Few people would've bothered to stop, let alone strip off and swim in the cold English Channel for the sake of a tiny creature.

He could hear Archie murmuring softly to the pup as he approached, the knife ready in his hand. Very slowly, he caught his arm around the junk, holding the ailing pup safe so he could cut away at the netting in which it was entrapped. It was a painstaking exercise, and as Archie sawed through the nets, Leo could see that the little seal was injured, the twine having cut into his skin.

Leo winced at the wounds he could see even from up on the yacht. He just hoped they'd get the pup to shore in time and safely to the sanctuary. With great care Archie pushed the netting away from the pup but still the animal just bobbed there, unmoving. It didn't protest as he gathered it to him and began to swim back toward the yacht, holding the pup to his chest.

Leo reached over the stern holding out Archie's shirt, ready to wrap the seal as soon as Archie passed the creature to him in case it struggled. But Leo wasn't sure the pup had much fight left.

"Nearly there," Leo said.

"He's not very well at all," Archie told him as he passed the pup over. "He looks half-starved."

Leo wrapped the seal and heaved him into his arms. He held him like he had his cousin's baby. Was he meant to? He wasn't sure, but he hoped he could warm the little pup with the heat from his own body.

"I suppose he's an orphan if he's so thin. Do you need a hand to get back in, Archie?"

"Yeah, I wouldn't mind." Archie held out his hand to Leo. "It's colder than it looks!"

Leo carefully laid the seal down in the cockpit, then he reached over the side and grabbed Archie's hand. "Ready? Up we go!" Leo pulled him up, dripping, onto the yacht.

"Thanks, Leo. I'm glad you're here," Archie said, slapping one wet hand to Leo's back. "How is he?"

Leo crouched down beside the little bundle and gingerly peeled away the shirt to reveal the pup. The infant creature blinked at them, twitching his whiskers. "We need to get to shore. Archie, I'll helm, don't worry. You get dressed. You must be freezing." Leo shook his head. "Sorry, I'm so used to being the cap—skipper."

"I'll be okay," Archie replied as he picked up his discarded trousers and stepped into them. "You get us home. I'll keep an eye on him."

Leo nodded. When he'd left Archie sleeping in that London hotel room, he'd never for a moment thought they'd end up like this, Archie shirtless, caring for an injured seal pup.

He tightened the sail, and the yacht was pulled along by the wind again. Then he called "Coming about!" and tacked around, the boom swinging across the yacht as they turned and headed to shore.

The sanctuary needed a new boat, Leo told himself, along with so much more. And that was why they had to keep up their lie.

The wind was with them and it wasn't long before the *Loveday* was back in the marina and Leo was motoring them to the berth. Liv and Rob were already there on the pontoon, waiting for them. The pup was still alive, snuffling although it was weak, thin lines of blood staining Archie's shirt from its wounds. As Leo brought them safely to the pontoon, Archie gathered the pup into his arms and rose to his feet with care.

"He's pretty weak," he called as he approached Rob and Liv. Then he told the seal, "You're in the best hands now."

"The vet's on her way. We'll soon get this little bloke back in action." Rob took the pup, who was automatically dwarfed in his arms, and laid him in the rescue harness, still in Archie's shirt.

"Let's get you back to the sanctuary," Liv cooed to the unmoving seal. Then she looked to Archie and Leo. "You two're quite a team. You've done really well but, Pops, put a shirt on!"

Leo glanced back at Archie's chest, then looked away again. "I found a cupboard full of *Aphrodite* crew T-shirts this morning, if there's any takers?"

"Dad lives on the boat, he's got a wardrobe full of chilled casual shirts with easy-to-roll-up sleeves downstairs," Liv reminded him as she and Rob transferred their patient into their little van. "And loads of wine, so you should definitely go and have a glass. You've earned it."

Rob got into the van, but before he shut the door, he said, "We'll let you know as soon as we have any news. Thanks for rescuing our little friend."

Leo hovered, wondering if he should go back to his boat or stay. "Do you fancy a drink, Arch?"

"Archie," he corrected, but at least it was with the ghost of a smile. "I need to get changed, but you can stay for a glass of something if you like. Good luck, little seal, hang on in there!"

"Thanks, Archie. Goodbye, little one!" Leo waved at the departing van. The pup would need all the luck it could get.

While Archie went into the cabin to change, Leo hauled down the sails, slipping their covers back on and tidying them away.

"Shipshape!" he said to himself as he went back to the cockpit.

It was then that he heard Archie call his name, followed by, "Do you prefer downstairs or on deck?"

"I'd love to see what—" *Don't say it. Don't say you'd love to see what* Loveday *looks like downstairs.* "Well, I've seen the deck. Why not the cabin?"

Leo swung down through the hatch and found himself in a cabin, all cozy with exposed wood. "This yacht is *so* nice."

It was exactly what he would have expected, a perfect combination of Liv and Archie. Homely, in fact, just the sort of place he could see Archie building with the sweat of his brow.

Don't think of that. Not for a moment.

"How has Liv never brought you over since you both got back from crewing?" Archie handed Leo a glass of chilled white wine. "Is this because my daughter spends every waking moment in coffee shops and seal sanctuaries?"

Leo took the glass. "Yeah! I meet up with her in town, usually, when I'm not away. And – don't take this the wrong way, but I never would've guessed you were her dad. She said, *he's a barrister, works at his family's chambers they've had for hundreds of years.* I had this picture in my head of this white-haired little bloke sitting in an armchair by the fire!" Leo laughed awkwardly. "I was a bit wrong there."

"Oh, you should see me in full sail, I'm a bit of a stage-hogger." Archie settled onto the sofa and kicked his bare feet up onto a polished driftwood coffee table. "I was thinking about earlier. Liv's told you how – You know me and her mum weren't a couple, don't you?"

Leo nodded as he sat opposite Archie on a padded stool. "Yeah, she told me all about that. You were best friends, and she wanted to have a baby. And you stepped in."

Archie took a sip from his glass. "I just want to be sure. You've only had male lovers. How can you be certain that – are you saying that Liv *turned* you?"

"Not turned, just made me realize I *could* find a woman attractive." *Except I don't.* Leo sipped his wine and said, "She's gorgeous. I don't just mean to look at, but on the inside as well. She'd do anything for anyone." *Even suggest becoming a fake bride.*

"Yeah, she would." Archie nodded. "We barristers are a suspicious bunch, always trying to whittle out an angle. For Liv's sake, I hope you haven't got one."

It's not just mine, Leo wanted to reply. *We're doing this for the sanctuary.*

"No, no, I don't," Leo insisted. "It just seems right. That's all. How does anyone ever decide when it's time to get married to *anyone*? Because it feels right, and it's such an unquantifiable thing."

"I've asked Liv to keep me in the loop with the arrangements." He took another drink. "And what're your plans after that? You're not going back to sea, are you?"

"I'll—I'll take shorter jobs if I do," Leo told him. "I've been having fun picking work around here, to be honest. I can climb a mast like a monkey, I'm in great demand!"

He nodded. "I think you and Liv need to have a conversation about that. As far as she's concerned, she's staying at the sanctuary. You wouldn't go crewing without her, would you?"

"No, of course not." Leo heard so much distrust in Archie's voice, but Leo couldn't blame him. "She's devoted to the sanctuary—I'd never take her away from that. And besides, I want to be with her. That's not going to happen if I'm being thrown about in a storm on the way to the Azores."

Archie nodded slowly, then drummed his fingers on his glass and mused, "No. No, it isn't."

"You know something, I'm glad we rescued the seal." Leo smiled. "The most important thing is that we got it to safety, of course, but you know, it's nice that we can be *the two guys who rescued the seal pup* instead of *the two guys who...*" Leo gestured helplessly. "*Y'know.*"

Why was Archie looking at him so closely, though? *"Always trying to whittle out an angle..."*

Was it possible he knew something was up?

Not another person to try and stop the wedding. It was bad enough having Conrad on his heels.

"You know, if there's anything wrong or anything you and Liv think I should know, you can talk to me," Archie told Leo. "Think of it as client privilege."

Couldn't a barrister keep a secret?

Maybe.

But Leo shook his head. It had to be watertight.

"There's nothing wrong," Leo said, and casually sipped his wine. "Why would you think there was?"

"Three reasons." He put his glass down, the better to count them off on his fingers. "One, you're gay. Two, this is not an insult, but you're not Liv's romantic type because, see point one. Three, you both tell you had a Damascene moment where you realized you loved each other, but I haven't seen any sign of real affection between you, and for the last three days Liv's left her engagement ring in the bathroom window and had to run back for it. But mostly one and two."

"Would that stand up in court?" Leo tried to sound flippant, but he was now rather concerned. *Would it?*

Archie picked up his glass and circled the wine that remained with a gesture from his wrist.

"I could probably sell it," he replied after some thought. "But I'd need to wear the gown to really make it fly."

Archie in a barrister's gown.

Leo started to slip into a happy daydream, imagining Archie holding forth, the gown flying theatrically behind him as he proclaimed on behalf of law and justice. *And to think he enjoyed being tied up.*

Oh, Leo, stop it!

"Look, really, if either of us didn't want to get married, we wouldn't be getting married, would we? We're going into this with our eyes open, Archie. It's what we both want."

And when Archie said casually, "Okay," Leo knew how it must feel to come up against him in court. He'd folded too quickly, too easily, for it to be anything but a front. "Shall we have a refill?"

"Yeah, wouldn't mind. Thanks." Leo wondered if this was a good move. Was Archie hoping to trick him and reveal the truth? Then again, the alternative was going back to the *Aphrodite* alone again and being the sole resident of Gunther's party palace was rather lonely.

Archie was going to be his father-in-law. His gorgeous, sexy father-in-law who liked being tied to the bed and gave the most wonderful hugs.

And he hasn't asked for his cufflinks back. But we mustn't talk about it.

Sitting there sipping wine, though, Leo remembered being in bed with Archie doing just the same thing, kissing, exploring, just being together.

I could've fallen in love with him.

Leo blinked as he glanced at Archie again.

I still could. And that might be rather awkward.

"Your mum's invited me over on Sunday," Archie confessed. "Should I go, or…?"

"Come over. Please." Leo swept back his hair, stiffened with salt from their sail. "Mum's looking forward to meeting you, and Dad is as well. It's a barbecue, if that's okay? Do barristers go to barbecues?"

"We do." Archie laughed. "We don't only eat twelve-course dinners in our clubs, you know."

Leo chuckled. "Do you all sit there in your wigs and gowns? Supping oysters and strange cuts of meat?"

"And passing the port, of course." He cocked his head to one side. "When we're not exchanging secret handshakes."

"And rolling up your trouser legs?" Leo shook his head, amused. "I have no idea what barristers get up to. When Brockett was reading the will, it was like a different language. And where does that extra-thick carpet come from?"

"Brockett!" Archie clapped his hands together and gave a cry of amusement. "It can't be the same Brockett I knew when I was in training. Brockett junior, maybe?"

Oh, crap.

"Maybe? He wears half-moon glasses. Very serious type."

"Oh, I know him." Archie chuckled. "Well I never, what a small world. He's the millionaire's solicitor of choice, you know. They like his sense of occasion. Specializes in smoothing the most crooked posthumous path."

Well, Gunther had certainly left one of those.

"He didn't seem phased that Gunther had left me his enormous yacht, and a tiny ship in a bottle! He must see all sorts of things. And never changes his expression from *this*." Leo did his best attempt at Brockett's blank expression. "Was he born like that or does he put it on? Maybe he's really gregarious and commutes on a unicycle?"

"I couldn't possibly say." There was that little mischievous smile again. "But you're in safe hands with him. You know, I thought he must've left Liv something because she's been filled with ideas for the sanctuary, none of them cheap. I suspect some of that might be coming out of my bank account!"

"Brockett seems a steady sort of chap..." Leo took a mouthful of wine. "Oh, has she? She's always coming up with ideas for something!" *What did I just say?* Leo had another sip. Then he remembered. "Rob's got ideas too. He knows a roofer, apparently, who'll work on the sanctuary for free if someone can provide the materials. Might not work out as expensive as all that."

"It runs in the family, you know. We're impetuous." He took a drink. "It's a Greville-Hall trait."

That didn't come as a surprise. Liv suggesting the fake marriage, Archie being tied up naked by a stranger. An impressive day of impetuosity from the Greville-Halls.

"I'd noticed!" Leo chuckled. "It's a good trait to have."

"Sometimes," was the reply, a wistfulness in that one word.

Leo could almost hear Archie's thoughts turning. *He's thinking about our night together.*

Leo drained his glass. He stood and held his hand out to Archie. "I better get going. Long day tomorrow folding spinnakers!"

"I really hope our little seal pulls through." Archie shook his hand. "I'm going to be thinking about him all day until I hear from Liv. Poor little fellow."

"I know. I will be too." Leo scrubbed back his hair again and said, "You were really brave. You didn't think twice, you just got in there and saved him. You're a really great bloke, Archie."

Archie blushed just a little, a soft flush creeping into his cheeks. Then he shrugged one shoulder and said, "It was teamwork. Don't ever say otherwise."

"All right, then. Teamwork. You take care." Leo patted Archie's arm, then he climbed the stairs up to the deck. He paused, then he turned and looked back inside. "Night, Archie."

"Cheerio, Leo," Archie said. He gave him a casual sort of salute. "I'll see you soon."

Leo saluted him too, then he headed off to his yacht. Something had shifted between them, and the world felt a little lighter for it.

Chapter Twelve

An outside broadcast van was parked outside the sanctuary, drawing curious locals like a magnet. Leo checked his hair again in his reflection in the van's window, then went through the gate into the sanctuary.

A cameraman waited for them by the pool, with a woman holding a microphone. She waved as Leo arrived. He'd never done anything like this before and he was awash with nerves.

"Hi, I'm Leo." He held out his hand to shake, knocking into the microphone.

She chuckled. "I'm Sharisa! Great to meet a local hero, Leo! We've already done some filming indoors with Liv and met the seal pup, so we've got some great footage. All we need is for you and Archie to tell us about the rescue."

Archie.

Leo glanced over to the buildings, where he supposed Archie was still inside with Liv. His gaze was still on the door when it opened, and Archie emerged.

He greeted them with a wave then strolled over to join the group.

"Hello, Leo." Archie laid his hand briefly on Leo's shoulder. "Spinnakers all safely folded?"

Leo did his best not to tremble at Archie's touch. He looked gorgeous in his casual, loosely buttoned shirt, and Leo hoped his shiver hadn't been picked up by the cameras. "Oh, yes. Tucked away for the night!"

"So Archie's going to be your father-in-law?" Sharisa asked. "Such a lovely angle to the story! And Daisy's so cute!"

Liv had sent Leo a text, explaining the seal was a *she*. A she named Daisy in honor of Liv's late mum.

"Yeah, me and Liv are getting married…" Leo ran his hand back through his hair, then wished he hadn't. Was it all sticking out, making him look like a scarecrow? *That'll look* great *on telly.*

The cameraman gestured to them to get into position, and Sharisa guided them to where they needed to stand before she stood beside the camera, the microphone held out at just the right angle for it to be invisible to people watching at home. There was a splash from behind as either Roxie or Cyrano dived into the pool, but Leo resisted the temptation to turn around and look.

"So tell us about the rescue," Sharisa prompted. "You two were out on Archie's yacht…?"

Archie looked entirely at ease, as though he did this sort of thing all the time. He nodded and replied, "We were out for an evening on the yacht, and Leo spotted what looked like a bit of a rubbish mountain floating in the water."

That was his cue, Leo realized.

"Yeah, I was up on the prow, securing a sail, and saw this fishing net ahead, all bundled up with plastic. But then I saw something move—just a tiny bit—and realized it was a seal pup that had got tangled up in it. So I shouted back to Archie, and he rang Liv. She said someone else had reported it earlier, but they hadn't been able to find the net again, so we had to take matters into our own hands."

"Brighton Seal Rescue does wonderful work, but all their funding is from donations, so their facilities are limited," Archie went on. "Liv wasn't going to be able to reach us very fast, so she asked us to bring Daisy on board and talked us through how to do it safely. Of course, we wouldn't have even attempted that without her telling us that we should."

"Yeah, you've got to be careful with wild animals," Leo said. And just at that moment, one of the seals barked at the top of their voices before entering the pool with a gigantic splash. Leo started to laugh. "As you can see! So...so Archie's a strong swimmer and he dived in while I held the boat steady."

"Archie, was it difficult to free Daisy from the net?" Sharisa asked. "How had she got caught, do you think?"

"I'm not sure *how*, but she was completely caught up. I didn't think that she was alive, but I managed to steady her so I could cut her loose and she gave a rather sorry little wave." Leo remembered it vividly, seeing the pitiful seal again in his mind's eye. "Getting her free wasn't easy and I didn't want to do any more damage to her, because we could see she was on her last reserves of energy. It was horrible proof of the problems we're facing with rubbish in the sea."

Sharisa nodded. "Yes, yes, very true. So how did you get her back to shore?"

"Archie swam back to the boat with her, and I wrapped her in Archie's shirt. I haven't held a seal before, but it was a bit like holding a baby." Leo smiled awkwardly. "Then we turned the yacht round and came straight back to shore."

"Which is where the professionals took over." Archie put his hand on Leo's shoulder and gave him a grateful smile. "It was Leo who spotted her. Without him I wouldn't have known Daisy was even there."

"It was a team effort!" Leo grinned. He remembered the slant Sharisa wanted for the story and said, "It was a good bonding experience for me and my future father-in-law!"

Sharisa said, "It's an unconventional start to a marriage, but it's great to see people pulling together for the sake of Britain's wildlife."

"And if anybody wants to follow Daisy's progress, they can visit the sanctuary seven days a week or keep up-to-date online." That was definitely a Liv plant, Leo knew, even as Archie said it. "There's always another animal in need."

"I'm sure they will," Sharisa said. "And you can donate to the sanctuary online at the address which you'll see at the bottom of your screens."

Archie glanced at Leo and smiled again. It felt as warm as the sun.

"Cut!" the cameraman called.

"Thanks, you two, you were great!" Sharisa said. "Fingers crossed for Daisy, and all the best for your wedding! Hope you and Liv have a fab day!"

Leo did his best to smile, but at his moment of triumph, he felt like an empty fraud.

Chapter Thirteen

A few days after their brush with fame, Leo headed for the marina's car park and Archie's MG, which was waiting for him. Liv wouldn't be going to the barbecue—she'd pretty much moved into the sanctuary. She was sleeping in the staff room when she wasn't caring for the seal. It was malnourished and dehydrated, with damage to its muscles and tendons and the bones in its flippers, as well as an infection from the wounds where it had been tangled in the net.

While Liv had been busy with the seal, Leo had been busy himself and booked their marriage at the registry office, as well as the Sea Scouts' hut for the reception and a slap-up buffet. In four weeks' time he would be a married man, and the sanctuary would have more money than they'd ever dreamed of.

And Conrad would have nothing except indigestion.

He waved when he spotted Archie. It was odd. He was half-dreading, half-looking forward to meeting him. Leo hadn't seen Archie since the evening they'd rescued the seal. Actually, he'd seen him often enough in his dreams, trying to pull Archie onto a boat, but their hands had slipped and the waves carried him away.

Don't be silly. Put on a smile for the barbecue.

"All ready for my dad's bad jokes and my mum's amazing puddings?" Leo called. He guessed that the vast bunch of flowers in Archie's arms was for his mum, but he wished it could somehow, by some miracle, be for him.

What a dream that would be. But he had to get over it.

"Ready." Archie nodded. "I wasn't sure it'd still be on without Liv, but you've got one very determined mum!"

"She keeps sending me photos of hats," Leo said. "It means Linda Maxwell's excited!"

The hood was down on the sleek vintage sports car. It looked perfectly suited for Leo's very own James Bond, even if he was about to become not a secret agent, but his father-in-law. Oh, why couldn't he drive a sensible estate car?

"I'd love to have a look at her engine one day." Leo gave the car an admiring sweep. Her bodywork was so shiny, so polished. "I can hear you going off to work in the morning. Such a gorgeous purr."

"I'll give you a tour of her one day. Hold onto these, they're for your mum." Archie handed the flowers over as in the distance Leo heard what sounded like the roar of a jet engine. His companion held up his hand to shield his eyes from the sun, then nodded toward the bright-red Lamborghini that was hurtling into the car park. "Looking at your yacht, I thought that was more your sort of car? Bit of flash?"

Leo sighed. He could see Conrad's smirk through the windscreen. "No, not my style at all. I know the *Aphrodite* is a bit OTT, but the only people who drive cars like that are annoying pricks."

"What's this I see?" Conrad called as the gull wing door opened and he climbed out. No pinstripes today, but tailored shorts and a slightly too-tight shirt instead, and yet another expensive watch, bulbous and oversized on his wrist. "Flowers from another bloke, eh? That's the least of what *I've* been hearing!"

"This a mate of yours?" Archie asked.

"Definitely not," Leo replied. He planted one hand on his hip and stared Conrad down. "They're for my mum, from my future father-in-law, who can't drive *and* hold flowers at the same time. And why are you here anyway? I've got nothing to say to you."

"I saw you and your bird on the news last night, yapping on about some sort of half-dead seal, begging for crumbs for her little sanctuary." He leaned his elbow on the roof of the car. "Sounds like they need money, right?"

"We're actually about to leave," Archie told him with icy civility. "So...would you mind awfully just clearing off?"

But Conrad stood his ground, staring at Leo. *Please don't say anything.*

"That right?" Conrad asked Leo. "I thought you were the one who needed the cash. But maybe it's her."

"It's a charity, for God's sake," Leo said. "And that rescued seal pup reminds people that the sanctuary needs help, all the time. It's not like seals have health insurance, is it?"

Conrad nodded slowly. Then he said, "You don't want me to tell your daddy-in-law the truth about you, do you? About this sham of a wedding? What'll you do if I tell him what I know?"

"I already know. I've discussed it with Leo's parents too," Archie said, much to Leo's horror. *You know?* "How could they keep it a secret? Liv and Leo have told me everything and I fully support them. A marriage is a marriage, that's all that matters ultimately."

"You know — the trust —" Conrad stammered. Archie folded his arms across his chest and nodded, a haughty tilt to his chin.

"We've got to go, Conrad," Leo said, getting into the car. By some miracle, Leo had managed to hide the wobble that threatened in his voice. "This has been delightful, but if we hang about here any longer talking to you, these flowers will've wilted before my mum gets to see them."

"You little fucking —" Conrad began, stamping his foot as Archie climbed in beside Leo and turned on the engine. It gave a familiar purr, as comforting as Archie's unexpected admission had been unsettling. Conrad was still standing there, his face as red as his car, as they cruised past and left him to his temper tantrum.

"He's a lawyer," Leo said, as if that explained everything. "He wants the *Aphrodite*."

"Does he really think we don't know you're bisexual?" Archie tutted and shook his head. *That's* what he thought Conrad's fury was about? Leo felt his panic begin to ebb. "Jabbering on about trust and sham weddings. I know you and Liv would confide in me if there were any truth in *that*."

He glanced toward Leo, then back at the road.

"I-it's *not* a sham wedding," Leo insisted. He clutched the flowers tightly, the cellophane crinkling in his fingers. "I've booked us in at the registry office, I've even arranged catering for the reception! And Mum's friend is making the cake."

"So the date's been set?" Archie took a deep breath. "When is it?"

Keeping his eyes straight ahead on the road, Leo replied, "Sixth of June. A Saturday. They had a cancellation at the Registry Office, so…that was good!"

Archie responded with a tight nod. So he had heard, even if he had nothing to say. What a happy marriage this was going to be!

"I'd like to pay," he said after a few minutes. "It's only right. I know Liv puts all her spare cash back into the charity and obviously I don't know what your situation is, but…she's my daughter."

"No, no, I wouldn't hear of it," Leo said, forcing himself to relax his grip on the flowers in case the stems snapped. "It's very kind of you to offer, but it's not an expensive do." *And we don't want you wasting your money on a fake wedding anyway.* "We decided against the big sit-down-dinner in a stately home sort of thing. You end up inviting lots of people you don't even like that much, and you always get chicken and roast potatoes for some reason. Our buffet'll be far more exciting. I've got my savings, it's really not a problem. But thanks anyway. I appreciate the offer."

"Liv won't take a penny — she'd rather I give it to the seals. She told me it was family only, and I respect that you don't want a showy bash, but…it's my only daughter's wedding." He darted a glance toward Leo again. "I want to pay. At least let me get dinner and the rings?"

Leo tapped his chin in thought. Maybe it would look less suspicious if they *did* let Archie pay for something.

But even so, it didn't feel right. Unless they paid him once the money had landed in Leo's bank account. "I'll have a chat with Liv about it. We just... We don't want to cause a fuss, you see."

"Would you rather I wasn't there at all?"

Leo hadn't been expecting that, nor the bitter note of sadness in Archie's tone.

"No!" Leo patted Archie's arm, then quickly withdrew his hand. "Oh, Archie, of course we want you to be there. It's just the paying side of things that we're a bit uncomfortable about. We're the ones who've decided to get married, we don't want to put people out. You're invited, and anyway, you *have* to be there to give Liv away!"

"You breeze about as though this is nothing." Archie tapped his fingers on the steering wheel, agitated. "We have our truce, I know, but inside — in my heart — I'm angry. Every morning I wake up to the sight of that bloody great yacht and know that you're on board. That Liv's going to be. And I resent her, and that's like a knife in me, because it's your fault."

"You resent her? Why would you —?" *Oh.* The temptation to reveal Gunther's clause was getting harder to resist. The whole, horrible mess had spiraled out of control. *But the marriage has to look real or Conrad will get the money. We can't tell anyone.* "Archie...please don't resent her. If I wasn't marrying Liv, I'd...I'd never have walked out of that hotel room."

"Even after everything you've done, all the bloody mess you've caused, I still want you. I think about you all the time, Leo," he admitted. "And I feel jealous of my own daughter. I thought about early retirement, running away, but I need to be here for her when you break her heart."

132

Here was the perfect moment for him to tell Archie the truth, but Leo was so used to telling the lie that he couldn't stop. And Conrad was circling like a shark, scenting blood in the water. There was no way for Leo to admit everything, even though Archie's low opinion of him hurt like a punch in the gut at the same time as his admission made Leo hope.

"I want you too," Leo murmured. "You were so brave the other day, so…so *good*. And I think back to that night we shared and… But we can't call the wedding off. We *can't*."

"We can't ever, *ever* be together again. It doesn't matter what happens with weddings and marriages, we have to just accept it." Archie took a deep breath. "I know I'm overprotective of Liv, but she had such a horrible start. Her mum died in front of her and every day since then, I've done everything I can to make sure she never has anything but good days. She's grown up, she's going to make her own way, but… She's the very best of me, Leo."

"Maybe that's why it's impossible not to love her," Leo said, his smile gentle. "You're such a great dad to her. I'll always look after her, I promise. And I know we can't be together again, I'd never ask that of you."

Archie took another deep breath, as though preparing himself to face a deadly foe. Then he nodded. "Prove me wrong," he implored. "And make her happy."

Leo nodded. "Oh, I'm going to make her very, very happy, you have my word."

Even though, in the process, he was breaking Archie's heart.

"This is Mum and Dad's house just up here," Leo said, pointing to a semi-detached house with new, diamond-paned windows. "The one with the ornamental well in the front garden."

Archie pulled into the drive behind Leo's father's Peugeot. Then he turned to Leo and asked with a smile, "Will I do?"

As Leo admired Archie's casual shirt with his customary rolled-up sleeves and unbuttoned neck, he wished it was different. He wished he had pulled up in the MG with Archie to proudly introduce him to his parents as his boyfriend.

But he couldn't.

"You look like the perfect father-in-law," Leo said. But as he started to get out of the car, the thought of seeing his parents in the same space as Archie at the same time dawned on Leo as the most terrifying thing he could imagine. But he had to go through with it.

Archie took back the flowers then they were at the door and inside. There were smiles and greetings and everyone was on their very best, very respectable behavior. They were one, big, happy family. Minus the bride, of course.

"Wasn't she great on the news? And you two as well!" Mike called from his station at the barbecue. "How's the seal pup getting on?"

"She's very poorly," Archie replied, pottering out to join Mike. "But she's in the right place to get better. Have you been to see the set-up there yet? Liv'd love to show you chaps round if you haven't."

"I've driven past a fair few times but never been in," Mike said. "I'd love to have a look around and meet the residents. Could even bring them some of these!" Mike liked to take his barbecuing to places barbecues didn't ordinarily go in English suburban back gardens. He held out a tray of sardines to show Archie. "What d'you think of them?"

"I think I'll enjoy them as much as Liv's seal would," Archie replied with a smile, before Mike embarked on what sounded like the start of a long list of questions about the MG. The parents, it seemed, were going to get along.

They sat outside on the patio, all chatting perfectly happily. The conversation turned, as Leo knew it inevitably would, to the wedding.

"Yes, yes, we've set a date!" Leo said. "Sixth of June. That's okay, isn't it? It's all arranged. Registry Office, Scout hut, buffet, and Auntie Sue said she could get the cake ready by then, so...so...yeah!"

Mike sipped his wine before saying, "That's only four weeks away, Leo. Are sure you'll get everything ready in time?"

"Yes—we already have!" Leo insisted. "It's not a royal wedding at Westminster Abbey."

Even though there's a queen walking up the aisle.

"And I can't convince either of them to let me get my checkbook out," Archie lamented. "So I'm going to have to spoil some seals rotten instead, I think!"

Mike laughed. "Nope, they won't let us pay either!"

Linda shrugged. "And Auntie Sue said she'd make the cake as a gift, but oh no, Leo here insisted on paying for it."

Leo glanced at Archie. Whatever was the man thinking as he heard Leo's parents talk about the wedding? But he was a barrister, he knew how to make his thoughts unreadable.

"I'm just glad that Liv's not a bridezilla." Archie laughed. "She's taken it all in her stride."

"You're lucky there, Archie!" Mike puffed out his cheeks. "Cor, dear. My niece, when she got married, she was a bridezilla, wasn't she, Linda?" Mike leaned back in his patio chair, hands folded across his stomach, and regaled Archie with an exhaustive anecdote involving five bridesmaids, two ring bearers, a cathedral-length train, three choirs and a steel drum band.

All the trappings that Leo and Liv's wedding wouldn't have.

"What about you, Linda?" Archie gave Leo's mum a rather mischievous look. "Were you a bridezilla?"

"Ask Mike." She laughed. "I'll say no, obviously!"

Mike chuckled. "One of the bridesmaids got a perm and her flower crown thing wouldn't fit on top of all the big hair she had! You cried down the phone about that! But I can't think of anything else. It all seemed quite placid from my perspective. What was your wedding like, Archie?"

"I've never had one!" Archie gave a comical pout. "Liv's mum and I weren't married. Our parents were a bunch of hippies, so...I was the gay best friend!"

The gay best friend, Leo thought. *History repeats itself.*

Leo's parents took a moment to process that. But having produced Leo, their surprise didn't last long, and they knew not to probe.

"Ah, I *see!*" Mike gave Archie a matey slap on the shoulder. "I apologize for assuming, Archie. Leo's told me off for doing that before!"

"Oh, God, don't apologize!" He laughed, entirely at ease. "Even for hippy kids it was an unusual way of doing it. Daisy passed away when Liv was four and it's been just us ever since."

I wish I could make this all stop.

But it was too late. And Archie had been hurt, and Conrad was up to something, and still Leo plunged on with his lie for the sake of a million pounds.

Archie, the single dad who'd taken a chance on a stranger.

If only I'd known.

"Hard work raising a child on your own," Mike said. "She's a lovely young woman, your Liv. And I'll be proud to be part of your family."

"Liv and I feel really honored to be welcomed into yours," Archie replied, swallowing hard. "More than you know."

Leo tried not to wince. *Poor bloody man.* He would've hugged him if he could have, promised him it'd be all right.

But there was nothing Leo could do.

And first they had to get this bloody barbecue out of the way.

Once the remains of the sardines were carried away, it was time for pudding. Linda had surpassed herself, making an enormous trifle.

"No sherry, as you're driving!" Mike quipped, rubbing his hands as the towering beast arrived at the table.

"Or not much." Linda laughed. "Just a taste. Archie looks like he won't mind a thimbleful!"

"You're a bad influence!" Archie teased. "I'll keep an eye on you!"

I wish it was different.

Leo daydreamed for a moment, imagining that he was introducing his boyfriend to his parents. And that his parents adored him, and all was right with the world.

"Mum and her cheeky sherries!" Leo laughed. "She taught me how to make pavlova, you know. It was her recipe I used the other night."

"We devoured it," Archie admitted, though he'd eaten less than anyone. It had seemed to be all he could do to swallow. "Why don't the two of you buzz over to Brighton one evening and I'll take you for supper? It's the very least I can do after this lovely spread?"

Mike put his arm around the back of Linda's chair and grinned at his wife. "We'd love that, wouldn't we, darling? Thanks, Archie, we will!"

"It's not often I get wined and dined by a barrister," said Linda. "Just try to keep us away!"

And when Liv and I get divorced, what happens then? Will they hate each other?

But all that money. Think of all that money.

"You're welcome back here for a barbecue any time you like!" Mike said to Archie. "And if she's not busy with the seals, bring your girl along too."

"We'd love to. Come and see the seals too, Liv's moved in while she looks after little Daisy!"

"Remember, I'm bringing them sardines!" Mike laughed. "You two rescuing the seal, though, I'm so proud of you. Must've been hairy, swimming up to a big old bundle of rubbish like that, not knowing what you'd encounter and whether you'd be able to get the pup out. Bloody brave!"

Archie made a show of waving the idea away. He looked toward Leo to declare, "I couldn't possibly comment!"

"He's being modest!" Leo now chuckled genuinely for the first time that evening. "He dived in and cut Daisy free. I spotted her and kept the yacht alongside until he'd got her out. He swam with a seal pup in his arms!" And Leo grinned at him with undisguised admiration.

"Anyone would've done the same." Archie patted Leo's shoulder. "And Leo spotted her, it was a team job really."

"You did the big job though." Leo remembered Archie standing on the deck, water droplets speckling his shoulders. That was *not* something to entertain while sitting on his parents' patio, so he thought instead of Daisy. "And even more of a team effort with Liv and Rob taking care of her. She's got the best team she could have."

Archie met his gaze and smiled. And Leo told himself that his heart didn't melt. But it did.

"Anything the sanctuary needs, by the way?" Mike asked. "I work for a marine stores company," he told Archie. "We've got ropes, we've got buckets, we've got..."

Leo didn't hear the rest of his father's words. He was trying to stop himself from gazing at Archie. But every time he looked at him, Archie was looking back at him. How could they ever pretend there was nothing between them?

Mike was still going. "We've got outboard engines, we've got wellies, look, I've run out of fingers to count them off on! And whatever you need for your yacht, Archie, I can use my staff discount."

"Thanks, Mike." He smiled. "And I hope you never need a barrister but...you know one if you do!"

"Well, funny you should mention that. Look..." Mike pointed over to the dark, impenetrable branches of their neighbors' leylandii hedge, looming over the fence. "I don't suppose I could cut them down and pretend it was an accident?"

Well done, Dad. Proving the Maxwell men aren't afraid to lie.

"Not a good idea." Archie laughed. "Give me a call. We'll talk it through."

"Thanks, Archie, I will!"

"You'll make his year—his decade—if you can sort that hedge out," Leo said. He knew how much his dad went on about it, and he grinned at his mum. "And Mum's too!"

Because we have to make this work, one way or the other.

Once Mike had finished his third bowl of trifle, the barbecue fizzled to its end. Leo helped carry the plates indoors, but his parents wouldn't hear of him doing anything more than that.

Leo and Archie said their goodbyes, and all the time Leo felt that uncomfortable mixture again, his feelings of excitement and dismay at the prospect of being alone with Archie. Even for the space of a drive.

They climbed into the car and, with a wave for the Maxwells, were on the road. The atmosphere didn't seem too heavy, thank goodness, but when Leo's phone buzzed, he couldn't help but worry what drama would be next.

Hope today went well. Daisy says hello, she's looking a bit happier tonight! Xxx

Leo looked up from his phone. "Archie, would you mind dropping me off at the sanctuary? It's more or less on the way. Just...I just want to pop in and see how Liv's getting on."

"Say hello to Daisy from me," Archie told him. "And thank your parents again, Leo, they're lovely people."

Without thinking, Leo patted Archie's knee. He tried to swerve away from the potential awkwardness by quipping, "And they're useful to know if you need a cut-price bucket!"

Archie gave a soft laugh and nodded, then turned his attention to the road as they sped into the sunset.

Chapter Fourteen

Leo didn't open his door at once, even though Archie had pulled up in the car park outside the sanctuary.

Leo turned in his seat and said, "Thanks for giving me a lift, Archie."

"That's okay." Archie turned to look at him, his eyes sparkling in the moonlight. "Will you two be all right getting home?"

"I'll get a cab, it's okay," Leo said. He still couldn't get out of the car. Archie's gaze had entranced him. He remembered that night again, Archie's kisses, the heat between them as their bodies united.

We want each other.

I'm still falling in love.

Leo let go of the door handle. For a moment, his hand rested on his lap but, haltingly, he brought it toward Archie's face. His stomach gripped with warning, but Leo ignored every voice inside him that urged him to stop and he brushed his fingertips against Archie's cheek as if touching him for the first time.

"You said you still want me," Leo whispered. "I still want you too, you know that."

"We can't…" Archie caught Leo's hand in his, holding it to his cheek. He closed his eyes and whispered, "I can't get you out of my head."

Leo rested his forehead against Archie's. "I'm so sorry. I've put you in such a horrible position, and I never, ever meant to. But the thing is, I can't forget what we did because you're the most wonderful man I've ever met."

"You knocked me sideways," he whispered. When he opened his eyes, his gaze locked on Leo's. "I could've fallen in love with you, Leo."

Leo's heart seemed to jump at those words. He cupped Archie's face, tracing Archie's lips with his thumb, and said, "Then do. Because I'm falling in love with you and there's not one thing I can do to make it stop."

"We have to. I can't do that to her—" Archie shook his head. "She's all I've got in the world."

"I wish it was different," Leo murmured. "I wish I didn't have to walk away from you."

"It can't be different, no matter how much we wish. Go to Liv." Archie caught Leo's hand and brought it to his lips. He placed a soft kiss on his palm. "Forget Hervey's."

Leo's skin thrummed where Archie had kissed it. He wanted him even more now. and his torment was like a knife through him as he forced himself not to reveal the secret that could have freed him to be with Archie.

"I can't. I never will. And nor will you. You magnificent creature."

"Stop it!" He released Leo's hand and it was like a physical pain, cold and burning all at once. "There's nothing between us anymore and there can't ever be. Go to Liv and forget what happened."

Leo turned away at once and fumbled with the door handle as he got out of the car. He didn't want to look back, but he did anyway. Before he shut the door, he whispered, "I'm sorry."

Then he ran for the sanctuary. Never before had its name been so apt for Leo. But he had to wipe away his misery before Liv saw it. Because she was his friend, she knew him, and she'd take one look at him and she'd —

What's that noise?

Leo let himself into the staff area, and as he opened the door to the staff room, where Liv had been camping out the past few days, he saw a sight that somehow seemed inevitable.

"Sorry, you two. Didn't mean to interrupt," Leo said. Liv and Rob sprang from each other's arms and broke their kiss as though someone had yelled *fire*, each trying to pat down their disordered clothes or somehow pretend nothing untoward had happened. Maybe a kiss was nothing compared to what had happened in that London hotel, but here in the low lamplight, in their nest of sleeping bags and pillows, it looked like the most romantic scene Leo could imagine.

"It's not how it looks," Rob said as he adjusted his T-shirt, trying to avoid Leo's gaze. "We were...we were...cold."

"And Conrad's been in throwing his weight around, and I got a bit upset and — Rob was just being a friend," Liv added, her voice filled with panic. "Honestly, Leo! You should see Daisy, she's looking almost chipper today!"

"Conrad was here?" Leo shook his head. *The source of all my bloody problems and he comes here and upsets my friend?* "What was he doing? I'm not surprised you were upset after that. It's okay, Liv."

She darted a concerned glance to Rob, who didn't quite *look* as if it were all okay. But what was his take on this? Did he feel about Liv the way Leo and Archie felt about each other? Was this ridiculous charade about to break another heart?

"Said he'd give the sanctuary more money than we'd know what to do with if you and Liv didn't get married." Rob folded his arms and his biceps bulged in a way that made Leo rather nervous.

I rather like my head sitting on my shoulders, Rob. It'd be a shame if you wrenched it off. Please don't.

"He said that, did he, the bollock?"

"Who is he, Leo?" Rob asked. "Liv said you know him."

Leo glanced at Liv, his eyes wide, trying to prompt her to say what she'd told Rob. She blinked, then stopped to pick up a cardigan, which she fussed with as she replied. Maybe it was easier than looking him in the eye.

"I told Rob the truth." She pulled the cardigan over her shoulders like a cape. "That Conrad likes me and he's jealous of you and me getting married. Conrad was horrible tonight, Rob ended up having to chase him off. I'm sorry, Leo, I shouldn't— It's just that Rob and I—"

Liv's lip quivered and suddenly tears were spilling down her cheeks. Her whole body heaved with great wracking sobs and she buried her face in her hands, gasping, "I'm so sorry!"

Rob took her in his arms and hugged her, rocking her from side to side. "It's okay. We're both worn out from staying up with Daisy. It's okay. Conrad's gone now. It's okay."

Leo dropped down onto one of the chairs. He had never felt so much of a fraud as he did at that moment, watching Rob comfort the woman he had told everyone he would marry because he adored her.

"You don't need to say sorry, Liv," Leo said. He got up from the chair and patted Liv's shoulder. "It's Conrad who's in the wrong. Not you."

"He said stuff about you, Leo," Rob told him. "Pretty nasty stuff. I won't have words like that being bandied about."

Still Liv sobbed, clinging to Rob. Leo knew he should've put on more of an act, played the outraged fiancé, but he found that he didn't seem to have it in him right now. This wasn't Liv playacting, this was real.

"Lots of homophobic twaddle, was it, courtesy of the *delightful* Conrad Beaucock?" Leo rolled his eyes. "Oh, Liv, darling. You wanted to do the right thing. A *good* thing. And I know it's hard. Believe me, *I know*."

Liv lifted her head and met Leo's gaze, her bloodshot eyes filled with panic. She gave a brief shake of the head, but Leo saw Rob notice. Then she mouthed, "Don't."

"What's going on?" Rob's suntan seemed to fade a few degrees as he looked from Liv to Leo and back again. "Something's going on, isn't it? Why *are* you two getting married?"

"We love each other," Leo answered, but he knew he sounded insincere.

Liv nodded quickly. She passed the back of her hand across her eyes, but another sob followed. Then she looked to Rob and whispered, "You've been so lovely to me. I'm sorry I'm such a rotten cow — I mean, I'm engaged and — "

The tears came again, and Liv hid her crumpled face into her hands once more.

"Liv, Liv, *please*." Hadn't Leo promised Archie he'd look after her? And here she was, sobbing so hard her heart would break. He couldn't bear to see any more woe caused by their lie. "Rob, can you keep a secret to save the sanctuary?"

"What? Of course, I'd do anything for this place. What do you mean?"

"Leo, don't," Liv implored. "I won't ever do it again!"

In the cheeky tone he used when he and Liv were ranking hot men who crossed their path, he said, "I don't blame you at all, Liv. Rob's definitely in the top ten. Look at those lips! I bet he's a really good kisser." In the campest voice Leo could muster, he cooed. "He looks the type!"

Despite her tears, she gave a sad smile. Then she blinked up at Rob and told him, "Ignore Leo, he's being silly."

"I'm not being silly, Rob. I'm being gay." Leo was gladdened to see that Rob's sole reaction to this was a raised eyebrow that seemed to say, *no shit, Sherlock.* "Rob, when Liv and I get married, the sanctuary will get the best part of one million quid. Got that? One million quid. Think of all the things that can be done here with that money. One million smackeroonies or however gangsters say it on the telly. Big bucks. *Mucho* money. Thing is, Rob, I haven't told you that, okay? But...if you and Liv want to be a couple, then it's fine by me. And if you want to name your firstborn, or even your second born, after me, go right ahead. But Conrad doesn't want the sanctuary to have any money. We call off the wedding, and he won't donate a penny. Why? Because the man's a gigantic bumhole who can't be trusted. So if you want to do your coupley things, that's great, but just make sure no one notices for the next few weeks or Conrad inherits the money by default and buys himself a new car and Daisy doesn't get a new swimming pool."

And Leo sighed with relief. That was one person he wasn't lying to, at least.

"You've got to get married for the sanctuary to get a million quid?" Rob wrinkled up his nose, puzzled. "*Seriously?*"

Liv sniffed and nodded. "All because Gunther didn't say 'married' instead of 'Mäuschen'." She dropped down into a chair, leaving Rob looking more confused than ever. "Why didn't he just say married?"

"Gunther? Mäuschen?" Rob rubbed his head. He looked like he was getting a headache.

"He left me the boat. I was his skipper," Leo said. "And he didn't know I'm gay, or maybe he did, but he wanted me to have my own Mäuschen in the next year because he thought I was lonely, and I'll inherit a million pounds if I do. To sweeten the idea of married life. His solicitors have translated Mäuschen to mean a wife, and so you see, I need to marry a woman. And Liv volunteered, because we'll give the money to the sanctuary." Leo remembered the sensation of Archie's gaze on him and he swallowed. "But bloody hell, Rob, it's hard!"

Rob sat down next to Liv and took her hand. "But your dad's a barrister, isn't he? Why can't *he* sort this out?"

"Because he's so happy for us getting married," she replied.

If only you knew.

"And now I've lied to him so long and so much about it, and — It'll break his heart if he finds out it isn't true! He's been on his own for ages because he's been so focused on bringing me up and this is how I repay him? We can't afford to take Conrad to court, so this seemed like the easy way to do it. But it isn't easy at all!"

Rob squeezed her hand affectionately, and Leo looked away for a moment.

"Okay." Rob nodded. "I can see why you'd think it was the easy route. And Conrad's a twat. But it's such a big lie to keep up. I'm not surprised you two don't look particularly happy. What'll you do once you're married?"

"Get divorced," Leo replied. "Once we've got the money. The only stipulation is that I marry a woman within a year. It says nothing about how long I need to stay married for."

He saw the slightest movement of Liv and Rob's joined hands as they tightened on each other before she said, "But we don't want to upset our parents by doing it too quickly and really it's all my fault because I just blurted it out in the lawyer's office. Conrad was raging, and I just thought...*oh shut up*! And then I just said it — *we're a couple* — and there was no taking it back after that. I wish I was more like Pops, he never jumps in with both feet!"

He jumped in with more than just his feet.

Leo sighed. "Yeah...I know you were trying to help, Liv, and I do appreciate that, but it might've been good if we'd had the chance to talk about it first before you announced we were getting hitched. It's all…bloody awkward."

Liv blinked then lifted her eyes and let her gaze settle on Leo.

"I was only trying to do the right thing," she murmured. The more she spoke, though, the more that murmur grew in agitation and pitch. "And trying to help. You could've said something right there and then, but you didn't! If it was such a stupid idea, why didn't you say weeks ago?"

Leo stared at her in surprise. He'd never heard her snap at him or anyone else before.

"How *could* I have said anything? Conrad was *right there*, if I'd wobbled at the idea of marrying you, that's it, no money! And maybe at the time it *seemed* a good idea. I wasn't thinking straight, I was too bloody surprised!"

"Well, at least you've got me to blame!" She kissed Rob's hand then rose to her feet. "Everyone says *oh, Liv's got it easy! Liv's got a rich old dad and a stupid hippy name. Liv never gets upset!* Well, I do! And I'm upset now! And I'm going for a walk!"

"Liv, I didn't mean it like that!" But Leo's protest sounded feeble as he realized he'd managed to upset yet another person he cared for.

"Liv, do you want me to come with you?" Rob asked her.

"I don't know what I want," Liv admitted. She gave a long, ragged sigh. "I really, really like you, Rob, but Leo's my best friend and the seals really need the money. If me and Leo go ahead with this marriage thing, Leo, will you still want to be my best friend? And, Rob, would you still go out with a divorced lady?

And maybe even have a little bit of an affair with a married one?"

"There's no question about whether or not you're my best friend, Liv," Leo said. Leo reached for her hand. "Of course you are. And you always will be."

Rob ran his hand back through his cropped hair. "I think you're ace, Liv. I'd do anything for you. And it's not *really* an affair if the marriage is just names on a piece of paper, is it?"

She beamed through her tears. "And little Daisy and her friends are the only ones who're really going to get anything out of it. Me and Leo aren't doing it so we can buy flash cars and all that. We just really, really want to get the sanctuary done up. I *know* Gunny wouldn't have minded Leo being gay, I just wish he'd been more clear in his bloody video!"

"I wish he had too. Then again, I'd've had to find a man who'd want to marry me!" And immediately, he thought of Archie. *Don't be stupid, you've hurt him and lied to him. Why would he ever want to marry you?*

But all Leo could think about was Archie, the lover, the hero.

"Are you two staying over?" Leo asked. "Only, I really need to get back to the marina."

Liv nodded. She squeezed Leo's hand. "Shall we walk you back?"

"No, no, you two stay here. Daisy needs you." Leo kissed Liv's cheek. Rob was a lucky man to have won Liv's heart. They saw him to the door, where Liv kissed Leo in return. Then, alone, he walked out into the night.

Chapter Fifteen

Leo walked along the prom, heading for home. The illuminations had come on along the prom, and the edge of the sky was tinted with the last of the sunlight. There were figures on the beach, couples holding hands, skimming stones.

He paused for a moment, his elbows on the railing, as he watched a figure coursing through the water to the shore. So free, so bold. They weren't someone who was weighed down by a lie that seemed to do nothing but hurt everyone in its path.

The figure rose from the water, and in the glow thrown by the pier, Leo saw something familiar.

He knew that body, and he'd seen speckles of water glittering against that skin before.

"Archie?" he called. It *was* him, he knew as soon as Archie lifted one sculpted arm and waved toward him.

"Leo?" he called, sounding rather perplexed. Then he stooped to pick up a towel from the pebbled beach. "What're you doing wandering about in the middle of the night?"

"I was…I was on my way home." Leo pointed along the prom toward the marina. "I was coming to see you."

Archie scrubbed the towel over his hair as he asked, "To see me? Do you want to come down here while I get dried off?"

Leo nimbly leaped over the railing and landed on the pebbles as neatly as a gymnast. Then he jogged in slow motion over the pebbles until he arrived at Archie's side.

"I wanted to tell you something," Leo said. He *had* to tell Archie now, because some sort of dam had broken inside him and it didn't help that the man who had stolen his heart was wearing nothing but swimming shorts, a sheen of water and a look of utmost, heartfelt concern. He couldn't lie any longer.

"*Please*?" Leo begged him. He looked back at the beach and the innocuous groups of people milling in the last of the daylight. "But not here."

After a few moments, Archie nodded. "There's something I need to ask you too. I've been doing a lot of thinking and— You're right. Not here." He slung the towel around his neck. "Are you okay to wait for me to throw my clothes on again and we can walk home?"

"I'm sure no one'd mind you going home in your shorts, but…" Leo grinned, even though his stomach was knotting up at the thought of what Archie wanted to ask him. "It's fine. I can wait for you as long as you need me to."

He watched as Archie dried himself, trying and failing not to notice the way the moonlight picked out the planes of his body. He did his best not to recall the shower they'd shared, but it would've been easier to ask the tide not to change. Leo noticed everything about Archie because he couldn't stop looking at him. And Archie kept darting glances his way too.

Once Archie was ready, they began their walk to the marina. Leo told him he'd seen Liv, but out here, where Conrad's spies might be lying in wait, no matter how much the truth was pushing against its bonds to be freed, Leo had to keep to the lie. He wasn't about to mention what he'd walked in on, and besides, it was up to Liv to tell her father about her new man.

"Daisy's doing really well," Leo told him. "I think maybe Liv will be coming back to the yacht really soon."

"But not for long," Archie said. There was a lightness in him, though, a sense of something that Leo couldn't quite put his finger on. "Swimming always clears my head. I'd never win a case without it."

"And it's pretty handy when it comes to rescuing seal pups!" Leo shoved his hands into his pockets as they went along. He wondered if he should ask, but he did so anyway. "So you've got a nice, clear head now?"

"We'll talk more about what's in my head when we get home," was his mysterious reply.

Leo did his best to make conversation, telling Archie about his time crewing with Liv. How much fun they'd had, and what a skilled sailor Liv was. None of this appeared to be news to Archie.

And all along, as Leo recalled days of sunshine and laughter, he wandered inside a bleak fog that had him entangled in its dismal clutches. He had no way of knowing what was about to happen. Would Archie be furious? Would he report him for fibbing to a solicitor? Was that even a *thing*? Leo had no idea how any of the legal machinery that churned and clanked in the background of everyone's lives actually worked. And that made it worse. He was navigating in the dark and had been since his call to attend Brockett's office.

When they reached *Loveday*, Leo followed Archie down into the cabin. Just as his presence had filled the sleek, modern hotel room, now it filled the cozy, homely yacht too. Leo was so aware of Archie that it felt almost instinctive. It was like they were somehow tuned in to the same wavelength.

"Drink?" Archie asked. "I'm going to be terribly boring and have a cup of tea, but if you'd rather have something stronger, just say."

"Tea's good, thanks. Milk, no sugar." Leo's heart thudded hard and fast. He summoned all his will to steady himself as the pressure of the truth inside him became harder and harder to bear.

"From the start, something's been off," Archie said as he busied himself at the kettle. "Not with you, with Liv. And when you said the name *Brockett*, things began to make much more sense. I love a puzzle, you see. It's how I make a living really."

Leo narrowed his eyes at him. Had he solved the puzzle, then? But Leo didn't feel relieved. He was more on guard than before, wondering what he and Liv could have let slip.

"You said you knew Brockett years ago. Why does Gunther's choice of solicitor make any difference?"

"That's not all I said." Archie handed Leo a steaming mug of tea. "I told you that millionaires like Brockett. Because Brockett specializes in tricky cases and knows every loophole in the book. He found most of them in the first place. "

Leo took the tea and closed his hand around the warmth of the mug. He was feeling lightheaded and needed something to anchor him. He met Archie's gaze as he asked, "Does that—does that include awkward clauses?"

"He's king of them." Archie blew over the surface of his tea. "If any relative of mine needed help with a creative clause, I'd give them Brockett's number."

"I see..." Leo swallowed. He was starting to sway on his feet and he clutched the antique barometer on the wall to keep steady. "I've got a question for you, Archie. Before I say anything, I want to ask you, what would *you* do for a million pounds?"

Archie raised one eyebrow. "And that's the last piece of the puzzle." He led Leo to the sitting room and took a seat on the sofa, all the time saying nothing. Leo felt as though he was waiting to hear his sentence, his heart thumping in his chest. "I wouldn't do anything until I'd spoken to a legal professional, for starters."

Leo sat down on the sofa too, parking himself into the corner. "I can't afford a legal professional. And you saw for yourself what that Conrad bloody Beaucock's like. He doesn't need a million, but he'd happily see the money go into barristers' pockets instead of mine, instead of the sanctuary's. Liv came up with the idea, getting married. And...it seemed the easiest thing to do. It's what Gunther asked for, after all." Leo clutched his mug even tighter and blinked back tears. All the hurt, all the lies, weighed like rocks on his conscience. "But it's not. A fake marriage is bloody hard."

"But... *I'm* a legal professional. Why didn't the two of you come to me?" Archie settled back into the cushions. "I didn't have the facts worked out but I had a feeling there was an angle to it. It's just not Liv. Believe me, if the two of you had been dating—let alone engaged—I'd have known about it. She wears her heart on her sleeve. And she wouldn't have been looking at Rob like she is either."

"We wanted to make the marriage look as real as possible," Leo tried to explain. "We didn't want *anyone* to know it wasn't. We just couldn't risk it with Conrad after us. To start with, it seemed like such a little fib, but it got more and more out of hand, especially once I discovered you're Liv's dad. I mean, how do I tell her what happened between us? I couldn't, not while we were pretending to be engaged. And it snowballed, and we didn't know how to put on the brakes." Leo sipped his tea, wondering if he should tell Archie that he knew very well how Liv felt about Rob. But wasn't it for the best that he did? There'd been far too many lies. "I know Liv likes Rob. They were — at the sanctuary when I got there, they were… Rob was *comforting* her because Conrad had turned up and offered money to the sanctuary if we called off the wedding."

"You silly bloody pair." Archie sighed and shook his head. "How did you ever think you could carry it off? A wedding!"

"It seemed so easy to start with," Leo said. "You just book in at the Registry Office, say *I do*, sign a certificate, and that's that. I've fulfilled Gunther's bloody silly clause, I get my million, I give it to the sanctuary, and me and Liv get a divorce." Leo ran his hand back through his hair. It *did* sound ridiculous, now he said it out loud. "But my mum's about to bankrupt herself buying a hat, Auntie Sue was going to make a six-tier cake with columns and gold leaf and God knows what, and…and worse of all, I've had to pretend I'm not gay. Everyone just looks surprised. *You* most of all."

"In case it's escaped your attention," Archie told him, "gay men can get married these days, you know."

"But to a *woman*?" Leo raised his eyebrows. "I mean, it's not like I don't think sexuality is a spectrum, because it is, but I tend to keep up one end of the spectrum with the guys."

"And the clause specifies it has to be to a woman?"

"How's your German? Gunther referred to his Mäuschen. It's how he always referred to his wife, and Brockett told us that's what Mäuschen means. A woman."

Archie laughed. "That's very Brockett! Did nobody think to *ask*? And not just assume?"

"Well...Conrad was there." Leo cringed at the thought of his nemesis. Why couldn't the bullies stay in the playground? It was bad enough encountering them at school, but now they were pouncing on him in adult life. "I just... I'd never been inside a solicitor's office, I have no idea how all this works. I didn't think I could risk saying, '*Oh, excuse me, Mr. Brockett, I'm gay. Is that a problem? Could I take it to mean a non-gender-specific spouse instead?*' Because Conrad would've straightaway said, '*It says wife, you're gay, no money for you!*' And unless I sell the *Aphrodite*, I don't have any money to contest it— certainly not against Conrad. He's loaded, and he's ruthless." Leo sighed. "It's just such a shame. Gunther didn't mean to put me in a tight spot. He basically thought I was lonely and as he was so happy with his Mäuschen, he wanted me to marry too. So he left me a million if I get married within twelve months of the will being read. Hence...*everything*."

"And neither of you thought to ask Brockett for some private advice? *Before* you started making wedding plans?" He wasn't laughing anymore, though. "You don't need to tell me who came up with the idea, it's got *Liv* written all over it."

Leo twiddled his thumbs. He didn't want to slight Liv, but then again, Archie *was* her dad. He knew her better than anyone. "Yes. You see, Conrad was shouting and being vile and accused me of manipulating Gunther, and...Liv meant well, I know she did, she just came out with it. *'Well, it's not a problem because we're getting married!'* And I thought, *Well, that might sort things out.* I dunno, it was almost fun to start with. Until...until I was lying there next to you, and I thought, *I have to walk away.* And I didn't want to, but I couldn't see how to keep up the lie if I stayed."

"And you really didn't know I was her dad?" Archie scrubbed one hand down his face. "You should've asked Brockett for guidance, Leo. It would've been the sensible thing to do, and confidential too. I need to think about this, but I think you, me and Liv need to sit down together."

Leo nodded. "I think we do. And honestly, I had *no* idea. She's never, ever referred to you as *Archie* before. It's always *Pops this, Pops that.* I hadn't even seen a photo of you. When you walked onto the yacht, I thought I was dreaming. Then it was a bit of a nightmare really, because you thought you'd had a fling behind your own daughter's back. I'm so, so sorry."

Leo couldn't even bear to think how much that must've hurt, and all he had done was to plunge the knife in farther by keeping up the lie.

"It's a lot to take in." That was the understatement of the century. Leo was silent, waiting as Archie regarded the surface of his tea. Finally, he said, "You certainly know how to spring a surprise. Or several surprises."

"Sorry. I've hurt you, and I…" Leo sighed. He did feel better now for telling the truth, but it was far too late. "And I don't expect you to forgive me. Really. But just please try not to hate me too much. It's all been such a muddle. I'm out of my depth."

"Well, that *is* true. This is a mess." Archie took a sip of tea. "And your parents don't know any of it? Weren't they even a little bit surprised?"

"Just a bit. But they're very accepting, so they're going along with it." Leo hid his face in his hands. "I feel so guilty. All these lies…Can't you just handcuff me and take me to the police station or something?"

Archie laughed and the tension seemed to lessen somewhat. Then he put his mug down and asked, "Do you want a drink? I think I need something a bit stronger."

Leo dropped his hands from his face. "I think I do as well! I was dreading telling you all this, but I knew I had to. Only I thought the sky was going to drop on my head." He peered around the curtain that covered the porthole. "So far, so good."

"What do you fancy? Glass of white? G and T?"

"G and T. I could do with the fizz!" Leo stretched his arms, then he shifted a fraction from his position wedged into the corner of the sofa. He watched as Archie strolled from the room and into the kitchen, leaving him alone. Archie didn't *seem* curious. If anything, he seemed less angry about this than he had been about the wedding, but that made a certain sort of sense. He hadn't betrayed his daughter after all, it was just a massive mess.

But he hadn't thrown Leo out, which had to count for something.

Leo saw a few family photos on the walls, a gap-toothed Liv with bunches, Archie carrying a small Liv on his shoulders, and a baby in a basket between Archie and a woman who Leo thought must have been Liv's late mother. She looked a lot like her daughter, but she was a brunette swathed in scarves and cheesecloth. There was teenager Liv with Archie on the deck of a yacht, then a photo that made Leo chuckle, showing Liv on the deck of the *Aphrodite*. It was a photo Leo knew well because he had taken it.

"I made it a double." Archie retuned to the room, ice tinkling in the two tall glasses he carried. "You know I can't get formally involved in this whole will mess, don't you? But I have a colleague who might at least be able to advise us. She's a wonder. Trained by Brockett senior, so she knows a few of his tricks. I know it feels like the marriage is the easy option, but it might turn out to cause a hell of a big problem if Conrad gets wind of what's going on."

It was good to think of Archie as an ally.

"If you think she's great, then she must be!" Instinctively, Leo patted his pocket for his wallet. "But how much would it cost? I mean, I could sell the *Aphrodite*, but I'd have to move back in with Mum and Dad if I did that."

"She won't charge for a bit of advice, don't worry about that." He passed a drink to Leo then settled onto the sofa. "Even barristers aren't *that* mercenary."

Leo sipped the drink, the scent of botanicals filling his nose. "Okay. But after that? If she thinks it could be challenged, how much does that all cost? I haven't got a clue, Archie, really."

A fortune.

"Let's not worry about money for now, okay?" *More than a fortune then.* "So the only reason they've assumed this is a woman is because he used the same nickname as his wife had? I mean, you could just as easily interpret as *you must marry someone nicknamed Mäuschen.* The frustrating thing is, that interpretation has basically set a precedent. It's given Conrad a foothold to say, *this highly experienced solicitor interpreted it as so, because it is so. Because Gunther meant it to be thusly interpreted.* Bloody Brockett! Too busy thinking about his golf handicap."

"Conrad didn't even know Gunther, not really. He wants the *Aphrodite* too, and that was unambiguous. Gunther *definitely* left her to me." Leo remembered something from the meeting in Brockett's office and said, "This might help, actually. When Conrad went off on one, and Liv retorted by saying we were getting married, Conrad said, not very nicely, that I'd taken advantage of someone with dementia. Do you think that might be useful to know? If it's the angle he might try to use? Because he could try to prove that the entire will should be ripped up if Gunther had dementia. But there's plenty of people who'd know he had all his faculties. All his girlfriends, for one."

Archie nodded, his expression thoughtful. "We might be getting ahead of ourselves, but keep hold of that thought. Those girlfriends might end up being very useful indeed, you never know." He took another drink. "I'll have a chat to Astrid tomorrow, see what she thinks. She's the will wizard, not me."

"I really, really appreciate this, Archie. Bloody hell, why didn't I just say something to start with?" Leo rolled his eyes. Then he noticed another photo, one he hadn't spotted to start with. Archie in a black gown standing in a very old book-lined room.

Leo hadn't ever thought of a barrister's outfit as being particularly arousing, but he hadn't seen Archie in his gown before. There was something irresistible about the hint of sternness the gown gave him, while there was still that sparkle in his smile.

But Leo forced himself to follow the path of the bubbles rising in his glass instead and hoped Archie hadn't noticed what he had found so fascinating. Luckily, he heard the soft chime of a mobile phone, and Archie's attention was caught by that. He took it from his pocket and said, "Message from Liv. Who's she engaged to now, I wonder?"

"Hunky Rob, I bet!" Leo laughed. "He'd get married in one of those T-shirts with a tie printed on it!"

Daisy's looking a lot happier tonight. She says hello Pops and Leo!

As Archie read the text, Leo heard his own phone buzz with an incoming message. She must have sent it to them both. He didn't take his mobile out though, because Archie had already moved closer, holding his phone so they could both see the screen. "Shall we have a look?"

Liv had no idea that Leo would be here.

"Yeah, go on," Leo said.

Archie smelled deliciously of the sea, briny and fresh. The very hint of it set off a longing in Leo that he did his best to ignore as he looked at the screen. Despite the low light, he knew straight away why Liv was so excited. Daisy, the seal they had rescued from the sea as she took what seemed like her last breath, was lounging with a look of something approaching satisfaction in her little room at the sanctuary. Her head was raised, her eyes bright and she was lazily waving one flipper as though greeting the camera. He could hear Rob's and Liv's laughter bubbling with excitement, and Liv declared, "A very happy patient on the mend!"

Leo gasped. It was the most adorable thing he'd ever seen, and he waved back at Daisy even though she couldn't see him. "I was so scared we'd lose her," Leo said. "Our little Daisy!"

"Just think...if not for you and that daughter of mine having no idea how to contest a will properly, we wouldn't have been there to rescue Daisy." Archie lifted his gaze and looked at Leo from beneath his eyelashes. "So maybe your lie wasn't so bad after all."

Leo looked back at him, his breath catching. *You are such a handsome man, Archie.*

"I'm sorry I ran away. I'm sorry I lied. *Can* you forgive me, Archie? Even a little tiny bit?"

"Forgive you?" Archie gave a rather embarrassed smile. "I think you're *both* a pair of noodles but...I'm just so relieved. I might actually sleep *well* tonight!"

"You couldn't sleep? It's all my fault..." Leo grimaced at Archie. "If I can do anything to make it up to you...any jobs you need doing on the boat..."

But it was there in the air between them, a thrumming like the tension as a storm rolls by, when the clouds turn dark and every color is twice as bright.

"Do you..." Leo touched one fingertip to Archie's biceps before trying again. "Do you still want me, Archie?"

"Do you really need to ask?" he murmured, giving Leo that little smile that was guaranteed to make him melt.

Leo slowly closed his hand around Archie's arm and half-closed his eyes as he felt the strength under his touch. "You do? I long for you, Archie. I need you."

Archie danced his fingertips down Leo's cheek. "Will you stay?"

There was so much warmth in Archie's voice, in his gaze. Leo slid his hand up to Archie's shoulder and circled his thumb against his firm muscles. "I'd love to."

He shifted just a little, just enough to press his lips to Leo's and kiss him. It was like the sun breaking after a rainstorm, bringing with it everything Leo had thought he had lost.

Leo explored him, remembering every sensation from the night they had spent together. Yet this was more intense, because it wasn't only a kiss but everything wrong put right. Archie still wanted him, and Archie had forgiven him, and those were the only two things in the world that Leo cared about at that moment.

The kiss didn't end, instead it grew deeper and turned into one of the smooches Leo had longed for. He let Archie ease him back against the sofa, his elegant fingers tangling in Leo's hair. Leo felt the scurf of salt on Archie's skin and the whole wonderful manliness of him, his strength and the firmness of his body. What could be better in all the world than to be wanted by this man?

"When I woke up and you weren't there…" Archie lost the words in another kiss. He skimmed his lips over Leo's jaw and lower, nuzzling at his throat. Leo felt the rasp of his evening stubble, rough against his skin, and he reveled in it. "I kept your note, but I couldn't stop thinking about you…"

Leo ran his hand through Archie's hair, moaning at the sensation of his lips as they ran across his skin. "It was the hardest thing I've ever done. Walking away from you. I saw you everywhere I went. I wish I hadn't left you…"

"It doesn't matter now," he whispered, his voice low with desire. "Come to bed."

Leo was so happy, he thought he might burst with joy. "There's nowhere else I'd rather be."

"Come on, Captain." Archie caught Leo's hand and rose to his feet. His eyes sparkled bright blue in the low light, but that wasn't *all* that caught Leo's attention. "Let me show you our cabin."

As Leo got up from the sofa, a very lewd memory burst in his thoughts. Archie, tied to the bed, naked and aroused and so very ready to be extremely naughty. Leo liked a man who embraced debauchery with such enthusiasm.

And to think I lost you, my perfect man.

If Leo had been challenged to describe Archie's cabin, he would've guessed at something cozy yet classy. He might've plumped for oceanesque blues and white, for family photos and varnished wood, fresh linens and soft pillows — and he would've been dead right. What Leo might not have expected was to see his own tie thrown over the headboard yet there it was, casually awaiting him and bringing back another flood of wonderful memories. Again Leo saw Archie naked, his arms tense, his chest sheened with the glow of perspiration, and his heart leaped in his chest.

And from his pocket, Leo produced Archie's cufflinks. He held them out on his palm.

"There hasn't been a day when I haven't carried these about with me," Leo told him. "Darling, I couldn't let go."

Archie took Leo's hand in his and closed it, bunching Leo's fist around the cufflinks.

"The first gift of many," he told him with a smile. "It was a wonderful night, wasn't it?"

Leo nodded. "The most wonderful night I've ever had." He brushed his lips against Archie's ear, teasing him, and whispered, "But I have a feeling we'll have many more."

This time there was no game playing, no carefully constructed roles, but an almost reverential silence that was broken only by their soft sighs and moans as Archie and Leo eased their clothes away and tumbled naked onto the bed. They were a tangle of limbs and kisses, fired by need.

Archie was a playground, to be re-explored and enjoyed. Leo roamed his touch over the body he had thought was lost but he had never forgotten. And was it his imagination or was Archie more real, more alive to him than he had been before? Now they were no longer strangers in an anonymous hotel room, but in Archie's own home. In Hervey's it had been all passion and lust, the *fuck* that he had longed for, but now, with their bodies joined in the moonlight, he knew that something had shifted. Tonight, safe in the haven of the yacht Archie had restored with his own two hands, they were making love.

Leo caressed Archie's face, gazing at his blue eyes, each thrust deep and slow and bringing them closer and closer together. When Leo kissed his cheek, he tasted the tang of salt from the sea on the body of his very own merman.

They wouldn't lose each other again, no matter what.

Leo and Archie tumbled into bliss as one, their bodies perfectly in sync and in tune, as natural as any instinct. As they came back down to earth Archie's embrace seemed tighter than ever, his kisses more filled with affection. Leo knew now that he'd been right...he *was* falling in love. Maybe he was already there.

They lay for a while, too breathless, too enchanted to speak. Leo touched his fingertip to Archie's chin, to his lips, to the tip of his nose. He was still with him, not a figment from a dream.

"I'm not leaving this time," Leo promised. "I swear to you, I won't."

"I get to wake up with you tomorrow." Archie smiled, his face alive with happiness. "I've missed you, Leo. I'm sorry I've been so snappy and bad-tempered, I didn't even recognize myself."

Leo brushed back Archie's hair and smiled at him. "It's okay. I must've looked like such a massive bastard to you. And I'm quite an honest sort of bloke really. I hated having to lie."

"I don't know quite how just yet, but we'll get it all sorted out." Archie kissed the tip of Leo's nose. "We barristers have all sorts of things up our sleeves, you know. Astrid's one of the very best."

Leo dropped a kiss to Archie's biceps. "You've got beautiful arms up *your* sleeves!"

"You've got a bit of a thing for my arms, haven't you?" As though to test the theory, Archie slipped his arm around Leo's waist and tensed the muscle to hold him close. How could he *not* have a thing for them when they embraced him like that, though?

"You're going to get me all excited again if you do that," Leo said, his voice soft. "But then again, *all* of you is wonderful. Every gorgeous inch."

Archie responded with a long, deep kiss. "Maybe I want you to get all excited," he purred."

"And if I do..." *If* was not quite word, as Leo's erection was blooming back into life as he spoke. "If I do, what would you like to do with me?"

"*Everything.*" Archie grinned, and as he trailed kisses down onto Leo's chest, he wrapped his fingers around Leo's erection and began to stroke.

Leo sank back in Archie's bed, sighing at every caress from that strong hand.

"I love how you touch me," Leo murmured. He felt Archie's breath on his skin a moment before he drew Leo's nipple into his mouth, teasing the tip of his tongue against it. Still he stroked at that same leisurely pace, taking his time.

Leo's heart rushed with anticipation at what he was about to ask. "Have you ever tied anyone up?"

Archie lifted his gaze to meet Leo's. He blinked once then said, "Not yet."

Leo saucily raised an eyebrow and asked, "Would you like you to?"

"Leo Maxwell!" Archie pantomimed shock. "Are you saying you'd like me to get toppy with you?"

"I might be..." Leo tickled Archie's ear. "You know, a barrister laying down the law with a very naughty sailor."

"Well in that case..." Archie cocked his head to one side. When he spoke again, his voice was stern. "Hands up, Captain, let's get you safely restrained."

A thrill shivered through Leo at Archie's order. "Yes, sir!" he said, and raised his arms, reaching back for the headboard. Archie shifted to kneel on the bed beside him and took Leo's tie from where it was waiting. He took one end in each fist and snapped it taut, flexing his arms.

Leo's hips involuntarily jolted. *Oh my bloody God.* "Archie, you're so hot, it's ridiculous."

"Perhaps you should visit me in chambers." Archie drew the tie tighter in his fist. "You look like you might benefit from a firm hand."

Leo groaned with delight at the thought. That photograph of Archie in his gown came back to him, and Leo began to think about all the fun they could have. Wouldn't it be fun to receive a hard spank from a stern, sexy barrister in his staid and traditional chambers? "Why, because I've been naughty? Do you barristers have certain methods for dealing with bad 'uns like me? Fiendishly sailing about the world, spreading mischief wherever I go?"

"Tell me what sort of methods you're hoping for." Archie began to bind Leo's wrists, tight enough to hold him but not so tight that it would be uncomfortable. "I hope they're suitably scandalous."

Leo bit his lip, picturing the scene and wondering if Archie would be game. Perhaps. "Would you spank me over your desk?"

"Darling." He smiled. "I'd love to."

"Then I am *definitely* coming to your chambers." Leo winked at him. "To consult you confidentially on a legal matter, of course."

"Of course." He lay down beside Leo. "I'll make sure I'm in my full regalia if you like."

"Now that I would definitely like." Leo ran his gaze up and down Archie's body. He was reclining like a figure in a classical portrait. All he needed was a vine wreath in his hair and a silver bowl of grapes. "Does your wig fall off when you get carried away?"

At Leo's words Archie smiled, his stern demeanor momentarily forgotten. "You want the wig too?"

"*Yes*," Leo purred. "I bet you look all stern and Establishment in it."

"Terribly..." He nibbled at Leo's earlobe. "Terribly stern. A pillar of the establishment in every sense of the word."

"A very keen, very solid pillar." Leo's hips jerked with need as he looked down and saw that Archie's erection had revived. "Impressive."

"Maybe I'll even cross-examine you," Archie mused. He skimmed his hand down Leo's chest and slid his arm around his waist to caress his bottom. Then he pressed the tip of one finger between Leo's buttocks and asked, "Tell me, Mr. Maxwell, exactly what you've been up to this evening. For the record."

Leo moaned with desire and for a moment couldn't reply. Once he'd regained control of his senses, he replied, "I went to the beach. And I saw this really hot guy swimming."

Leo glanced at Archie and saw again the droplets of water over his broad shoulders.

"Tell me about him." He added a second finger, stroking deep within him.

Leo pulled against his bonds, his breath stolen from him by the pleasure Archie was giving him. "He...he's very handsome. Broad shoulders. Big blue eyes. Lives on a boat. Works in the law but I think he's quite naughty underneath."

"Did you want him?" He caught Leo's ear with his teeth again. "Does he make you hard?"

"I did want him," Leo panted. "I wanted him to have me on the pebbles. I just have to think of him and I'm hard."

"He wants you too," Archie assured him. Then he kissed Leo, the touch filled with hunger and desire. He was as fierce now as he had been gentle before, his tongue stroking against Leo's.

As much as Leo had enjoyed tying Archie up, it was just as fun being tied up too, giving himself over to Archie and being possessed by him. All Archie's ardor and longing was pouring out into his passionate touch, and Leo kissed him back, just as hard and deep.

"Do you want me to fuck you?" Archie purred against Leo's lips.

"*Yes!*" Leo begged him, breathlessly. "Yes, fuck me, please fuck me."

Leo watched Archie prepare himself in what looked like a leisurely manner, but he could see the urgent need in his lover, recognize the effort it was taking Archie to give the appearance that this was no effort at all. And Archie was his.

Leo pulled against the tie, and joked, "You teasing bastard, leaving your captain all tied up and waiting…!"

"I'm sure you'll get your own back." Archie moved over Leo and kissed him again. He urged Leo's leg around his waist, teasing him with the very tip of his erection. "How much do you want me?"

Leo nodded toward his erection. If there was any sure way of showing how much desire he had for Archie, it was that. "*This* much."

"That much," was Archie's fruity reply. Then he gave a thrust of his hips, uniting their bodies again.

Leo cried out with joy. He lifted his legs and crossed them around Archie to hold him close. "You bloody gorgeous fucker, you," he murmured.

Archie grinned and gave another hard thrust. "Say that again, you naughty thing."

"You..." Leo pushed against him. "Bloody!" He tightened his legs. "Gorgeous!" He pushed again. "Fucker!" And Leo lifted his head and licked Archie's sideburn in one sinuous movement. He'd never heard a sound quite like the one that Archie made then, somewhere between a whimper and a moan. An expression of pure, unbridled lust. His blue eyes fluttered shut for a moment and he arched his neck, parting his lips.

"*Captain*," Archie exclaimed, reaching down to take Leo's erection in his hand. "You're fucking beautiful!"

"That's what I like hear!" Leo tried to quip, but his voice was hoarse with passion as Archie took him in his hand. "Oh—oh, Archie, bloody hell, you're fucking amazing!"

And this was only the first—or second—night of their lives together. This overwhelming pleasure, this sense of everything being just right, was their life now. Then it was all kisses and sensation, their bodies driving each other into bliss.

Leo shivered with intense joy as he reached his peak, and Archie was there with him. Leo moaned his name, or at least tried to, as his body thrust against Archie's until all his pleasure was spent.

A moment before Archie sank against Leo he reached out and untied the tie with a flick of his wrist. Then he snuggled onto Leo's chest, massaging his shoulders with confident sweeps of his hands.

Leo pressed a kiss to Archie's neck. "You enjoyed that, didn't you? We're going to have a brilliant time, Archie. If...if you want to?" *This isn't just sex, is it? It felt like a relationship.*

Archie rested his chin on Leo's shoulder, an affectionate light dancing in his eyes. He drew the tip of one finger up Leo's chest and asked, "If I want to? As an engaged man with a charming fiancée, I don't suppose you're in the market for your very own barrister, are you?"

"Oh, but I am. It's quite all right, you know." Leo started to kiss him, then he stopped. "We'll have to tell Liv, won't we? About us. I hope she won't mind too much."

"With the way she and Rob look at each other? I don't think she'll be too disappointed."

Leo trailed a bead of sweat down the side of Archie's face and caught it with the tip of his tongue. "What will she think of you having a younger man?"

And there was another of those low gasps. Leo would never get tired of hearing that sound.

"Especially one as hot as you? I think she'll be surprised!"

Leo chuckled as he wrapped his arms around Archie. "Aren't gorgeous specimens hurling themselves at you all the time?"

"Somewhere between restoring the yacht, having a career and — most importantly — bringing up the best daughter anyone's ever had, *ever*, I sort of ran out of time to have a love life." He propped his head up on his palm. "What about you? Is there a string of older men feeling terribly jealous of me?"

"Going away for months at a time isn't very conducive to relationships." Leo smiled, though,

174

because as lonely as his itinerant life had been sometimes, it had brought him to Archie. "I'd come back, and they'd have moved on to someone else. Or if I met someone while I was crewing, it never lasted. Long-distance relationships are tough. And I didn't — although I was offered — have any flings with men who'd hired me as a captain. It didn't really seem right, even if it was an invitation to sleep in the best cabin."

"You and I... You know, if you want to go back to sea, back to being the captain, I wouldn't stop you." He kissed Leo's cheek. "Obviously I'd rather you were here with me, but you have to have your dreams. I'm not that sort of guy."

"On my last trip, I'd been wondering, actually..." Leo hadn't told anyone this. Not his parents, not Liv. "If I still want to do it. Maybe it's time I try something that wouldn't keep taking me away for ages. It gets lonely, you know. And I wouldn't want to go away for two months and not see you."

Archie nodded. "So what's the plan?"

"There's a sailing school in Newhaven," Leo said. "I thought I'd see if they have a vacancy for a captain. I'll teach people how to sail a yacht or a dingy or a rowing boat, I don't mind! I could go freelance, if there's demand for it. *Know your fo'c'sle from your mainsail,* that sort of thing."

"Liv used to tell me that boat of yours was a bit of a pleasure palace," Archie said, nuzzling a kiss to Leo's shoulder. "She said your boss was famous for his parties? Have you thought about making something out of that? You could hire her out, be Brighton's very own *Great Gatsby!*"

"I could, couldn't I! If I don't have to sell her..." Leo shrugged. "You know, on some yachts I had to wear uniforms, like an entirely white outfit with shiny buttons and a hat. I could get one of those again. Wouldn't be a bad way to make a living. We could just pootle up and down the coast so there wouldn't be any of that hard sailing where you're keeling over and it's freezing cold and the waves are coming at you."

Archie gave a low, rather heated sound of acknowledgment. He walked his fingers down Leo's chest and paused at his navel.

"So...this uniform? Are we talking *An Officer and a Gentleman*?"

"That sort of thing, yes. A bugger to keep clean, but..." Leo chuckled. "Archie, are you thinking what I think you're thinking? You'd like to be tied up by a man in a white officer's suit? You are a brilliant sauce, aren't you? If you're good, I'll let you wear my hat!"

"I would *love* that!" Archie beamed. "Captain, we're going to have a hell of a time, you know!"

Leo saluted him. "Oh, yes, we bloody well will, your honor!"

Chapter Sixteen

"*I'll* sort out breakfast, you've got a busy day ahead," Leo said as he tightened the belt on his toweling dressing gown. He stared about at Archie's galley kitchen, so compact, and yet a mystery to him. "Although...I'm not sure where everything is."

"Then you'll have fun finding out!" Archie scrubbed at his wet hair with a towel and pottered through into the kitchen after Leo. He caught him around the waist and kissed the back of his neck. "I don't want to go to stuffy old chambers!"

Leo linked his fingers with Archie's and said, "Well, I'll come to visit you soon, and they *won't* be so stuffy then. What do you have? Toast, cereal? I feel like I know you really well but I don't know things like...what do you like for breakfast?"

"Tea, toast and tons of strawberry jam," Archie told him. "I'll talk to Astrid today, and we'll get you an appointment set up to see her. What's your schedule for this week? When're you around for meetings?"

Leo homed in on a china pot and discovered the bread lurking in it, so he got to work with the toast and Archie's grill. "Well, you know me, Arch. A high-flying, busy executive like me, it'll be hard to fit it in! I can move stuff around, it's not a problem. I've got a list of jobs that need doing, but no one's breathing down my neck. They're just glad that *someone*'ll do it for them before summer kicks in."

He opened a tin with a ceramic seagull sitting on its lid and discovered the home of Archie's tea bags.

"Would it be terribly naughty if I wore your tie?" Archie tilted his chin to peer at Leo, his smile mischievous. "And you need to take my phone number, or how will you send me suggestive messages when I'm supposed to be working?"

"Wear my tie?" Leo found the fridge behind its disguised door and rummaged for the jam. "Yeah, if you like! I bought it especially for that meeting with Brockett, you know. I thought, *people will take me seriously in this*. I hadn't realized it'd be so good for…light bondage."

"I've got a lot of ties. Maybe we should try them out." Archie's words were a tease. He put his arms around Leo again and pulled him into a kiss. Leo put the jam jar down on the side and hugged Archie tight as their kiss deepened. Would Archie ever get to work at this rate?

"*Wow*."

That didn't sound like the radio. It sounded like Liv. And she didn't sound happy.

"I don't— Oh my *God!*"

"Shit! Liv! Shit, I'm sorry!" Horror-struck, Leo tried to step back from Archie but there wasn't any room to move. She really hadn't needed to walk in on them like that. A nice chat with her dad would've softened things.

"Pops?" she asked, her eyebrows raised. "Is this a joke?"

"Can everyone just stop walking in on each other snogging?" Leo said, and his face broke into a smile. "Sorry, this wasn't a good way to find out, was it?"

But Liv looked furious. She walked over and slammed the fridge door then said, "This is my fiancé, Pops, how could—" Then she shook her head and sighed before whispering, "I'm sorry, Leo. I can't do it to my pop. We have to tell him."

Faced with the collapse of her spirited act, Archie smiled. He reached out and knocked her arm with his fist. "I already know, darling. It turns out we've all been wrapping ourselves in knots for weeks when we should've just told the truth. Do you want some breakfast, and we'll get everyone on the same page?"

"I'm making toast and tea. There's loads," Leo offered. Yet Liv was looking at Archie a little suspiciously, then she grabbed Leo's arm and put her lips to his ear.

"Is *this* the silver fox?"

"Erm…" Leo glanced awkwardly at Archie. "We're best friends, we tell each everything! Well, pretty much."

"How much—" Archie caught himself then shook his head. "Don't tell me, I don't want to know!"

Liv scrubbed Archie's hair and assured him, "Neither do I. So, you two met…what, after the will reading? And you didn't get each other's numbers. Which is why Pops was in such a grumpy mood for the next couple of days!"

"That's it." Leo nodded. "I went for a drink to toast old Gunther, and who should walk in but this gorgeous man? I had no idea he was the legendary Pops. You'd made *Pops* sound like he shuffled about in slippers!"

"And I'd always pictured Leo as a grizzled young salt. Called *Max*," Archie confessed. "Not *this*!"

"A grizzled young salt called Leo!" Leo chuckled as he tweaked Archie's nose. Liv shook her head and went over to the toaster as though this was the most normal thing in the world.

"How's Daisy?" Archie asked.

She turned to look at them, her face lit by a beaming smile. "She's on the mend. We don't know if she can be returned to the wild for a bit, if ever, but she's going to live and that's thanks to you two young lovers."

"You're working the magic twenty-four-seven," Leo said. "Daisy looked like she was on her last legs, but we weren't going to give up on her. And she's going to live because you and Rob wouldn't either."

Her smile grew even wider, then she said, "Look, I'm not going to pretend that you two being a thing isn't a shock, okay? But it's not the worst one I've ever had. The only thing I really need to know is, am I still engaged?"

"Maybe…maybe just for now," Leo said. He glanced to the porthole but the galley's curtain was firmly closed over it. "Your dad's going to speak to a colleague to see what our chances are."

"And next time, come to me first," Archie instructed. "Before you make wedding plans. And that goes for both of you."

Leo batted his eyelashes at Archie and pouted. "I'm sorry, darling. We won't do it ever again."

"Toast's burning," Liv informed them with a look of long-suffering good humor. "I don't know. Pops steals my fiancé *and* burns my toast. Can things get any worse?"

"Sit down, both of you." Archie kissed Leo's cheek. "And Leo can get us all up to speed while I make more toast!"

Leo sat down with Liv and went through with her what he and Archie had discussed regarding Gunther's bequest. He wasn't sure if he was hopeful or not, but one thing was for sure—Leo wasn't going to lie to the people he loved any longer.

Liv took it all in her stride and soon, with her questions out of the way and the truth finally aired, they were all looking at photos of Daisy instead. Seeing the little pup only galvanized Leo all the more to get the bequest Gunther had intended for him. It wasn't about money, it was about making a difference.

"Since we got on the news with Daisy we've had loads of interest," she told them. "People seem to have really taken the story to heart, which is brilliant. We're getting donations and lovely messages from all over the place. I mean, it helps that two such lovely blokes did the rescuing bit. And Rob looking like Thor in a T-shirt doesn't do any harm either."

"Sorry, but I didn't hear you mention yourself in any of that," Archie told his daughter. "You're the one who keeps that place going, and don't forget it. Leo, I don't know if Liv ever told you, but she worked there for no pay at all when she was a girl. She only agreed to go off crewing because they ran out of cash to pay her."

Liv nodded, her ponytail bobbing. "True. I saved up enough crewing to not have to get paid much when I got back. And it helps that Pops is super generous too!"

"I was coming to that..." He knitted his fingers on the polished top of the table. "I know that the money from Gunther is a matter of principle for the two of you. But barristers — particularly barristers at Bedford Court — don't come cheap, even on mates' rates."

Leo sighed. "Should we just go through with the wedding, then? If we can, and hope bloody Conrad doesn't find out anything to stop it?"

"If you're going to have to spend a fortune in fees to fight the case, we have to weigh up whether it's worth it, that's all I'm saying." He was right, of course, but it seemed so unfair. "Principle is one thing, but common sense is another."

"But Conrad's *such* an —" Liv looked down as her phone pinged. Then her mouth fell open. "Oh my God. You will not *believe* this!"

Leo tried to read her expression, but it didn't look good and he was filled with trepidation. "Dare I ask?"

"An email from *a well-wisher*. To the sanctuary account. Dear Loveday," she read, her eyes scanning the screen. "I thought you should see this before you go through with your marriage. My condolences. You must be heartbroken."

With that, she held up her phone so Leo could see the image on the screen.

And there on the screen Leo saw himself and Archie in the MG, parked up outside the seal sanctuary. There was no mistaking the ardour in their gaze, nor the romantic gesture of Archie kissing Leo's hand.

The sky really was falling down on Leo's head now. *This isn't fair. None of this is fair.* "I knew someone was watching! Oh, bloody hell, why wasn't I more careful? Is this Conrad's work?"

But something had changed in Archie's face. Liv seemed as stricken as Leo, but not Archie. He had that steely look again, his jaw tight and his eyes flashing.

"Oh, the game is *on!*" He slapped the palm of his hand down on the table. "If he wants a fight, he might've just got one!"

Leo glanced at the photo of Archie in his barrister's gown, his expression intent and as hard as granite. Was Conrad Beaucock about to meet his match?

Chapter Seventeen

Once Archie had returned from work that evening, he drove Leo back to his parents' house. There was no barbecue now, and Leo wasn't sure much would be left of the mountainous trifle, but it was only right they were told the truth as well.

Mike opened the door. "Didn't expect to see you too back again so soon! Fancied more of my sardines?"

"Dad, can we pop in for a sec?" Leo glanced over his shoulder but, unsure if anyone was watching, he lowered his voice, "For a word?"

Mike frowned. "Are you okay, lad? Come on in." As he beckoned them in, he called into the house, "Linda, kettle on! We've got guests!"

Mike closed the door behind them and led them to the lounge. Leo's school photos were still arrayed across the mantelpiece, as well as his parents' wedding photo featuring the bridesmaid with the enormous perm. Mike gathered up the pages of his newspaper, which he seemed to have covered every surface with.

"I was trying to find the sudoku. They keep moving it," he said by way of explanation as he shoved the pages aside. Mike offered the armchair by the window to Archie and sat down on the sofa. "I hope no one got food poisoning? What with you being a barrister, Archie, that could be awkward!"

"Unless you're committing major corporate fraud, you don't need to worry about that," Archie assured him with a matey slap to Mike's shoulder. He offered a bright smile to Linda too, when she appeared in the doorway. "We're so sorry to just drop in like this."

"Oh no, anytime you like," she assured them. "Tea's mashing, and I'm wondering what's happened to bring you here? So put me out of my misery."

Leo decided to go in gently. "Have you bought a hat yet?"

"A hat? Why— Oh, Leo, don't tell me you're gay again!" She threw up her hands. "What did I say, Mike? Didn't I say it was a surprise? I knew this'd happen!"

Mike shook his head. "That or he's going to ask you to get a damn silly perm. What is it, son?"

Leo dropped down onto the edge of the coffee table. "I—I always have been gay. It's just, you know how Gunther left me the yacht? I'd inherit a million pounds as well if…"

"If…?" Mike leaned forward in his seat. "If…?"

"If I get married. And the solicitor decided Gunther meant I had to marry a *woman,* so Liv suggested I marry *her,* and we've been pretending to be a couple, and I lied to you, and I'm so sorry." Leo lowered his head and sniffed back a tear.

He felt Archie's hand on his back, soothing him. But what would his parents say to this new, unspoken revelation? He could hardly imagine.

"You silly thing," Linda said gently. "Why didn't you tell us? I thought it was funny you marrying a girl, but...why didn't he just leave you the money if he wanted you to have it?"

"Because he thought I was lonely and he wanted me to settle down. And he's right, I *am* lonely sometimes, going out on the yachts for months at a time. He was so happy with his wife, you see, and he kept going on about his missus and...the solicitor decided that's what he meant. I needed to have a missus too in order to inherit it. Not a mister, which is far more my style."

And Leo gave Archie a grin. The way Mike cleared his throat and fidgeted indicated that Mike might just have worked out what was going on. Linda, however, still looked none the wiser. Instead she crossed the room and ruffled Leo's hair, as though he were her little boy again.

"You'll find your mister one day. And he'll be lucky to have you!"

Leo glanced at Archie again. "There's...there's something you should know." Here, Leo decided to edit the truth a tiny bit. "I've spent so much time with Archie of late, and...the thing is...he and I..."

Mike coughed loudly, but once he'd settled down Leo finished.

"Me and Archie are a couple."

After a couple of moments' silence, Mike said, "Another surprise!" He held his hand out to Archie. "I'm glad. You seem like a decent sort of bloke, Archie. Welcome to the family. Again."

Archie seized Mike's hand and shook it as he admitted, "I'm glad you approve! I know I'm not as pretty as my daughter, but I hope that isn't a deal-breaker."

Linda was silent for a few seconds, as though she was processing the information. Leo waited for her verdict, silently praying that she wasn't about to hit the roof. It didn't happen often, but Leo didn't lie often either.

"So…" She frowned, but it was a thoughtful frown rather than an angry one. Maybe even a touch confused. "A couple? But you're not engaged? Or are you?"

"No, bit too soon for that." *Although I wouldn't mind one bit.* "I just couldn't go on lying to you. It wasn't right. I should've trusted you, and I didn't, and I'm so sorry."

"Come on, Leo," Mike said, in the affectionate voice he'd used so often in Leo's life. When he'd fallen and skinned his knee, when he'd been picked on at school, when his dinghy sank in the regatta and he was disqualified. "If someone offered me a million to get married — well, I already am, but I'm not surprised you decided to do it. Lots of people would."

Linda nodded. Then she winked. "Especially if he looked like Archie!"

Leo shook his head. "Unfortunately, Gunther didn't say, '*Leo! Find a handsome barrister, marry him, and I'll give you a million quid!*' But seeing as Archie *is* a barrister, and this is all a bit legal and not my area at all, Archie's ridden to my rescue."

"I've got a colleague who specializes in wills and trusts," Archie explained. "She's agreed to make some inquiries and see if there's anything we can do. At the moment we're really just waiting to hear her verdict, but fingers crossed it can all be resolved painlessly. There's someone else we have to think about, you see.

Leo, do you want to clue your folks in on the Beaucock factor?"

"Yes, yes, I'd better." Leo rubbed his hands together. "Right, there's this prat called Conrad Beaucock —" Leo paused while his father roared with laughter. Once he'd finished, Leo went on. "He's a distant relative of Gunther's and he reckons he should inherit the *Aphrodite*, and he pretty much feels that if I don't marry a woman, *he* should get the million pounds. He keeps popping up like the world's most unpleasant jack-in-the-box, and he's trying to catch me out. And I'm fairly sure he's got someone to spy on me. He thinks I'm gay. I mean, we know he's right, but if you think anyone's watching the house, or someone asks you anything about me and Liv... Can you just not say anything? And try to remember what they look like so we know if they reappear?"

"That's a thought," Archie mused. "Leo, ask around your mates. Find out if anybody's been showing an interest."

Linda gave a firm nod too. "I said to Mike yesterday I'd had a message on Facebook from someone who said they'd been on the crews with you. There wasn't a profile photo so I blocked it. I've had half a dozen since you got engaged."

Archie had that look in his eye again, a gleam like a cat watching a mouse.

"Next time, Linda, if you don't mind would you make a bit of small talk?" He raised his eyebrows. "I'd bet you that million that they're going to be asking questions about Leo. *'Has he got a boyfriend right now?'* That sort of thing. Conrad's trying to build evidence that the engagement's a sham. And it is, but for the most honorable reasons. It's for the seals, you know."

"Seals?" Linda exclaimed. "Now you've lost me."

"What, rubber seals?" Mike scratched his chin, frowning. "We've got loads in the warehouse, what's getting married and a million quid got to do with them?"

"No, the seal sanctuary," Leo explained, and he clapped his hands together as if they were flippers and did his best impression of a barking seal. Lightbulbs began to go on above his parents' heads. "I've got that enormous, daft boat, and a million quid? I mean, it's nice, but wouldn't it be great to do something wonderful with that kind of money? The seal sanctuary needs as much dosh as it can get, and I thought, *I'll get that million and give it to the sanctuary.*"

"Oh, you're such a sweetheart!" Linda put her arms around Leo and hugged him. "I'm glad you've finally got a proper, sensible boyfriend. I bet Archie won't turn up in hot pants like the last one! I didn't know where to look!"

"Yes..." *Although Archie could carry it off with* those *thighs.* "It was a very hot day, after all. But you two do understand, don't you? Why me and Liv had to lie? We didn't want to, we felt horrible, but we thought, *all we need to do is get married, and we get all that money for the sanctuary.* Only it's not very easy, is it?"

"We understand," his mum assured him. "I'm not happy about it, but I know why you did. The wedding's off, I assume, Archie?"

Archie looked at Leo. *Is the wedding off? Probably. Maybe.*

"I don't want Leo and Liv to marry," Archie replied. "Not because I'm his partner or her pops. It's because Leo deserves that inheritance for being Leo, not for having a marriage certificate that doesn't mean anything. But I'll stand by his decision, whatever it is."

Leo didn't say anything at first, but he took Archie's hand and held it gently. He'd been so callow, pursuing the marriage against all the odds, but he'd never stopped to think of it in that way. "Gunther wanted me to be married to someone I love as much as he loved his wife. You're right, I can't inherit that money based on a fake wedding."

Archie met his gaze and smiled. Then he told him softly, "I think I'd have got on with Gunther."

Chapter Eighteen

What a treat, Archie driving us into London on a lovely spring day.

And it would have been perfect if Leo hadn't had to pretend there was nothing between them. More than once Leo had to stop himself from brushing against Archie. He couldn't squeeze his thigh or his knee because who would believe *that* was innocent?

I'm so tired of pretending.

But maybe Astrid would have good news?

"How do you feel?" Archie asked as they idled in a long queue of Monday morning traffic. "I don't want you to be nervous."

"I am a bit." Leo smoothed down his tie, one his parents had given him for Christmas, with a pattern of anchors embroidered on it. He was wearing his tweed suit again. With an awkward laugh, he admitted, "I feel so out of place. And I'm worried I won't understand anything."

"She won't try to bamboozle you." Archie gave him a winning sort of smile. "Would you like me to come in with you or would you rather be alone?"

"Could you come in with me? I'd feel better if you were there." Leo did his best to return Archie's smile as he said, "It's a bit overwhelming, really."

"Of course," he promised. "I just want you to think carefully about whatever advice she gives, okay? Don't bankrupt yourself to make a point to Conrad Beaucock. Agreed?"

"Yeah." Embarrassed, Leo swept back his hair. "When this all started, he got on my wick so much that…maybe it wasn't just getting the money for the sanctuary that was motivating me. I just didn't want him to win."

But how quickly would contesting the will burn through a million pounds? It wasn't as if Leo had the money to pay for it anyway and even if he did…maybe Archie was right. But he'd wait and see what Astrid said before he made a decision.

Bloody Conrad Beaucock.

"He wants the yacht too." Leo sighed. "So even if I said, *okay, I'll sell the* Aphrodite *so I can pay the fees –* Well, I'd be a bit stuck if someone in a wig decided he should have that too as well as the money."

"From what you told me, it doesn't sound as though there's any risk of losing the yacht. It's important not to get the details confused," Archie advised. "You have to be guided by your head in this sort of thing, no matter what your heart says. Everyone in my job has seen somebody take a matter of principle to court and lose their shirt and their house for the sake of winning their case. I don't want you to do that."

"I won't, don't worry," Leo assured him. "As much as it'll be annoying to see that pillock crowing, I just...well...I can always look in the other direction, can't I? And it's not like I'm losing that million exactly. I've never had it. It would've been nice all the same, but..."

Archie was silent as they drove on, deeper into the city. Leo watched the Monday morning commuters hurry past and saw the sun glint off the Thames as they drove over Blackfriars Bridge, the cries of gulls overhead reminding him of the calm waters of the marina. Then Archie turned the car into a narrow cul-de-sac and drew in alongside the curb.

Only he would have a secret parking spot right in the heart of London.

The Georgian houses rose up around them. Somewhere, a siren shrieked and voices called. But there was something quiet and cloistered about this place, and Leo was reminded of the silence of Brockett's offices.

"Here goes," Leo said as he got out of the car. *Bedford Court Chambers.* Professional home of the Greville-Hall family for centuries and the place where his fate might be decided. And it suited Archie down to the ground.

Leo felt more confident than he had walking into Brockett's offices. At least he now had a vague idea of what to expect, and with Archie beside him there was a sense of familiarity to the place even though he'd never been to his chambers before.

The wood-paneled offices were deceptively quiet. Rather like a swan gliding over the waters, Leo suspected that under the chambers' calm appearance, intense work was in full swing. He followed Archie through the building, past impressive paintings of barristers past, the sense of past and present coexisting in harmony somehow palpable.

"I'll drop my things in my office," Archie told him as they strolled. "So you can see my little corner of London!"

Leo brushed his palm against the panels as they walked along. It was like being below decks in an old ship, and it smelled of wax polish. "This place is great! It's nicer than Brockett's office! He's got magnolia paint in his corridor!"

"He suits his offices, though, don't you think? Deceptively humble, so his ultra-rich clients think they're getting a bargain." He paused at a large, paneled door. "And here's mine!"

With that he pushed the door open and stood back to let Leo enter.

Leo gasped in amazement. It was beautiful, like a room in a museum or a country house. It was paneled like the corridors, with leather-bound books in the alcoves beside the marble fireplace. There was a desk by the window, larger and older than Brockett's, although it had the same green-shaded lamp that seemed to be standard issue for people working in law. Everything looked so of a piece that Leo didn't at first spot the computer on Archie's desk, and it made him chuckle. The room didn't strike Leo with fear or reverence, but perhaps it was because it felt so very *Archie*. Then, on a coat stand in the corner, he spotted the black drape of what Leo assumed was Archie's gown. And although it shouldn't have, it gave Leo a frisson of excitement.

"I'll picture you here at your desk while I'm back at the marina, patching up sails!" Leo laughed.

"And I'll picture you patching up sails at the marina and feel terribly envious." Archie put his briefcase down on his desk. "That sounds like much more fun than I'll be having."

"You never really talk about your job." Leo wandered over to the bookshelves and ran his finger along the spines without reading their gold-leafed titles. "Is it top secret, or is it just not very exciting?"

"I specialize in corporate fraud cases, so exceptionally rich people hoping to get richer." Archie put his arm around Leo's waist. "And I do my best to make sure they don't. They'd eat Conrad for breakfast and spit out his bones."

"I don't suppose you could arrange that for me?" Leo grinned as he walked his fingertips up the front of Archie's suit. "Are you very stern with them?"

"Sometimes." He kissed Leo. "Have you got a bit of a thing for stern barristers?"

"Not until I met you..." Leo gazed at Archie and unfastened the top button of his jacket. "But now for some reason the thought of a stern barrister really turns me on."

Especially one who could also be as gentle and affectionate as Archie. Not to mention as silly or as spontaneous. He was exactly what Leo had always wanted.

But Leo had to banish all thoughts of stern barristers from his mind as Archie took him up the stairs to Astrid's office. Leo wasn't holding out for a miracle. At least this time, though, he'd get an expert opinion and would understand where he stood. He wouldn't feel like he was groping about in the dark anymore.

"Good luck," Archie told Leo as they paused at the door. He patted Leo's back. "She won't steer you wrong."

Leo rapped three ponderous knocks to the door, and a voice rang out, "Hello!" And Leo nearly fell forward through the door as it sharply opened.

This, then, was Astrid. A tall woman in a black skirt suit, with white-blonde pixie-cut hair and pillar-box-red lipstick.

"Mr. Leonard Michael Maxwell…" she said, mock seriously, before changing her tone to say, "Or Leo, as I'm told, and…now who's this you've brought with you? My goodness me, it's our Archie! Take a seat, take a seat!"

She beckoned them into a room that was a lot like Archie's, except the wood panels were painted a light sage green. Sunshine poured in from between opened shutters, and the lamp on her desk glowed.

Astrid stood beside a small drinks machine next to her desk. "Tea, coffee, hot chocolate, fizzy water, everything but champagne, I'm afraid. What'd you like?"

"Tea. Just milk, please," Leo said as he sat down at Astrid's desk. He was perturbed by how bouncy she was, as if she'd ingested nothing but neat sugar for breakfast. Was this a way of sweetening the pill so his disappointment wouldn't be too crushing?

"You do know there are people in this building who exist solely to make drinks for clients?" Archie asked with a warm smile as he settled into a seat. "Good weekend?"

"The best!" Astrid chuckled as she turned to make the tea. "Spent most of it lying flat on my back in the park with a book. And…a certain person. Don't worry,

Leo, Archie's my Agony Uncle, he knows all about the *certain person*. I was asking for man advice from him on the subject the other week. And it seems you were right, Archie. He *does* like me after all." She brought a mug over to Leo and gave Archie a wink.

"Does this mean...?" Archie gave a look of shock. "Astrid, is this love story going to have a happy ending?"

"I think it might..." She sat down behind her desk and put on a pair of round tortoiseshell glasses that had been waiting for her on a stack of buff files. Astrid clasped her hands on her desk and said in a stage whisper, "We're going to his cottage in the Cotswolds at the weekend!"

Archie leaned forward and whispered, "So when do I meet him?"

"Soon." Astrid took a slim file from her stack and laid it on the desk in front of her. Leo couldn't help but notice that the label on the front read *MAXWELL*, and it sent a stab into his gut. "I *have* suggested that after we go to his cottage, for my treat we pop down to Brighton for a weekend. I don't suppose we could swing by the *Loveday*?"

"Oh, do!" Archie grinned. "We'll go for a sail, take a picnic?"

"Absolutely! That would be *so* splendid, thank you, Archie! I'll look forward to that." Astrid smiled at Leo. "So...you have a slight problem with a certain Mr. Beaucock, I believe?"

"Erm..." Leo put his half-drunk tea down on the edge of Astrid's desk. "I suppose Archie's filled you in?"

"Yes, he has," Astrid replied. "And I think it's a very, very interesting case. Archie has said that we don't want long-drawn-out legal wranglings, and I understand that. But I do think it's worth taking it before a judge."

"Yeah, but Brockett's already decided," Leo said, recalling Archie's words of warning. "And won't a judge cost money?" He glanced from Astrid to Archie. The humor had gone from his lover's expression now, to be replaced by a serious look. After a moment Archie sat back in his seat.

"It feels winnable to me," he said.

Astrid nodded. "Oh, yes, it does to me too. And I think it's an important case, as well as an interesting one. So much of the law is down to interpretation, but interpretation relies on context. Did Mr. Schreiber say *wife*? No, he did not, he used his pet name for *his* wife — his spouse. Brockett might've interpreted it to mean wife, but I believe it could just as easily be interpreted to mean any spouse, husband *or* wife. Brockett has read gender into something, looking through his own heteronormative spectacles, I would imagine."

"It's good to hear you say that," Leo said. He reached for Archie's hand and clasped it.

Astrid's eyes widened for a moment, before asking, "Archie, were your thoughts running on a similar track?"

He nodded. "Yeah, they were. The will is watertight to me, I don't see any chance of Conrad getting that overturned, but the interpretation of the wording of the trust? That's another matter. I assume Beaucock's argument is going to be that, as a man who was married and loved the company of women, Gunther *obviously* intended for the condition to be interpreted as marriage to a woman. Brockett assumed that was the case for starters, and that's valuable to Beaucock." He squeezed

Leo's hand. "If we get the right judge, we could put this to bed very quickly. If we get the wrong judge...you already know."

Astrid gave a world-weary sigh, nodding as she opened the file. "I know very well. Now, Beaucock. I personally would love to stop him getting his hands on this money. He is an unprincipled, devious, selfish man and he doesn't deserve a penny. You've had several run-ins with him, Leo, haven't you?"

Leo nodded.

"Same here," Astrid said. Her playfulness evaporated as she explained, "He and I trained together. He...well...he seemed to think that because I'm a woman, I would of course find him irresistible. Alas for him, I have taste. I turned down his offer, and I thought everything would be all right—he didn't pester me. But oh, no, I hadn't bargained for the way he would get his revenge. He mounted a bizarre campaign against me, spread rumors, exaggerated the truth until it bore little relation to reality, on and on it went until I was nearly taken before a disciplinary board for professional misconduct."

She glanced from Leo to Archie.

"I nearly lost everything—at the beginning of my career. His name was never brought up in connection with what had happened, but I knew he was the source of certain rumors. I suspect he thought he'd got away with it, caused mayhem without me knowing he was behind it. I never had it out with him. Not long after that, I was called to the bar and came here, to Bedford Court, and Conrad and I moved in different circles. I rarely cross his path now, but from what I hear on the grapevine, he's still just as awful as he ever was."

Leo sensed a certain shift in Archie, just a hint of tension when he asked, "This previous clash, it's nothing he could use to muddy the waters, is it? Because he seems the type."

"No. It involved a forged signature, and I hadn't done it, and could prove I hadn't. As far as I know, they never found out who'd done it. Conrad's name was never connected with it, so he can't claim I'm not independent. You see, it's not just *that* which makes me dislike him. He twists the law for his own purposes, he does it all the time, turns justice on its head and buys himself another ridiculous car, and I'm not the only person who would very much like to stop him for a change. So that's why..." Astrid's smile returned, and she said, "Leo, I know you're concerned about the costs involved in contesting the clause of this trust. There's such an important point to be made here about gender and modern relationships, and I would like to take the case on *pro bono*. You wouldn't have to pay a thing."

"*You* are a one off, Astrid," Archie told her, his voice filled with enthusiasm. Then he turned to Leo. "Before you decide, you should probably be aware that this is the sort of case the press are likely to love, especially if Gunther's lady friends get involved. How do you feel about that?"

"I dunno, I suppose I could always sail into international waters...!" Leo chuckled. "Astrid's right, the whole gender thing... Brockett assuming a man marries a wife, not a husband. It needs to be in the press, don't you think? It's the twenty-first century. I *know* it's not a foregone conclusion that we'll win, I know that... But Conrad'll be out there right now somewhere trying to find some arcane law to stop the wedding anyway. It's all such a mess, and I feel really horrible for the sanctuary, but think of the publicity they'll get!"

"Then it's up to you." Archie lifted Leo's hand and kissed it. "Do you want Astrid to go ahead and challenge the interpretation of the trust and take Conrad head on? The first step's mediation, but I don't think Conrad's the mediating type."

Astrid rolled her eyes. "No, he's not. He's going to relish this, you know that?" She rubbed her hands together and said, "But I'm going to relish it even more!"

"Leo?" Archie asked.

"Will he...will he say I'm a liar?" Leo was aware that his voice sounded small, like a frightened child's. "I did lie to people, and I feel really bad about it, you know, with the fake wedding."

Astrid tapped the cover of the file with her scarlet-painted nails. "He might try to impugn your character, yes, but the core of this case is the interpretation of Mr. Schreiber's clause. You getting halfway to a marrying a woman isn't material to that. It will be brought up, though, but it's worth wondering what the average person on the street would think. Someone offers a single person a million pounds if they marry a woman—who wouldn't? And no matter what mud-flinging Conrad attempts, you've got Archie, you've got your family and friends. And the very fact you're sitting here fretting about the fact you lied tells me you're a decent person. Conrad Beaucock isn't."

"This is Astrid's speciality, not mine," Archie told him. "But I think the truth of this case is so compelling that we should be confident in telling the story. The motive was honorable, even if the means were a little dishonest."

Leo felt himself blush. "Yeah...sorry."

"Archie's right," Astrid said. "This *needs* to go in front of the public. And I will be so proud to represent you. So you might want to go away and have a think before you decide anything, but here's my card. Get in touch with any questions you might have." Astrid slid a neat business card across her desk to him.

Leo took it. "I will. Thanks, Astrid, I really appreciate this. I...I'll think it through. I want to say *yes* right now, but...jumping right in is what got me in trouble to start with."

"And remember, if this ends happily in mediation then the job's done." Archie gave Leo a reassuring smile. "But I'm with you all the way."

Chapter Nineteen

Back in Brighton, Leo's first task was to tell Liv the wedding was off. He'd left Archie in his chambers and come back by train, then walked from the station to the sanctuary. There was usually a little queue to get in these days and today was no different, as a gaggle of schoolchildren were being shepherded through the gates by Rob and one of the many volunteers.

"Rob, is Liv about?" Leo called.

Rob nodded and pointed toward the pool. "She's at the pool. I'll give her a shout."

Leo trotted after him into the sanctuary. The Plexiglas box for collecting donations was looking pleasingly well-stuffed, and on it was a little photograph of Daisy, her flipper raised in a greeting. A speech bubble had been affixed to the photo in which someone—Liv, Leo guessed—had written, *"Thanks, friends! Xxx"*

And there she was, the celebrity herself, her head poking up above the water of the pool. Leo forgot all about lawyers and wills and Conrad Beaucock for a moment and watched along with the other visitors as Daisy paddled along. She didn't move as smoothly as Roxie and Cyrano, but after what had happened to the seal pup, Leo was glad to see her moving at all.

He spotted Liv and waved to her. "Liv, have you got a sec?"

"Hello, darls!" Liv jumped to her feet from where she was kneeling beside the pool and headed toward Leo. "Come and see Daisy hanging out with her mates!"

Leo let himself into the enclosure and stepped carefully to avoid a fish head that one of the seals had left on the grass.

"She's swimming!" Leo rubbed his hands with glee. "Oh, Liv, you and Rob have done something amazing."

Liv beamed and took his arm. "She's never going to be able to live in the wild, so she's officially our mascot. Which means she permanently occupies a spot here, so we desperately need more space. But have you *seen* the donation box? People have really responded to her story. They were pulling for her when she was struggling."

"Your celebrity resident!" Leo took a deep breath. "Look, about the wedding. I've just got back from seeing Astrid, the will person. She thinks I've got a such strong case, she'll represent me for free. Your dad thinks it's winnable. But there's still a risk it won't go our way and we'll—the sanctuary—will lose the million. Thing is, if we don't contest the clause then Conrad will make trouble anyway with the wedding, and I know how much the sanctuary needs the money, Liv. I know how much this place means to you. But we have to cancel the wedding."

Liv glanced back toward the pool, where the three seals were swimming without a care in the world. Then she nodded. "We'll manage. It's the right thing to do."

"We've probably got more chance of getting the money this way. Conrad knows the wedding's not real, and he just can't be trusted." Leo winced, thinking about Astrid being subjected to Conrad's campaign, and he wondered again at how someone as nice as Gunther could be related to someone so irredeemably horrible. "He'll do *something* to prove the wedding's not real, and we'd end up in court anyway. But thanks for being a good sport. It might've worked and all gone off quietly if it wasn't for Conrad bloody Beaucock."

"So…you and Pops? You're not going to fulfill the marriage clause yourselves?" She winked. "I can't call *you* pops as well!"

"We haven't been dating very long!" Leo chuckled. *Dating isn't quite the word.* "But I do really, really like him, and if it came to it…maybe one day he and I might get hitched. Would you mind if I was your stepdad? I know it might be a bit weird, but I won't tell you off for coming home late or force you to eat your greens!"

Liv shrugged then patted his arm. She'd forgotten her engagement ring again, Leo noticed.

"I think it'd be lovely. Pops deserves a good bloke and so do you. And you look so cute together." She grinned. "Of course, this is taking a bit of explaining to my mates, but they all know my folks were hippies. When it's not weird that your dad's dating your own ex, you know you've reached peak Brighton."

"So Bohemian, and I don't own any tie-dyed kaftans!" Leo laughed. "Although I do in a sense — some of Gunther's are in a drawer on the yacht! If you want to hold a jumble sale for funds, you just let me know! But all that aside... Astrid warned me that the media might be interested in the case, so...I thought it was only fair to tell you because you'll probably be dragged into it at some point. Are you okay with that?"

Liv jerked her thumb backward toward the pool. "If it brings in the pennies, the more the better. Just...look after Pops? He's such a sweetie."

Leo nodded. "Don't worry, your dad's in safe hands. I'd never hurt him Liv, I—" *I love him.* "I really care about him."

"You go together much better as a couple than we ever did." Liv's eyes sparkled with the same mischievous glint as her dad. "I'll just have to content myself with my lovely, muscly, seal-crazy Thor!"

"He's pretty crazy about you too!" Leo noticed how Rob, who was talking to the schoolchildren, kept darting affectionate glances Liv's way. "I'm so glad you found your dream man in the end. He's perfect for you."

She blushed beet red. "And you and Dad will look spectacular on a seal-themed Pride float. I can see it already!"

"As long as we don't have to dress as seals!" Leo glanced over to the gate, where another crowd of visitors was waiting to come in. "You're busy, I better leave you to it."

Liv rose to her tiptoes and kissed Leo's cheek. "You'll always be my best friend, Max. I really love you, you know. And if I need to talk to Astrid or anyone else, I will."

Leo gave her a hug. "I love you too, Liv. Thanks for being such a brilliant mate. You take care."

Leo headed out of the sanctuary and started the task of canceling their fake marriage. He went to the

Registry Office and saw their name vanish from the list of forthcoming weddings. He rang the florist and canceled the small order of buttonholes and a bouquet and rang the caterer to cancel the buffet. He canceled the booking with the Sea Scouts but gave them the money for the booking anyway as a donation. Then he rang Auntie Sue, who at that moment was getting into the car to buy the ingredients for the cake.

"It's a long story," Leo told her. "You'll hear all about it soon enough."

Then he went round to see his parents, who seemed relieved that the wedding wasn't going to happen.

But it all left Leo at sea. He'd been so focused on the wedding that now it wasn't happening, the waves seemed to be teetering before crashing in to fill the void. Instead of a wedding, there were going to be legal proceedings, and even with Archie's reassurance, it was still alien to Leo. There were no caterers or florists or generous aunties to negotiate, only legal professionals in their world of paneled wood and leather-bound books.

It was then that his phone rang. The number was central London and, somehow, he had a sixth sense that it was going to be something to do with the case. Surely it was too early for them to have an answer?

In his most polished voice, he answered, "Hello, Leo Maxwell."

"Captain Maxwell, this is Jason from Bedford Court Chambers. Mr. Greville-Hall has asked me to give you a call with a view to setting up an appointment with him."

Leo was on the verge of asking if Jason had made a mistake, but something in his words sent a smile to Leo's face. *You wonderful bastard, Archie!* "Ahhh...

Right, an appointment. When is Mr. Greville-Hall free to see me?"

"He does apologize for the short notice, but he has an appointment at six o'clock this evening?" *Does he, now?* "We can send a car to collect you."

Leo had been entertaining visions of another train journey, but a car? Archie was pulling out the stops. "Excellent. Can you send the car to pick me up from the marina?"

"Of course. It'll be with you at three-thirty."

"Thank you, Jason. Thank you very much."

Chapter Twenty

The car pulled up in the road outside Bedford Court Chambers. Leo smoothed down his suit as he climbed out and headed to the door. His heart pounded with anticipation. Archie summoning Captain Maxwell? Leo would give him his very, very best captain.

He went into the building and told the receptionist, "Captain Maxwell. I've got an appointment with Mr. Greville-Hall at six."

"Of course." She tapped at her computer keyboard. "He says you're welcome to go straight up."

"Thank you!" Leo said with a nod and headed upstairs. He'd managed to resist the temptation to send Archie a text on his journey up, anxious to avoid spoiling what appeared to be a little game for them. He tapped on Archie's door. "Mr. Greville-Hall, Captain Maxwell here. You summoned me?"

"Come in!" Archie called. There was a deliciously stern edge to his voice, just as Leo had hoped.

Leo opened the door and found himself staring at Archie in his gown and wig. Desire shot straight to his groin, but he assumed his most insouciant manner and said, "Mr. Greville-Hall, you called me away from important business. I assume this is urgent?"

He closed the door behind him, then came a little farther into the room, arms folded.

"Captain Maxwell." Archie looked every inch the patrician in his wing collar as he sat behind his desk, his expression that haughty one that he deployed every now and then. "I understand you're often employed on *important business*. Perhaps that's what financed the super yacht you came by so conveniently?"

"What are you to trying to imply, Mr. Greville-Hall?" Leo raised an eyebrow. "Are you insinuating that I might have been dabbling in *illegal practices*?"

"Secret liaisons in five-star hotels?" Archie put his hands on his hips. "With men of questionable repute?"

"You forgot to mention the enormous cocks." *Is it getting hot in here?* Leo loosened his tie. He was close to needing to loosen his trousers too. "But there's nothing illegal about that, is there? I only tie up my lovers if they ask nicely."

Archie walked around his desk and closed the space between them. He seemed even more imperious now, but there was still a glint of naughtiness in his blue eyes. "And what else do you do? If they ask *nicely*?"

"I let them fuck me..." Leo purred, and ran his finger down the front of Archie's suit. "Hard."

Archie gazed down, watching the progress of Leo's finger. "You look like the sort of rogue who *would* like that sort of thing. Tell me what else you like, Captain Maxwell."

Leo reached the top of Archie's trousers and cupped his erection through the fabric. "I want to be spanked by a stern, hard man."

"You're just what I expected from a sailor." Archie reached his arm around Leo's waist and clasped his hand tight against Leo's bottom. "A thoroughly bad lot."

Leo grunted at Archie's contact. "And you, an upstanding pillar of the establishment?" He tightened his hand around Archie's erection. "Manhandling a sailor in your chambers? Do you want me naked, Mr. Greville-Hall? I bet you do."

"Lock the door," Archie commanded. "Then strip."

With that, he turned, the gown billowing as he made his way to the window and closed the blinds with a satisfying *snap*. That done, he settled back into his chair as though he were about to set to work. And he was, in a way.

Leo turned the key, then he went back to the middle of the room and unfastened his tie. He held it out at arm's length and let the strip of silk fall sinuously to the floor. Then he unbuttoned his jacket and threw it over the back of a dark-green leather sofa, before sending his shirt after it. Leo slowly drew down his trousers and pulled off his socks, leaving him wearing only his shorts, straining to contain his erection.

He tucked his thumb into his waistband and, with his head tipped to one side, he peered at Archie through his fallen fringe. Teasing like a coquette, Leo asked, "*Everything* off, Mr. Greville-Hall?"

"*Everything*, Captain Maxwell," Archie instructed. "I like to know exactly what I'm dealing with."

Leo turned his back on Archie, peering over his shoulder at him as he drew off his shorts. He threw them aside and they drifted down to land with the remainder of his abandoned clothes, then he placed his hands on his hips and turned to face Archie again, naked and aroused.

"Mr. Greville-Hall, are you going to examine me?"

"Captain Maxwell, you can count on a very thorough going-over." Archie was doing his best to keep up his stern, detached act, but Leo thrilled at the hitch in his lover's voice. He thrilled too at the unmissable erection in Archie's immaculate trousers when he left his seat and came to stand before Leo.

Muted footsteps went by in the corridor. What a wonderfully naughty man he was, sending a car to collect Leo for after-hours fun in his office.

"I think you should show me your cock, Mr. Greville-Hall." Leo ran his tongue over his lower lip. "You don't want to keep a beast like that all cooped up, surely?"

He heard Archie's breath catch again, then Archie took Leo's hand in his and brought it down to his zip.

"I think *you* should do it, Captain. You're no stranger to taking orders, I hope?'

"Not at all. And this is just the sort of order I like." Leo slowly brought Archie's zip down, then he slipped his hand inside and with care brought out Archie's cock through the opened zip. "There, that's more comfortable, isn't it?"

And not to mention fucking hot.

Because there was Archie, fully dressed as if he were about to face a judge, with his large cock lewdly poking out from his sober suit.

And this very literal *pillar* of the establishment was Leo's to enjoy.

"Tell me, Captain," he purred. "Do you run a tight ship? Plenty of discipline?"

"Of course," Leo replied, his gaze fixed on Archie's erection. "Only way for a captain to succeed. Sometimes you have no choice but to crack the whip." Then he lifted his head and looked Archie square in the face. "And sometimes you have to accept discipline yourself."

Archie allowed himself the barest hint of a smile. In one move he took Leo's cock in his palm, holding it as though testing the weight. He dropped his voice to a low growl and said, "I think you need a little discipline right now."

"I do." Leo turned his head and ran his tongue from Archie's jaw up the side of his face. "Stern men taste good," he murmured.

That never failed to get a reaction, and from Archie's answering gasp, it seemed that today was no different. He lifted his hand from Leo's bottom and brought it down in a gentle slap against him.

"Do that again," Leo said, his lips against Archie's ear. "Do it again, hard."

"Bend over the desk," Archie instructed urgently. "Let me see that arse."

Leo stepped slowly over to the desk, the expensive carpet thick and soft under his bare feet. He placed his palms flat against its surface, his feet shoulder-width apart.

Leo looked back at Archie. "How's this for a display, Mr. Greville-Hall?"

There was that hint of a smile again when Archie purred, "Perfect, Captain Maxwell." Then he strode over to the desk and caressed his hand down over Leo's bottom. "Ready, Captain?"

Leo couldn't manage anything more of a reply than, "Mmmm..." He braced his arms, the polished wood of the desk smooth as sin under his hands.

Archie kissed the nape of his neck, the gesture a loving one. A moment later he brought his hand down onto Leo's bottom, dealing out a sharp spank.

Sensation rocketed through Leo's body and he moaned with joy. The heat from Archie's spank stayed on his skin for some moments.

Oh, this is glorious! Naked in Archie's chambers, bent naked over his antique desk.

"How was that?" Archie stroked his hand over the place where he had spanked, soothing Leo. "Would you like another?"

"Fantastic," Leo murmured. The softness of Archie's palm as he caressed him was a wonderful companion to the sharp heat of the spank from the same hand. "Yes, go on, give me more."

Without replying, Archie drew back his hand and spanked Leo again. He followed the spank with another, punctuating each with a soft, affectionate stroke.

With each spank, Leo groaned, teetering on the delicious edge between pleasure and pain. And each spank made him more aroused, the world falling in on him and Archie and pleasure and nothing else.

"Again!" Leo begged him.

"Captain Maxwell," Archie exclaimed as his palm landed, his tone deliciously fruity. "You're outrageous!"

Leo grinned at him over his shoulder. "And so are you, you sauce! Spanking a naked man over your desk" — his gaze to fell Archie's unflagging erection — "with *that* poking out of your trousers?"

"I'm a highly trained and professional barrister." He leaned forward and kissed Leo's ear. "And I'm desperate for you."

Leo took one hand from the desk and reached back, running it through Archie's hair and sending his wig flying. The scent of Archie's cologne filled the air around them, and Leo gasped with need. "Have me, then. Over the desk, on the floor, in your chair, over the sofa, against the wall, oh, Archie... I *want* you."

"Right here." Archie flicked his tongue against Leo's ear. "Like this."

"How are you ever going to get a moment's work done again at this desk, Mr. Greville-Hall?" Leo chuckled. From behind he heard the telltale sound of a condom wrapper, his heart pounding with anticipation. When he'd imagined them fucking over this desk, it hadn't seemed like the sort of thing that could ever actually happen, yet it was about to.

"You can pay me back with a night aboard your pleasure palace," he told Leo. "Make it as decadent as you like, Captain."

"Our very own two-person party in that very big bed." Which Leo hadn't yet shared with Archie because they kept falling into bed on Archie's boat. "I didn't think you'd dare to do this, you know. Over your desk. It's so fucking hot. *You're* so fucking hot!"

"And I'm all yours." Archie closed his hand over Leo's hip and entered him with one powerful thrust. "God, Leo, you're glorious!"

Leo moaned, clutching the desk with one hand, his other in Archie's hair. The rasp of Archie's clothing against his bare skin was so illicit it only sent his pleasure higher. "You feel so good, so, so fucking good..."

"Leo," he gasped, moving his hips hard. Leo was vaguely aware of feet passing the door again, the respectable world outside going on around them. Inside there was only Leo and Archie, though, their bodies united and moving as one.

"I love you." The words spilled from Leo's mouth and he couldn't put them back in again. But it was true. He did. He loved the brave, caring man who was willing to be naughty to please him. To please each other. And he wanted nothing more than to be with him.

"You—" Archie paused for just as long as it took to say, "I love you too, you know."

"You marvelous bloke, Archie! I adore you!" Leo turned his head, trying to capture Archie's lips for a kiss. It was an awkward maneuver but with Archie's arm around his waist, they somehow managed it. Then Archie took Leo's erection in his hand and began to jerk his wrist in time with their thrusting hips, catching every moan in another kiss.

So many sensations were rushing through Leo, pleasure and a glorious warmth from being loved. From being *whole*. He moaned with every one of Archie's thrusts, his pleasure building and unspooling, taking possession of him, his body and his soul.

"Leo." He moaned, thrusting harder, carrying them both into bliss. What a feeling to be loved by Archie. In every sense of the word.

Leo shuddered against him, sighing with joy as Archie took him to his peak. He was a sweaty, happy mess, trying to kiss Archie, touch him somehow as pleasure shivered through him.

"I love you," Archie gasped. "I really do, Leo."

Leo twined his fingers with Archie's where they rested on his waist. "We're so lucky we found each other. You're fantastic."

"I've got a surprise for you," he murmured in reply. "We're not going back to Brighton tonight."

"We're not?" Leo hadn't expected that, but he should've known what the impulsive Greville-Halls were like. "Where are we—? Hang on, how many guesses do I get?"

"The classic *three*." Archie kissed him. "I bet you'll get it in one though."

"Hmmm…" Leo tapped his chin, pretending to think. "Well, I don't see any sleeping bags in your office, so are we going to the Hervey by any chance?"

Archie laughed. "Yep! I hope you don't mind, but I had Liv steal your toothbrush and some essential bits and bobs. We've got a table booked for dinner too. All you need to do is enjoy the evening."

"You think of everything." Leo chuckled. "Gimme a big hug, Archie, your naked man loves you."

Archie took Leo in his arms. "And I love my naked man!"

Leo held him tight. He wasn't thinking any more of the illicit thrill of those barrister robes against his bare skin, but only of being in the arms of the man he'd fallen for. *My gorgeous, lovely Archie.*

He was more precious than any amount of money.

Chapter Twenty-One

After a very nice shower at the chambers, Leo was almost respectable again. But he couldn't resist trying on Archie's wig.

"How do I look?" Leo clutched his lapels and intoned, "*Exhibit A, m'lud!*"

"It suits you!" Archie had changed out of his robe and bands and into a smart blue suit. Leo's tie was around his neck, offering them a little reminder of their first night together. "That was certainly the most enjoyable meeting I've ever had. I just felt like, I don't know. You've been through the mill these past few weeks. I wanted to give you a night away from it."

Leo took the wig off and carefully set it down on Archie's desk. He patted Archie's arm. "That's so kind of you. Especially as...well...you haven't had an easy time either because of all this. I wish I'd been brave enough to tell you everything earlier. But I just couldn't."

"Today must've been tough, even if the wedding wasn't real." Archie adjusted his tie one last time. "Astrid should have an answer on the mediation for you soon. Then we can move forward."

"I feel like such an idiot," Leo admitted. "But what can I say? It seemed like a good idea at the time."

"It was an act of spontaneity that was almost worthy of the Greville-Halls themselves," Archie chuckled. "We've got a car booked to take us to the hotel. Ready to go?"

Leo nodded and picked up his overnight bag, then he took Archie's arm.

The car was waiting for them behind the chambers, and soon they were heading through the evening streets of London. It was still busy, but Leo didn't pay much attention to the hurrying traffic. He leaned back against the leather seat and played with Archie's hand.

If Conrad challenged them, and Leo knew that he would, then all of this would come out. The world would know about the lie, about Liv and Archie and every bit of it. Would Gunther really have wanted *that* if he had wanted Leo to be happy and content? But Gunther hadn't thought that far ahead, and Conrad wanted that money, so if Leo had to fight, he would.

The car pulled up outside the Hervey and a man in livery opened the door for them. Leo didn't feel like a fish out of water anymore at such a grand place. He walked up the steps to the hotel, brushing his fingertips against the back of Archie's hand in a gesture that told him, *If I could get away with holding your hand right now I would.*

But he didn't plan to give Conrad any more fuel.

Archie checked in and had the bag sent up to room four-two-three while he and Leo were escorted through to the restaurant. It was the sort of place Gunther used to visit during their island stopovers, with low light and gentle music, soft chatter and glittering chandeliers. Their table looked out over the Thames, and Leo had a feeling that this was all thanks to Archie.

"Do you think I could get a job on one of those?" Leo joked, pointing to a boat chugging along the Thames. It seemed to be carrying a party in full swing.

"Do you think *I* could?" Archie laughed. "Looks more fun than chambers on a Monday morning!"

"You wouldn't earn a tenth of what you're on now, though!" Leo sipped his wine. He had no idea how much Archie earned, but he knew it was far more than a humble skipper on a floating Thames party palace ever would.

"I don't really like discussing money," Archie said with the laid-back air of a man who had plenty of it. "But I've been building up a little bit of a fund. My *round the world* fund. We're not quite there yet, but how would you feel about it in a few years? Would you be my skipper?"

"Of course I would." Leo reached for Archie's hand over the table. "I'd even wear that white uniform with the brass buttons for you. And with any luck, I'll have some money coming in if I rent out the *Aphrodite,* so we wouldn't need to eat into your fund too much." Although Leo suspected that the rent he'd get would be peanuts compared to the money Archie must've saved up.

"I need to see Liv settled first, though, I'm that sort of pops!" He gave a bashful shrug. "What do you think about Rob?"

"A gentle giant," Leo said. "He seems more like son-in-law material than I ever did. He'll make Liv really happy — well, he already *is*."

Archie nodded. He reached out and topped up their wine glasses. "Happy endings all round!"

As Leo sipped his wine, his attention was caught by a loud bark of laughter from another table. He peered around an ornamental urn and to his horror, he saw Conrad.

Conrad was dining with two other people, and Leo realized he recognized both of them. One, from television and newspapers, was a footballer in one of the top clubs. And the other was a woman he'd last seen sunbathing on the deck of the *Aphrodite*. It was Marisol, one of Gunther's Eurobabes.

Maybe it was a coincidence. Leo hoped so. Hadn't Conrad said he worked with footballers avoiding speeding tickets? And after all, Marisol had been dating, sort of, Gunther, and if she'd married him, would've been related to Conrad.

She should be glad she isn't.

Leo whispered to Archie, "It's Conrad. With one of Gunther's girlfriends. And a footballer. At that table over there."

"Probably one of Conrad's motoring clients. Teflon Con, indeed." Archie peered around the urn too, then darted back. "Knowing what you do about the young lady, is that something we should be suspicious of? Or does seeing her with a footballer feel like a natural progression?"

Marisol laughed and shook back her mane of dark hair.

"I don't think it's too much to worry about. It goes with the territory, I think," Leo replied. "I bump into footballers on the yachts sometimes, that might be how she met him. Or at a champagne pool party somewhere."

Archie peered over again. "I've never been to a champagne pool party, you know. Are they fun?"

"Not really." Leo shook his head. "They all talk about their shoes and their plastic surgeons. There was some bloke telling me to get implants in my *legs*. And someone else wanted to know who'd done my lip-plumping and they wouldn't believe me when I said they're real. Gunther loved those parties, though, but you would if you love being surrounded by bosomy women in small bikinis."

Leo glanced around as he saw someone in the corner of his eye. It was Marisol, in her form-fitting, long red dress swishing toward the river view. Leo wasn't sure if he should say hello or not, but before he'd quite decided, Marisol had spotted him.

"Leonito!" She flung herself at him, wrapping her arms around his neck. "How are you, the little captain? And who is this gentleman?"

Marisol unpeeled herself from Leo and batted her huge eyelashes at Archie.

"Erm...Marisol, this is Archie. He's my very good friend. And Archie, this is Marisol. She was Gunther's girlfriend." Leo knew from experience that it was never wise to say they were *one of* Gunther's girlfriends. "We're just having dinner."

"Lovely to meet you, Marisol." Archie took Marisol's hand and gave a polite nod of his head. "I've heard all about Gunther from Leo. I'm sorry for your loss, he sounds like a hell of a chap."

"He was a wonderful man. I was so very, very fond of him." Marisol's eyes misted up. "I miss him terribly.

Did you know, Leonito, he has left me an apartment in Marbella? It is not so far from my *abuela's* village. Is that not very, very kind of him?"

"*Very* kind," Leo said. "Did you know he left me *Aphrodite*? If you ever want to come out for a sail, let me know."

"Perhaps I will! It is a shame his cousin is not so nice." Marisol gestured back toward Conrad's table with a flick of her head. Contempt dripped from her every word. "Do not worry, I shall not tell him you are here. Tonight, is celebrating a job well done."

Archie grimaced, then his smile reappeared. "Leo's right, come down and see us in Brighton. Lots of perfect selfie ops!"

Remembering how excited Marisol used to be when dolphins swam alongside the yacht, Leo said to her, "You should come to the seal sanctuary!"

"I would love to see them! I will come soon." She brandished her phone. "Telephone number, Leonito, then I will visit you."

Leo recited his number to her, and she tapped at her screen with her perfect long nails. Archie took out his wallet and retrieved a small business card. Leo recognized the little cartoon seal it bore from the T-shirt Rob had squeezed himself into so soon after he'd arrived.

"This is the seal sanctuary that my daughter manages." He handed her the card. "She's potty about them and we're all going the same way."

"Liv, you remember her? Archie's her dad," Leo said.

"Eh! That is so sweet, of course I remember Liv! I will come and visit soon, I promise." Marisol shot a glare at Conrad's table and hissed under her breath,

"Very, *very* soon. Now — selfie. Goodnight, Leonito, goodnight, Archie!"

And Marisol sashayed off to the verandah to take her own photo.

"I get the distinct impression she's not very fond of Conrad," Leo whispered. "Or her boyfriend?"

"She looks like the sort of lady who'd know how one goes about turning a luxury boat into a party boat business," Archie mused. Then he patted Leo's hand and asked, "Ready for bed, darling?"

"You might be onto something there. Marisol would know exactly what to do," Leo said. He pushed aside his empty bowl. "But now, bed beckons."

And from the glint he saw in Archie's gaze, Leo knew they wouldn't do much sleeping. And even better than that, he knew that Archie loved him. No matter what happened in court, if his case ever got there, Leo had already won.

Chapter Twenty-Two

"I'm sorry I can't stay," Leo said as he and Marisol headed toward the pool where the sanctuary's three seals were swimming. "I've got a really important appointment."

"I don't mind. I will see you soon on the *Aphrodite*. I hope all goes well!"

I bloody hope so too.

A few weeks had passed since Leo had met Astrid, and he was due in London that afternoon for mediation with Brockett. Astrid had told Leo in advance that all the signs were good that Brockett would acknowledge Gunther hadn't necessarily meant that Leo should take a wife. And that made Leo very happy. Especially as his dear Archie had made time in his diary to come with Leo for moral support. Archie would do anything for Leo, just as he would do anything for him.

But they needed Brockett to agree in writing before they could go a step further.

Marisol paused by the fence and watched Cyrano pull himself out of the water. "They are so handsome. And look, there is Liv!"

Marisol's gold bangles clanked as she waved. Liv waved back then called, "Mari, do you fancy helping with feeding time?"

"I would love to!" Marisol said, as Leo opened the gate for her. She rained continental kisses down on Leo, then sprinted toward Liv in her silver trainers. "Fish for the seals!"

Cyrano tipped back his head and barked with glee.

"Pops is outside waiting for you," Liv told Leo. "Good luck!"

"Is he?" Leo beamed. "And there was me thinking I'd be getting a train. See you later, Liv! Bye!"

Leo headed out of the sanctuary, and saw Archie outside in the road. A surge of love for him rushed through Leo at that moment. He might've only seen Archie that morning, but the unexpected lift to London, when he was starting to fret about the meeting, took almost all of his fears away.

"Thank you, thank you, thank you!" Leo exclaimed. It was hard not to absorb Marisol's effusiveness. "Archie, you're fab."

Archie leaned across from the driver's seat of the MG, its top already down. Thinking he had already been to London that morning, only to come home and ferry Leo all the way back to the city, gave Leo a new jolt of confidence.

"Going my way, guv?" Archie called. "Hop in!"

"We're off to London Town!" Leo replied, trying his best Cockney accent. He climbed into the car and patted Archie's leg. To anyone watching, it might've seemed a jokey gesture, but Leo and Archie both knew it wasn't.

As they drove, Archie asked, "Do you think we need to keep up this pretense? If we're going in there all gay guns blazing, why're we hiding?"

"I suppose you're right," Leo said. "I've been so used to being cautious. Just in case. But if Conrad *is* watching us, then he'll know we always sleep on the same yacht. Fire up your gay guns!"

"You've officially entered mediation with an argument that marrying a man is as valid as a woman." Archie reached over and patted his knee. "I think the secret's probably already out, you know."

Leo awkwardly brushed back his hair, but the breeze took it and swished through it again. He gave up.

"You're right, everyone must know by now." They pulled up at the last set of traffic lights before leaving Brighton, and Leo leaned over and kissed Archie's cheek. "There we go! The first of your many public displays of affection from me!"

"I love you." Archie beamed. "And I don't care who knows it! Let Conrad give it his best shot. He won't get past Astrid *or* me."

"I love you too." Leo rested his hand on Archie's thigh, and on they drove to London.

Chapter Twenty-Three

They must've looked a formidable bunch, Leo, Archie and Astrid, as they strode through the corridors to Brockett's office.

Astrid knocked on his door.

"Mr. Brockett, it's Astrid Baxter."

He opened the door to them with the same placid smile that had greeted Leo that spring.

"Come in, do." He stepped forward and peered along the corridor. "Has Margaret offered you tea?"

"She has, thank you, she said she'd bring it through," Astrid replied. "And thank you, Mr. Brockett, for agreeing to this meeting with my client and myself. Mr. Maxwell's partner is here too in a personal, rather than professional, capacity. I believe you've already met?"

Brockett gave a look of pantomimed surprise, then beamed a welcome smile.

"Archie, welcome to my humble office. Rather less fancy than you're used to, eh?"

"I've very happy memories of this place." Archie shook his hand. "And all I hear about you is great things."

Brockett waved his hands dismissively. "That's not my golf handicap, I'm sure! Ah, Margaret! Just in time!"

It was a world away from Bedford Court as Margaret laid out the cups and tea service with studied care. Just like the solicitor himself, it all felt very timeless.

"I believe you've had time to talk this matter through with your partners?" Astrid asked as she took one of the seats by Brockett's desk. Leo took the middle of the three seats and Archie sat beside him, Leo holding his hand.

"I have indeed. I've discussed the situation with Herr Schreiber's executors and his estate's assorted legal representatives. Of which there were *many*."

Astrid nodded. "Yes, I'm sure there are. And was a consensus reached regarding my client's concern regarding the interpretation of the clause?"

"There was indeed." Brockett picked up a rich tea biscuit and placed it on the edge of his saucer, relishing his moment in the sun, no doubt. "A unanimous one."

Leo tightened his grip on Archie's hand. *Here's the moment. Here it comes.* Instead of waiting for Astrid to reply, Leo asked him, "So what did you decide? Do you agree with Astrid?"

"You see, it's not a question of agreeing with Astrid as such." As Brockett spoke, though, Leo got the impression that Astrid wouldn't let the preamble go on too long. "Rather, there are delicate legal matters that must be considered. One must examine the evidence and the wishes of the deceased. One can't tread too heavily on such matters."

"And you've had several weeks in which to do that, Mr. Brockett. So…" Astrid gestured with her pen. *Come on, Mr. Brockett!* "And the decision is?"

"On behalf of Herr Schreiber's estate, legal representatives and executors, I do have an answer." He opened a drawer and took out a buff folder. Even from here, even before he opened it, Leo could see that it only contained one sheet of paper. "Your request to reinterpret the wishes of Herr Schreiber in such a manner that you might benefit from the bequest should you enter into a same sex marriage" — Brockett blinked at Archie over his spectacles, then looked back at the paper — "is unanimously accepted and agreed to. As far as we're concerned, the matter is duly concluded."

Leo hadn't realized he was holding his breath, but now he puffed out all the air trapped inside him and flopped back against the chair. Astrid patted his shoulder, laughing. She was obviously relieved too.

"That's brilliant! That's *so* brilliant!" Leo hugged Archie's arm. "Isn't it brilliant?"

"Leo Maxwell's a great big pooft — " Conrad's words faded into silence as he burst through the door, an envelope held above his head. Then he muttered, "Poofter."

"*Poofter?* Are you twelve?" Leo had turned in his seat. He tried very hard to repress his need to retort to everything Conrad said, but the man reawoke in Leo the young lad who'd stood up to the bullies at school. "Don't you knock?"

"What on *earth* are you doing here?" Archie rose, and Leo, with a little fizz of heat, got a sudden idea of what it must be like to face Mr. Greville-Hall in court. He seemed a little taller, a lot posher. And far more stern. "Mr. Beaucock, explain yourself?"

Margaret appeared in the doorway behind Conrad, stammering an apology that Brockett dismissed with a kindly shake of his head. Then Archie said, "Speak, Mr. Beaucock."

Leo glanced from Archie to Conrad. Emboldened by the outcome, Leo said, "Go on, Connie, what were you so desperate to tell everyone that it required you to burst uninvited into someone else's meeting?"

"I've got evidence that your engagement's a crock of shit," Conrad sneered, though Leo could tell that he was wrongfooted already. "And you're shagging your bird's dad!"

"You're several pages behind, Mr. Beaucock," Archie told him curtly. "Ms. Baxter is handling Mr. Maxwell's affairs and Mr. Brockett is, of course, handling the late Herr Schreiber's. You're in the business, you know the way things're done. Or you *should.*"

"Quite so," Brockett agreed. Then he looked to Astrid and asked, "If Mr. Beaucock requires anything further, Ms. Maxwell, I trust that you and I will liaise accordingly?"

"Yes, of course." Astrid rose from her chair to shake Brockett's hand. "I'm very glad this issue has been resolved so amicably."

But there was a challenge in Astrid's voice, perhaps not meant for Brockett.

"It's been a pleasure." He smiled as he shook her hand. "Mr. Beaucock, would you mind awfully contacting me through the proper channels? We're in rather a delicate meeting, so..."

Conrad looked utterly confounded then. After a moment he nodded, jabbing his finger toward Leo. "This isn't done," he said. "We'll see whose balls are biggest."

"I think you'll find it *is* done," Leo remarked, lifting his nose just slightly into the air. "Brockett and Co. have decided that if I take a husband, rather than a wife, I can still inherit. So I'm a rather lucky poofter, aren't I?"

"Then we're taking this to court," Conrad said. "And you'll lose the lot."

Oh, fuck it.

Astrid sucked air in between her teeth as if she were a plumber assessing a burst pipe. "Are you sure you want to risk it, Conrad? You wish to challenge the decision of the legal representatives and executives of Herr Schreiber's estate? Do you plan to challenge the legal definition of marriage as well, while you're at it? Is that *wise?*"

"Yeah, I do." Conrad told her. "Because I'm normal, get it? I'm a normal, red-blooded man and I'll see you all in court. Especially you, gay boy."

He would have turned on his heel and strode from the room, had Margaret not pulled the door to on her departure. Instead he turned on his heel and walked into the door, then managed to stumble out into the corridor and away with the remains of his dignity.

Leo pressed his lips together, trying very hard not to laugh. But once he was sure that Conrad had gone, out it came, in a roar of hilarity.

"Sorry—so sorry, Mr. Brockett," Leo said, once he'd recovered enough to speak. "But thank goodness for your door. It's given me a much-needed excuse to laugh."

"If he takes this to court, we're going to go straight through him. We'll win," Archie assured Leo. "Astrid'll brush him off like dust."

Astrid nodded, but Leo spotted signs of strain around her eyes. "I'll do my very best, I promise you, Leo. I can't do more than that."

Chapter Twenty-Four

Leo and Archie headed into the court's buildings, Leo clinging to Archie with his arm around his waist. Although *walk* perhaps wasn't the best way to describe it, as they were carried along by the eager crowd of reporters who'd been waiting outside. The sheer noise and the pressing bodies, the flashes popping in Leo's eyes and the microphones shoved into his face should have been terrifying, but Archie was with him, protecting him. His broad figure seemed to do more to clear the route ahead along the pavement than the phalanx of police who were trying to keep order.

There were cameras behind, cameras on either side, and cameras in front. Leo kept wondering what would happen if one of the reporters tripped over. Would the whole lot of them collapse in a heap and leave them alone?

And they were shouting, their voices merging into an incomprehensible din.

"Leo, Leo, what are your chances of winning?"

"Leo, do you think Conrad's homophobic?"

"Are you really going to donate all the money to a seal sanctuary?"

"Leo, give your boyfriend a kiss!"

Leo knew to ignore them and keep going, but it was a world away from Sharisa and the Brighton local news.

"What a bloody madhouse! If I were advising Conrad, I'd have told him not to represent himself. This is a world away from motoring fines for footballers," Archie told Leo as they entered the building. He took Leo's hand, making no effort to hide what they shared here in the place where Leo's fate would be decided.

Astrid was waiting for them in her barrister's gown. Her bright red lipstick had been replaced with a far more somber shade, but her smile was still as bright.

"Hello, you two!" she said. "Bit of a scrum out there?"

"Bloody ridiculous, but we were expecting it," Archie told her, brushing it off in a way that Leo decided might be well worth taking on board. "Hello, Astrid, any clues on the judge yet?"

"I've heard rumblings," Astrid replied as she led them toward the spiral stairs in the middle of the enormous glass and steel atrium. "My cousin was in his golf club yesterday and heard something. It's old Langston-Rowe, he said."

Leo wasn't sure what the sound of acknowledgment Archie made signified. Not exactly an optimistic cheer, but not a groan of horror either. He turned toward Leo and told him, "He's very establishment. Lives to the letter of the law, so... If nothing else it'll be interesting to follow his thinking."

"The letter of the law?" Leo winced. "That's not too good, is it?"

"To the contrary. The letter of the law can be rather surprising at times." He kissed Leo's cheek. "It *was* written by chaps in wigs, after all."

"And you're not just talking about drag queens." Leo chuckled.

"I would imagine Conrad won't be too pleased when he finds out," Astrid said in a low voice. They had reached the top of the stairs, and Astrid guided them past several very ordinary-looking, plain wooden doors. Leo hadn't been expecting the place to look like an office block, but it was exactly how it appeared. "Here we are! Court number one."

A woman in a black gown pushed open the door for them. It was a very strange room, not like the old wood-lined courtrooms Leo had seen on television. It just looked like a boring meeting room, rendered somewhat terrifying by the empty red chair at the top of the room sitting underneath the Royal Coat of Arms.

Archie had talked Leo through court etiquette on several occasions, even using boat bric-a-brac to explain how the court would be laid out, but Leo still wasn't entirely sure where he was supposed to sit.

"Will you stay next to me, Archie?" Leo asked. "I'm sure they won't mind."

Archie looked to the usher for confirmation, which was given with a friendly nod. He tightened his grip on Leo's hand almost imperceptibly and together they followed Astrid to a long desk, which faced the red throne.

"It looks a lot more intimidating than it is," Archie whispered. "And if you picture Langston-Rowe singing *Agadoo* at his chambers' Christmas bash twenty years ago, he won't seem half so frightening either. I may even have photos somewhere."

Leo laughed behind his hand, then he noticed Astrid stifling her laughter as well.

"You have *got* to show them around the office…" she said as she laid out her files on the desk.

"And that's Conrad's side?" Leo asked, trying to keep a wobble out of his voice as he pointed to the empty desks beside them. Archie nodded.

"He'll have to behave in here. There are some judges who don't take well to the sort of grandstanding Conrad likes, and we've got one of them." Archie glanced toward the door. "If Conrad actually shows up."

He wasn't outside primping for the media, was he? Relating a sob story to tell the world that a devious sailor had tried to rob him of his rightful inheritance?

The answer came a moment later when Conrad swept into the room at the head of a legion of sharp-suited male assistants. Each carried a briefcase, though Conrad's hands were empty. He strode across the court toward his desks, glaring at Leo as he did.

"This is going to be fun," Conrad told his entourage, receiving a few theatrical sniggers. "Watch Teflon Con blue ball the lot of them."

Leo somehow managed to stop himself from rolling his eyes, and only just managed to stop himself muttering, *Oh, do sod off, you silly wanker.*

Astrid crossed the small distance between them, her hand outstretched. "Good morning, Mr. Beaucock."

He looked down at her hand, then ignored it as he decided, "At least I'll have something cute to look at while I win this case."

Astrid sighed, shaking her head as she went back to her chair.

Moments later, the door at the back of the court opened and an usher intoned, "All rise."

Leo's heart was in his throat and he held ever tighter to Archie's hand as he saw a tall man in a dark blue gown with red tabs at his neck enter the room. His lips were pursed as he headed to the chair at the front.

Can't go back now...

Leo kept his gaze on Langston-Rowe because out of the corner of his eye he could see a smirk of enormous proportions on Conrad's face. But he was still holding Archie's hand and Astrid had the determined look of a woman about to go into battle. He knew which side he'd rather be on.

Langston-Rowe laid down his files and, before taking his chair, scrutinized everyone in the room, lips still pursed like a headmaster trying to work out who was talking during assembly. Then, at last, he sat down.

The usher called "Be seated," and everyone took their seats. Leo glanced quickly at Archie and gave him a grin, trying to tell him, *I'm all right really, I'm not scared at all.* But he was fairly sure Archie could see through it.

Langston-Rowe folded his hands on the desk and unpursed his lips to say, "I have sat in judgement on Chancery cases for many years, but never have I seen a crowd outside the court as I have today. This case is somewhat under the media microscope, but that does not change what occurs in my courtroom. Due procedure will be followed, and I will not suffer any parties who may play to the gallery of the press." He took a pen from his pocket and laboriously unscrewed its cap. Then he smiled, although there didn't seem to be much humor in it, and he said, "Shall we begin?"

Chapter Twenty-Five

Leo basked in the sunshine on the deck of Archie's yacht, a gin and tonic in hand. He laid his head on Archie's lap, and bit by bit the sense of unreality he'd felt melted away. He didn't belong in a courtroom, but a boat was his natural habitat.

"I'm glad we don't have to go back for a while." Leo opened his eyes and smiled up at Archie. "Thanks for being there."

"Where else would I be but next to my man?" Archie stroked Leo's hair. "I'm glad you didn't insist on sitting through every minute of it. Much nicer soaking up some sun, don't you think?"

"*Much* nicer! And home at last." Leo mused for a moment before saying, "I feel a bit bad leaving Astrid on her own, but it seems like she's enjoying the challenge!"

"That is a woman rightly in her element." He took a sip from his glass. "I wouldn't want to go against her, and I consider myself *fairly* good at what I do!"

Leo chuckled. "Do you think Langston-Rowe likes her? Does he like *anyone*? He just looked so... disapproving."

"That's a judge thing. They practice that face in mirrors."

Leo laughed. "I can't imagine what it's like to get paid for looking grumpy all day. Then again, I'd look grumpy if I had Conrad stuck in front of me. Who were all those people he brought in? Did he hire them from an extras agency?"

"Team Teflon. You don't think Conrad does any of the legwork to find those loopholes for his footballers, do you?" Archie reached across to put his glass down. "You and I and Conrad are going to be in the papers soon, you know. The whole world's going to know that I'm the fellow on Captain Maxwell's arm, and I could *not* be happier about it."

Leo reached up, caressing Archie's arm on his way to stroking his face. "I love you, Archie. You're a babe. And you mean everything to me."

"I've got some time off due. How about I bank it for after the ruling, and we go off on one of the yachts for a bit? You choose which one."

Leo gasped. "That would be amazing! I suppose we can't take the *Loveday* out otherwise we'd make Liv homeless. But I'd love to see how she sails without rescuing a seal!"

Archie looked thoughtful, or the version of thoughtful that Leo had learned to recognize as a plan being formulated.

"I'm sure Liv won't say no to housesitting the super yacht so we can head off on the *Loveday*." He raised one eyebrow. "What do you say!"

"Yes!" Leo cheered. He pulled himself up from Archie's lap to kiss his cheek. "A holiday on the *Loveday*. Brilliant!"

Archie put his arm around Leo's waist, the mirth gone from his face as he studied Leo's gaze. For a long moment he said nothing, then he whispered, "I love you so bloody much, you know."

"I adore you, Mr. Greville-Hall." Leo brushed the tip of his nose against Archie's and slowly brought their lips together. If he'd known a year ago that he'd be at the forefront of a court case that the media was trying to turn into a cause célèbre, Leo would have found a sunset and smiled into it. He would have run a million miles from it, but that was before Archie. With Archie, the court case was part of life, but it wasn't the lurking terror it might once have been. Maybe that was part of growing up.

"Good evening!" a voice called.

Reluctantly, Leo broke from their kiss. When he looked along the pontoon, he saw Marisol striding toward them in designer ripped jeans and a crop top, with Liv beside her.

"A lovely night for a kiss!" Marisol called again.

"What night isn't?" Archie asked. "Come aboard, ladies, it's gin o'clock!"

"Gin?" Marisol laughed. "Don't drink all the gin without us, Archie, we're coming!"

She took Liv's hand to balance as she climbed onto the yacht, then once she was aboard in her platform espadrilles, she reached back over for Liv. As the two women safely clambered onto the deck, Liv said, "We've been thinking about you all day. How did it go?"

"I don't know!" Leo replied. "Erm... Conrad brought enough assistants to fill a football team, but Astrid was phenomenal. She didn't look scared of him or the judge or anything at all. And I dunno if it's been on the news, we've been avoiding it, but there were all these cameras and reporters outside the court."

"We saw it on Twitter," Liv said as she poured out two very generous measures of gin and tonic. "You two looked super cute going into court. Every time someone's come to the sanctuary to ask about you, we've stuck a collecting tin under their nose!"

"We have made lots of money!" Marisol threw up her arm and her bracelets jangled. "And horrible Conrad! I hate that sneer on his face. I do not like him at all. But then, he got on very well with my ex, so...two very horrible men!"

"Are you staying in Brighton, Marisol?" Archie asked. "Have the seals charmed you into giving up the jet set?"

"I have found a very nice apartment, so I am staying for a while. Who knows, I might stay a long time!" Marisol sipped her gin, then stretched out on the deck like a cat. "I need a rest after dating Mason. Do you know, he *was* speeding? I was in the car! Then he said he was not. Does he think I am stupid? I said I would not lie. But somehow...Conrad got him off the charge."

"Didn't he get it chucked out?" Archie asked. Then he shrugged. "I admit I might've done a bit of digging on Mr. Beaucock, just to see what we're up against. I've picked out a pattern here and there."

"What sort of pattern?" Leo asked. This was the first he'd heard about Archie looking into Conrad's business. "Is he up to something dodgy?"

Marisol nodded. "I think he is," she said. "What did you find out, Archie?"

"Nothing concrete," he admitted. "Loopholes are loopholes, I can't do anything about them, but... I've called in one or two favors—legal secretaries are wonderfully helpful if they dislike their boss enough— I have a feeling that he offers a sort of *express service* for those who can afford it."

Marisol pushed herself up. She sipped her gin, before saying, "I think—and I don't know how— someone *else* got the points. I overheard him talking to Conrad on the phone. Mason said, *"I wasn't speeding, I don't have points!"* Then he laughs. *"Not me, anyway!"* You see? Then we go to Hervey's for dinner because Mason is celebrating. And I had to pretend I did not know what they had done."

Leo saw Archie's eyes light up. "That's what I thought! Some of Conrad's clients—the richest and those who can't avoid a ban—consult him then miraculously remember that a completely random third party was actually driving. I think for the right price, Conrad will sell on the offenses. Probably a few thousand for half an hour's work. It's easy money, even in the legal profession!"

"And illegal, right?" Leo asked. "I didn't even know people did that."

"Look at it like this," Archie said, filled with enthusiasm. "You have nine points and you stand to lose your license. I can represent you in court for tens of thousands of pounds *or* you can bung me five grand, and I'll get some shady chum to say they were driving and that's that!"

"*Really*?" Leo shook his head. He'd known Conrad was devious, but he'd had no idea what he'd been getting up to. "That's dreadful. There's all these dangerous drivers on the road thanks to him. He can't get away with that, surely?"

Archie tapped his fingertip against his chin. "Maybe I'll look into it a little bit more. I've no time for a dodgy lawyer, there're too many of them knocking around as it is!"

"Mason is still friends with people he knew at school," Marisol said. "Could it be one of them?"

"And Conrad likely has a willing pool of people happy to make a quick buck too." He picked up his drink. "I'll get some of our people to ask around. It may come to nothing, but...if it unsettles Conrad, it's all to the good. We may be on the side of the angels, but that doesn't mean we can't play the odd backhand."

Leo touched his glass to Archie's. "I'll drink to that!"

"Cheers, Captain," Archie replied, giving his lover a saucy wink.

Leo quirked his eyebrow. "Cheers, Mr. Greville-Hall!"

Chapter Twenty-Six

Summer brought back the fair-weather sailors, and Leo was kept busy with more and more odd jobs, climbing masts, fixing engines, threading rope. Sometimes he would be engrossed in a job and it was only when his thoughts drifted that he would remember the question of his inheritance was the topic of debate, not only in a London courtroom but in the media too.

And at those moments, when the difficulties and complexities of legal wranglings broke in on Leo's humdrum reality, he was always grateful that he and Archie were together. It didn't scare him now or overwhelm him because Archie was his anchor.

Not only did Archie demystify what would be happening in the court, but when Leo curled up with Archie in bed at night, he was loved and protected. And he was home.

And whatever was going on in that courtroom couldn't touch him.

Sunday morning had passed in a lazy haze of lovemaking and now, as Archie made coffee, Leo lay back against the feather pillows and stared at his notepad. Astrid had steered things for the long weeks of the trial but in the coming days it would be Leo's turn in the spotlight. The witnesses and experts had spoken, from Brockett to Marisol and everyone in between, but before the ruling was made, Leo would face Langston-Rowe and make his own submission to the court. He knew what he wanted to say, that love was love wherever you found it, that Gunther had wanted Leo to be happy, to know the singular wonders that came from being in someone's arms, but how could he say that to a man like Langston-Rowe? He had to put it into a speech if it was going to make an impact, but how did one even begin to make a speech out of love?

Leo looked up from his notepad as Archie returned with a tray. His hair was a disordered mess from the night before and Leo decided it suited him.

"I've written a title." Leo turned the pad around to show Archie. "It says *My Speech*. And there's some bits I've scribbled out. I just don't know how to...you know, how to put it. It's all up here." Leo tapped his head. "But it won't come out *here*." And Leo shook his pen.

"I found croissants." Archie settled onto the bed and put the laden tray down between them. "What's the message you're trying to get across? Let's start with that, because not everything needs a soliloquy. Unless you charge by the hour." He gave Leo a wink, then picked up one of the croissants.

"I just... I want to say, *Gunther was my friend, and he wanted me to be happy*, but..." Leo helped himself to a croissant. He couldn't resist the pastry a moment longer. "That doesn't sound like a speech, does it? It sounds like the toast at a wake!"

"What mattered to Gunther most of all, do you think? What lesson should we take away from his life? A life that seems to have resulted in no enemies and a crowd of friends going back to primary school at his funeral, all of whom had nothing but the happiest of memories?"

Leo bit into his croissant and chewed pensively. "Erm... Well...loving people. That was the most important thing. I suppose the lesson is...be kind. Accept people..." Leo put the notepad aside. "You know I never told Gunther I was gay? Thing is, I never told him because I kind of got the impression he knew. And it didn't bother him a bit. He accepted me for who I am. The guy who skippered his yacht."

Archie kissed his cheek. "And *my* captain. Besides, I've got plenty of bizarre forenames already, so if I have to add *Mäuschen* to the collection to sidestep the condition, we can always do that too." He gave Leo a cheeky grin. "One more crazy name wouldn't hurt."

"How bizarre are they?" Leo laughed. He'd seen Archie's initials on an official-looking envelope that had been addressed to him, but he'd never asked before.

"*Quite* bizarre." AMS Greville-Hall was as far as Leo knew. Archie was easy enough, but MS?

"The *M* isn't Michael, like my middle name, is it? I'm named after both my grandads, and my dad, because he was named after *his* dad. So...where did your names come from, Archie Marvin Simon?" Leo got the giggles at that guess and laughed uncontrollably, repeating the names.

"If you think Marvin and Simon are bizarre, you're *never* going to guess. Give me a kiss and I'll tell you?" Then Archie looked thoughtful. "Actually, give me three kisses. One for each name. And one extra, because one of the names is two words."

"All right... You can have all the kisses you want, then you tell me." Leo cupped Archie's face and kissed him slowly and lingeringly on the lips. "One..." Leo said. Then kissed him again. "Two..." And again. "Three..." And again. "Four."

Archie studied Leo's face as they parted, his smile more mischievous than ever as he drew in a theatrically deep breath and told him, "Archibald Mungo St. John Grenville-Hall. Try saying that after a few glasses of bubbly!"

Leo raised his eyebrows as he repeated, "Archibald Mungo St. John Greville-Hall? Wow. That's quite a collection of names you've got, Archie. Were you named after your grandads as well?"

He nodded. "Mum and Dad came up with Archie, but Mungo was Mum's Pop and St. John was Dad's. And Daisy named Liv *Loveday*, which is wonderfully in keeping with the unusual theme, don't you think?"

"Just a bit!" Leo chuckled. He traced his fingertip across Archie's shoulder. "So, Archibald Mäuschen Mungo St. John...!"

Archie picked up the notepad and put it on the bedside table. "Let's have a day off? Forget court, forget speeches, and let me spoil you rotten."

Leo slipped his arm around Archie and snuggled close, brushing croissant crumbs from Archie's chest. "Spoil me? You already are."

"Good." Archie held Leo tight. "Because that's what I'm here for."

Chapter Twenty-Seven

"So this looks like it's going to be the last day." Astrid beamed at Leo even though she looked rather tired. They were sitting in a waiting room at the court building, with a pile of files next to Astrid. "How are you feeling, Leo?"

Leo squeezed Archie's hand as he said, "Nervous."

"I know you guys have spent hours going through this, and I know we'll win," Archie told them. "And Marisol tells me that the press and Twitter — for what it's worth — are on our team. Any last-minute prep we need to hear, Astrid?"

"There's no need to be nervous, Leo. Langston-Rowe wants to hear your statement, so the floor is yours. You have every right to be talking. And I get the impression Langston-Rowe is on our side, but we can't be complacent." Astrid patted Leo's shoulder. "Finish strong, Leo. That's the best you or I or anyone can do."

"Got your sob story ready?" Conrad and his entourage strode through the room. He balled up his fists and rubbed at his eyes, putting on a pathetic voice.

"Ooh, sir, give me the money because my rich sugar daddy might close the bank of Archie. Please, sir, I need it to buy poppers and Babycham!"

Archie smiled and commented breezily, "We certainly don't need it to pay off any speeding fines. Or convince our shady contacts to take them. Do we, Conrad?"

He narrowed his eyes and asked, "What's that mean?"

"Nothing." Archie shook his head. "Not. A. Thing."

Leo watched Conrad carefully. That sneer of his was twitching at his lips.

"He'll have plenty to think about when he gets back to the office," Archie confided as Conrad went back to his entourage. "The Solicitors' Authority take a very dim view of their members committing fraud to cover up their rich clients' speeding points."

Astrid collected up her folders. She nodded toward the courtroom and said, "There's a bad smell out here. Shall we, you two?"

Leo's inner twelve-year-old wanted to waft his hand in front of his nose and say, *Smells like a bad loser to me.* But he didn't. Instead, he rose to his feet, smoothed down his suit, flicked off lint that wasn't there, and gave Conrad a slight, unconcerned glance. "Yes, let's get going. We've got a case to win."

"What did you mean about shady contacts?" Conrad asked. He was more than ruffled, Leo could see, and that made Archie look even less concerned as he stood and took Leo's hand. "What did you mean?"

Archie blinked. "Nothing you need to worry about. See you in court."

Leo felt as if he'd added an inch or two to his height as he, Archie and Astrid walked into the courtroom. He didn't feel all at sea as he had done on his first visit to the room. It seemed smaller than it did before, unthreatening and familiar.

"Just be you and speak from your heart," Archie whispered. "I wouldn't tell any of my corporate clients that, by the way."

Leo swept back his fringe and grinned at him. "From the heart...right... I can do that."

Once the court was in session again, with Langston-Rowe pursing his lips, and Conrad sneering at his desk, Leo felt as if he'd never been away. But this was crunch time now, and as the time drew nearer for Leo to give his speech, images popped into his mind of the seals at the sanctuary, of the cracked concrete around the pool and the roof tiles Rob had hammered back into place, and the extra patients who were turning up and who Liv and Rob made room for as best they could. But they were at capacity, on the verge of turning seals away.

They needed the money, and there was a principle at stake too. Would Langston-Rowe rule that *love is love*?

But first there was Conrad. Conrad in his sharp suit and Rolex, barely even looking at Leo as he rose to make his own closing statement. On and on it went, a litany or legalese that Leo couldn't hope to understand. It seemed like a one-man *This Is Your Life* he was conducting for himself, listing his achievements, his meteoric rise and his money. God, he valued money.

More than family, apparently.

"I never met Mäuschen," Conrad finally admitted after forty-five minutes of autobiographical rambling. How had he never met her? Gunther had been married to his late wife for decades. "You may ask why. I'll tell you why. Because I was too busy achieving. Gunther knew all about achieving. *That's* what he cared about. He sailed around the world on his super yacht and he could only do that because he made money. He wanted money. He loved money. And women too. He didn't want Leo to marry *anybody*. He wanted him to marry a woman because that's what a rich man should have, and Gunther knew it too."

Archie cleared his throat and looked skyward. Conrad glanced around him, then narrowed his eyes.

"He had the yacht, the money, the women. And if Leo is worthy to take his legacy, he should honor that. And he can't. Leo Maxwell is a practicing homosexual." Conrad seemed to think that was news. Far from it. "He lied, he faked his engagement, and he did it to get money. I've already got money *and* girls, so you know that's not why I'm here. I'm here to uphold the name of my uncle. I may not have seen him for thirty years, but *I* am his blood. And that's why *I* deserve his legacy. Thank you."

Langston-Rowe sat very still, his gaze never wavering from Conrad for several long moments. Then he gave a sharp nod and said, "You may take your seat, Mr. Beaucock."

There was silence as Langston-Rowe made some notes, his pen moving slowly. Leo's mind had gone blank, but he looked at Archie and the sight of him there beside him made Leo feel brave. Feel loved.

And that was what Gunther had wanted for him, Leo was certain.

"Mr. Maxwell, your statement, please. Speak nice and clearly, if you would."

"*I love you,*" Archie mouthed. He squeezed Leo's hand.

"I love you too," Leo whispered. He kissed his hand and pressed it to Archie's arm. Then with a deep breath, Leo got to his feet.

"I tried to write this down in advance to prepare, but...but it didn't really look right on paper. So...so I'm just going to tell you, if that's all right?"

Langston-Rowe nodded and gestured for him to continue.

"I spent a year working with Gunther, skippering his yacht. The *Aphrodite's* not a small craft by any means, but you really get to know a person when you're stuck together at sea. He was one of the best. One of the nicest guys I've ever met. His yacht was full of people. Women, men, everyone in between and beyond. He just loved people. I was saying to Archie the other day, I never told Gunther I was gay because I thought he knew. I wasn't the only person on the yacht who wasn't straight, and Gunther didn't seem concerned. He accepted people as they were, and who you loved, it didn't matter to him. But what *was* important to him was love.

"I know a lot's been said about the women on his yacht, but it wasn't just...if I may say so, *sex* with Gunther. He was affectionate, adoring, and he loved his girlfriends. He said to me once — it was near the end of my time sailing with him, and we were on deck watching the sunrise — he said, "*Don't ever be lonely, Leo. It's a long life if you're alone.*" And I knew, deep down I knew what he meant. I am — I was a captain-for-hire. Never in one place long enough to love anyone. And I think it made Gunther sad.

"When I was called to Brockett's office after Gunther's death, I had no idea what to expect. He left me a beautiful ship-in-a-bottle that his wife had once given him. I was so touched by that, it meant so much to him. Because, you see, it represented to him the love he and his wife had shared, back before he was a success, back before he really had *anything*. I couldn't believe it when he left me the *Aphrodite*, but I was even more amazed when he left me all that money too.

"I believe, in my heart, Gunther wanted me to be happy. To be loved, and to love in return. He mentioned his Mäuschen because she was the love of his life. He wanted me to find the love of *my* life too. And with all that money, I wouldn't need to be a captain-for-hire anymore. And yes, I...I was going to marry my best friend because I thought that would fulfill the clause. But..."

Leo glanced at Archie. "But someone very wise, someone very dear to me, made me see that that wouldn't have fulfilled the clause at all. Just as Mr. Beaucock says, Gunther didn't want me to marry just *anyone* – but Gunther didn't mean *marry a woman*. He meant *marry someone you love.* Knowing Gunther as I did, I'm sure that's what he meant. And I think all this...all this palaver would've upset him. He wasn't litigious. He was a kind, gentle, affectionate man, and he only wanted to see more love in a world which really could do with more. That's all I wanted to say. Thank you, your honor."

And Leo sat down again and took Archie's hand. *Oh God, that was awful.*

Langston-Rowe watched Leo for a moment and Leo felt so uncomfortable under his stare that he turned and smiled at Archie. There was something calming about Archie's face that immediately made Leo relax.

"How did I do?" Leo whispered.

"Perfect," was his lover's verdict as, across the court, Conrad gave a derisory cough. He leaned forward to look at Leo, a sneering smile of victory on his face before he settled back.

Langston-Rowe made his notes again. He shuffled his papers and smiled. And this time, it seemed to be a genuine look of amusement on his face.

"Well, that concludes what has been a very interesting few weeks. I confess I have encountered many disputes over the years, but I think this one will lodge in my mind as one of the more...compelling. We have heard many people speak to us about the late Mr. Schreiber as we have tried to decide what the late gentleman intended. We must do our best to honor the last wishes of the dead. It is a service we can and should all render to them, out of respect...for much-loved friends, or relatives we rarely had the time to see. Having reviewed all the evidence, having given it all much, much thought, having heard Ms. Baxter's arguments on behalf of the defendant, and having heard Mr. Beaucock's own representation — along with a supporting cast — I have made my decision."

Silence fell, a silence so total that Leo could have sworn he could hear every process in his body.

"I find that Mr. Schreiber's clause should not be interpreted that, as a requirement to receive his legacy, Mr. Maxwell must marry a woman. There are no boundaries to gender when it comes to marriage under the laws of this country, therefore, there can lawfully be no requirement that a stipulated marriage is to a particular gender. I find therefore that Mr. Maxwell may inherit Mr. Schreiber's legacy provided, of course, that he *does* marry. But, Mr. Maxwell, as undoubtedly touching as your statement was, you did not mention any intention to marry. And if you do not marry, the legacy is forfeit."

Cold terror sluiced through Leo. *What? No! Not now! Not now we're so close! Oh, bloody hell, why didn't I say something?*

"I'll take that!" Conrad laughed, looking toward Leo again. He was grinning like a Cheshire Cat, a winner simply because Leo had forfeited the legacy. He'd never wanted it anyway. He'd just wanted to keep it from Leo.

Leo glanced at Astrid, who was pressing her fingers to her forehead, her head bowed.

We're lost. Oh, bloody hell, we're lost.

Leo turned to Archie. Archie with his calm blue eyes and his broad shoulders and his arms that Leo loved to get lost in.

"If I may, M'lud?" Archie asked Langston-Rowe, rising to his feet as he said, "I may have additional evidence."

Langston-Rowe tutted as he leaned forward, his hands clasped. "This is a rather late hour, Mr. Greville-Hall. But please, if you have additional evidence, I am willing to hear it. It has been an unusual case, after all." Once again, Langston-Rowe slowly unscrewed his fountain pen and sat poised to listen.

"Thank you, M'lud. I hadn't realized it was relevant until now." He nodded his thanks and turned to Leo. *Evidence? What—* Archie reached into his jacket and took out a small velvet box, then dropped to one knee. "I was going to do this at dinner, but…Leo, I love you and I wonder, would you do me the honor of becoming my husband?"

"Oh, come on!" Conrad bellowed. "Fucking hell, man, get this courtroom under control!"

"Order!" Langston-Rowe bellowed, his face red. Leo jumped. "Order in the court! I will *not* be disrespected in my courtroom with language like *that*, Mr. Beaucock. You're in contempt of court and you will be spending an hour in the cells for your outburst." Then he smiled as he looked to the other side of the court and said, "As you were. Mr. Maxwell, do you have an answer for Mr. Greville-Hall?"

"Yes." Leo nodded as tears rose in his eyes. *A real marriage, based on love, just as Gunther would have wanted.* "It's yes, Archie. I love you!"

"I'll even sign a prenup," Archie joked as he opened the ring box. Inside it was a band of silver shaped to look like an eternal coil of rope. "And you can call me Mäuschen if you must."

"*Mein Leibling*," Leo said. "I love you, Archie."

Archie threaded the ring on Leo's finger, where it fit perfectly. He rose to his feet and swept Leo into his arms. "I love you, darling." Their kiss might've gone against the etiquette of the courtroom, but Leo found that he didn't care anymore. As they broke for air, Archie said, "Thank you, M'lud."

With Leo's hand safe in his, Archie took his seat again.

Langston-Rowe seemed just a little flurried now as he rearranged his papers. "Indeed, I believe that I can take that as an intention to marry. And therefore, Mr. Schreiber's legacy is not forfeit. I rule that Mr. Maxwell, on the day of his marriage once both he and Mr. Greville-Hall have signed their marriage certificate, is entitled to the sum of money promised to him by Mr. Schreiber. I believe that resolves the business of this case. Good day to you all."

Langston-Rowe rose from his seat.

"All rise," the usher said.

And as Leo stood, he half-expected to hear The Wedding March play.

Epilogue

Leo took Archie's hand as he climbed on board the yacht.

With a cheeky smile, he said, "Welcome aboard the *Loveday*, Mr. Greville-Hall. I am Captain Leo, your skipper for this voyage."

And not just a skipper in oilskins and a jumper. Leo had managed to track down a pristine white captain's uniform complete with brass buttons and a cap. Which Leo was deliberately wearing at a jaunty angle.

"Hello, Captain." Archie laced their fingers together. "I'm off on my honeymoon. But you already know that."

"Well, isn't that a coincidence? I am too." Leo drew their joined hands to his lips and kissed them. "And we're going to have a fantastic time."

"My new husband's a millionaire, you know." Archie put his arm around Leo's waist. "Or he was for about five minutes. Now I know some *very* rich seals instead."

"I did tell Liv and Rob that they should install a wave machine, but they don't think that's a good idea." Leo pouted. Archie — Leo's husband, he reminded himself in wonder — kissed the pout, turning it into a smile.

"Let's get out to sea," he murmured. "Then I'd love to see belowdecks, Captain. What do you say?"

"I say yes! Oh, and look what I found." Leo passed Archie the newspaper he'd picked up earlier. He unfurled it to reveal Conrad on the front, his sneer rather muted now.

JAIL FOR TEFLON CON.

"Now that's a nice wedding present, don't you think?"

Archie glanced down at the headline. "Maybe he'll learn a trade while he's inside. Something useful," he mused. "Now, set sail for the sunset, Skipper Leo. We've got a wedding night to enjoy!"

Leo gave Archie a hug, touching the tip of his nose to Archie's. "And a whole lot of nights and days after that!"

"There's only one answer to that." Archie kissed Leo again and whispered in the fruitiest, most decadent tone he could muster, "Aye aye, Cap'n."

Want to see more from these authors? Here's a taster for you to enjoy!

The Reluctant Royal
Catherine Curzon & Eleanor Harkstead

Excerpt

Joe took another sip of tonic water. He wished it contained gin, because being the only sober person at the table was hardly his idea of fun, but as he watched the bottle of champagne being passed around, he knew he didn't really want any alcohol anyway. He couldn't go back to work the worse for wear. Not after months of sick leave. Best foot forward, as his dad would say.

And it wasn't only his decision not to drink that made Joe an oddity at the table. These were all Wendy's friends, out for her birthday. Solicitors, legal types, who'd spent most of the evening already talking shop. Joe looked on, his mind on other things. Would he cope on his first day back? Would they trust him to ever do a good job again?

"So, Joe, we're taking bets on who you're going to be coddling next week!" Wendy put her second bottle of Prosecco on the table and settled into her seat. Her leg brushed Joe's momentarily and she shifted, putting air between them again. "Izzy thinks one of the Fergie duo. Barnaby's bet his bonus on Wills and Kate. I think it's going to be the queen. The top job for a top bobby!"

"I don't know yet." Joe shrugged. "Maybe one of the corgis?"

"I bet you do know, and you're teasing us!" Wendy's friend Jemima brayed. "Have you signed the Official Secrets Act?"

Joe turned the plastic stirrer through his fizzing drink, rattling the ice cubes against the glass. He didn't pester Wendy's friends about confidential matters, so why did they think he was fair game? "As you know, if I had, I wouldn't be allowed to say."

"Whoever it is," Wendy told them, "let's hope they don't put my poor old hubby in hospital again! He's getting too old to play the action hero!"

Wendy's friends laughed, and Joe tried to look happy, but he really didn't want to be reminded of the accident. The headlamps coming straight for him in the evening darkness — and after he'd pushed the Duchess of Albany out of the way, there had been no time for Joe to leap aside. Just that crushing pain as the car slammed into him. Joe had slumped over the bonnet and found himself eye to eye with the idiot who'd just tried to deliberately run down the duchess.

"He's not that old!" Verity giggled. She patted Joe's leg and he tried not to flinch. "And still in fine form, too, Wendy, you lucky thing!"

"Lucky old me!" Wendy's smile looked like a grimace. How would she know what form her husband was in when it had been over six months since they'd so much as kissed, let alone more? She refilled her glass and whispered to Joe, "For God's sake, have a real drink."

"Come on, you know I can't," Joe replied. "I can't risk it. First day back and all that."

"It's my birthday." Her pink lips grew thin and she drew in a deep, sharp breath, as sharp as her fresh blonde bob. Then she put her lips to his ear and hissed, "Stop showing me up, Joe, have a drink."

"I'm drinking a stunt gin and tonic. That's enough." Joe held up the glass. It had the brand name of a well-known gin printed down its side. "They do tests, you know. I want to be nice and clean when they poke through my bodily fluids, thank you very much."

"Barnaby!" Wendy subtly turned away from her husband, the centre of attention all over again. He was dismissed, just as he had been so many times over the five years of their miserable married life. "So, we're all dying to know how your Tokyo merger's going. It's all everyone's talking about. Tell us all the latest from the front line of big money!"

Joe sat his glass down on the table. The last thing he cared about was Barnaby and his bloody merger, which he'd heard snippets of for weeks as Wendy had made business calls at home. Barnaby this, Barnaby that, *'Barnaby's going places.'*

So am I.

Joe nudged his seat back and stood to leave. Verity glanced at him, as if she was surprised he was going, but her attention turned to Wendy and Barnaby. Joe wasn't sure where he'd go, but he needed fresh air. He wanted to be away from loud drinkers, away from Wendy's carping. His head was pounding and as he stepped outside the pub, a car drove by close to the kerb. He instinctively jumped back, pressing himself against the wall behind him.

Calm down, Sergeant Wenlock, he told himself.

The night was cold, as cold as the pub had been hot, and Joe took a deep breath of autumn air. London tonight seemed even more surreal than ever, the streets a curious mix of the same well-dressed professionals who filled Wendy's group and those who had embraced Halloween, escaping the real world in the form of cats and devils, vampires and aliens, some already stumbling, others only just starting out. And there in the middle of them was Joe, who would rather be anywhere else but there.

Maybe Joe should've thrown aside his tweed jacket and sensible open-necked shirt for a costume. He'd have made quite a good Frankenstein's monster, maybe, though that said, when he'd first been taken to hospital and had plaster casts and bandages in places he hadn't thought possible, he'd have been a brilliant cursed mummy.

Joe decided to go for a wander. Once he was working again, he'd have little time to call his own. He'd take his freedom when and where he could. Music blared from pubs and bars, people laughed, taxis pulled up and disgorged their passengers. And up ahead, someone was shouting.

Bloody people, can't hold their drinks.

"Don't you ever, ever bloody do that again! Do you hear?"

It was a man's voice up ahead. Joe could see two figures, one in a black suit with a skeleton painted on it in white. He was wagging his finger — jabbing it — at the red-headed woman walking beside him in heels so high Joe wondered how she didn't fall flat on her face.

"It's so important to me, so fucking important, and all you have to do is just nod, and instead, you're pissing about, making a fucking joke of yourself!"

"I'm sorry!" Her voice sounded almost desperate and she recoiled from her companion's stabbing finger, jerking away as though it were the blade of a knife. She hurried after the skeleton when he stalked onwards, scooping up the silken hem of her shimmering red evening gown to follow. "Don't be angry, I'm sorry!"

"I'm sorry!" he mimicked. Joe could almost see him in profile. The man's face was disguised by makeup that turned his face into a skull.

Seemed a bit rich for him to be accusing someone of making a joke of themselves.

"The man's an investor in my film, and I wanted him to know that I'm serious about my art, and then you're there hanging over my shoulder, interrupting and gobbing on about God knows what!" The man clenched his hands. Even they were tricked out in skeleton makeup. "Why do you wind me up like this? You do it on purpose, for fuck's sake, then it's all I'm sorry! Well, you bloody well will be!"

"He was laughing too," the woman said, a fresh note of desperation in her sing-song voice. No, not desperation. Fear. "He was having a good time, you're not thinking straight! Just—please, don't be like this!"

"My thinking's perfectly clear!" The man gave a long sniff then, and Joe knew exactly what was going on.

The drugs are talking.

The man stopped where he was and raised his hand at the woman. The way she flinched back told Joe that this wasn't the first time it had happened. As she drew away, he saw her makeup clearly, a glamourous sugar skull in a rainbow of colours that nearly took his breath away.

"Please don't," was all she said.

Joe increased his pace. The man's raised hand trembled but in a split second he slapped the woman across her painted face.

Joe ran.

He was on the couple in only a few steps, and interposed himself between them. He didn't look back at the woman, but could hear her frightened breathing just behind him. "That's enough. Time for you to go."

"And who the fuck are you, James Bond?" the man sneered.

"I'm not going to stand around and watch a bully like you slap a woman." Joe clenched his fists, resisting the temptation to give Skeletor a taste of his own medicine.

"A woman? That's a fucking joke. *She's* a drag queen—a bloke!"

Joe turned to look at the woman.

A bloke?

Was she?

It was hard to tell under the exquisite layer of paint—she looked more like a china doll than anything remotely masculine. She blinked her large dark eyes and lifted one lace-gloved hand to her face, then whispered, "It was my fault, really—"

Joe shook his head. He turned back to face the skeleton. "I saw what you did. All these other people in the street saw what you did too." Joe extended his hand, indicating the crowd of onlookers who'd paused for a bit of unexpected entertainment. "Bloke or woman, I don't care, no one slaps anyone on my watch."

You're not on duty now, Sergeant Wenlock!

Joe ignored the little voice at his ear. He was going back to work, wasn't he? He protected people. And that's just what he'd do.

PUBLISHING

Sign up for our newsletter and find out about all our
romance book releases, eBook sales and promotions,
sneak peeks and FREE romance books!

About the Authors

Catherine Curzon

Catherine Curzon is a royal historian who writes on all matters of 18th century. Her work has been featured on many platforms and Catherine has also spoken at various venues including the Royal Pavilion, Brighton, and Dr Johnson's House.

Catherine holds a Master's degree in Film and when not dodging the furies of the guillotine, writes fiction set deep in the underbelly of Georgian London.

She lives in Yorkshire atop a ludicrously steep hill.

Eleanor Harkstead

Eleanor Harkstead often dashes about in nineteenth-century costume, in bonnet or cravat as the mood takes her. She can occasionally be found wandering old graveyards, and is especially fond of the ones in Edinburgh. Eleanor is very fond of chocolate, wine, tweed waistcoats and nice pens. She has a large collection of vintage hats, and once played guitar in a band. Originally from the south-east, Eleanor now lives somewhere in the Midlands with a large ginger cat who resembles a Viking.

Sign up to receive their newsletter at
https://curzonharkstead.co.uk/newsletter/

Catherine and Eleanor love to hear from readers. You can find their contact information, website and author biographies at https://www.pride-publishing.com